Tell Me No Secrets

Tell Me No Secrets

Lynda Stacey

Gripping edge of your seat reads!

Published 2018 by Choc Lit Limited
Penrose House, Crawley Drive, Camberley, Surrey GU15 2AB, UK
www.choc-lit.com

A CIP catalogue record for this book is available
from the British Library

ISBN 978-1-78189-416-3

FSC
www.fsc.org
MIX
Paper from
responsible sources
FSC® C018072

Printed and bound by Clays Ltd

For my wonderful mother, Pauline.
You were taken from us far too soon
and far too many years ago.
There isn't a day that passes that I don't miss you
and every single day I wish that you were still here
to read my books and to drive everyone just a little
bit crazy, by constantly talking about them!
xx

Acknowledgements

I'd like to take this opportunity to thank Jane Lovering.
She's been the most amazing friend. She has picked me
up on so many occasions, dragged me along kicking
and screaming, fed me numerous mugs of coffee and
on more than one occasion convinced me to carry
on. I really don't know what I'd do without her and
I'm sure that without her help and encouragement,
I still wouldn't be published. So … thank you!

A huge thank you as always goes to my husband, Haydn.
He's the one anchor in my life, the one person in the world
I could not live without and even though my writing
means that he ends up spending many evenings watching
TV without me, he's been encouraging throughout.

To both Kathy Kilner and Victoria Howard who
both read my manuscripts repeatedly. You've both
helped me, critiqued my work and supported me
daily. Its friends like both of you that keep me going
on days when it would be easy to do anything
else except for the writing. Thank you xx

To Jayne Stacey, Cynthia Foster and Vivien Norton. You
have all read this novel, given critique, believed in me,
supported me and encouraged me to continue. Thank you.

To my amazing editor, what would I do without you? I
loved every minute of working with you. You were the best
and I couldn't have wished to work with anyone better.
You helped me add the sparkle and shine. Thank you xx

And finally, I'd like to thank the team at Choc Lit for believing in me. They are amazing and always supportive, even when replying at stupid o'clock at night. All emails end with lovely smiley emoticons and I can't imagine what it would have been like to take this journey with any other publisher. So to you, the thanks come from every millimetre of my heart!

Special thanks goes to the Tasting Panel readers: Elena B., Dimi E., Ruth N., Yvonne G., Stacey R., Isobel J., Samantha E., Thatsany R., Melissa B., Kathryn B. and Bianca B.

Thank you so much, xx

Chapter One

'How many times do I have to tell you, don't phone me here.' Rob's voice echoed up the stairs, making Kate jump out of bed. He sounded angry and Kate didn't like it. She crept onto the landing, where she stood and waited, not knowing whether to go down, stay put or go back to bed. 'Not a chance. I'm not doing it. Now, you stick to your plan, and I'll stick to mine.' Kate held her breath as she heard the kitchen door quietly close and the mumbled voice continued.

'Rob,' she shouted. She inched her way down the stairs. 'Rob, is everything okay?' Her feet were cold and she hopped from foot to foot, wishing for just a moment that she'd thought to put her slippers on as she'd jumped out of bed. 'Rob?'

The door handle snapped down and the kitchen door jerked open. 'What?' he bellowed, making her jump backwards.

'I ... I heard you on the phone, is all okay?' she questioned, and nervously pulled at her pyjama top. She'd heard whispered conversations like this before. Each one had been in a hushed voice. Each one as secretive as the one before and each one had showed her a side to Rob that she didn't like.

'It's just work. Go to bed, I'll be up soon.'

'Okay.' He was lying to her. That was obvious. 'Come on, Rob, how long will you be? It's just ... I start my new job tomorrow ...' She tried to play on his conscience. '... You have remembered that, Rob, haven't you? I could do with an early night, and I hoped you might join me.' She pushed for an answer knowing that the phone was still in his hand, hidden behind the door.

1

'Kate, stop nagging and go to bed.'

The kitchen door slammed shut in her face and Kate pouted. She wasn't nagging and what's more, she wasn't stupid; she'd heard his words and knew that he was up to something, but once again, she didn't know what.

Sighing she went back upstairs, climbed into bed, and picked up her unfinished glass of wine. She took a sip and looked over at the impeccably positioned photo. It stood on her bedside table, silver framed, perfectly polished. The photo had been taken the year before, at their engagement party in September, a time when they'd both been happy. Rob was hugging her so close and looked so good. But then, Rob always looked good. Why wouldn't he? He always seemed to have the perfect tan, an amazing body, figure-hugging shorts and a smile that could be seen for miles. Unlike her, who in comparison was far too scrawny, with long auburn hair and pale freckly skin that burnt far too easily.

Everyone had said that opposites attract, but Kate still wasn't sure. Of course, she'd thought so at first. Things had moved quickly, Rob had bombarded her with romance, love and affection and all at a time when she'd needed it the most. But recently, he'd changed. He'd become distant, cold and, dare she admit, just a little on the aggressive side. It was as though from the moment she'd agreed to him moving in with her, he'd become far too comfortable and seemed to do or say whatever he wanted, in whatever tone he liked. And the normal politeness of a new relationship had disappeared overnight.

A million questions ran through her mind. Who had been on the phone? Was it a girlfriend? Had he met someone else? Did he regret meeting her, or was it that he'd simply stopped loving her? She wouldn't have been suspicious if there had only ever been one call, but there hadn't and now her mind was working overtime.

Kate shook her head. She wouldn't blame him if he'd found someone else. After all, what man in their right mind would want to love someone who looked like her? A single tear dropped down Kate's face as she closed her eyes and tried to decide what to do. Did she go down, confront him, ask him the questions that were spiralling around her mind, or did she go to sleep, curl up in the duvet and once again pretend that she didn't care?

It was seven o'clock when her alarm clock burst into life. Its constant buzzing drove her insane, but she didn't dare switch it off. She couldn't sleep in; not today. But she was struggling to wake herself. She knuckle-rubbed her eyes and finally slapped the alarm clock into silence as she slid her leg over to the left-hand side of the bed, her toes searching for Rob.

His side of the bed was cold. She should have known he wasn't there due to the lack of snoring, but for a few seconds her hand inched across to where her fiancé should have been sleeping.

The empty space in the bed encouraged her eyes to finally open. She peered at the duvet. It was perfectly straight, even the decorative cushion still lay where she had left it the night before and she slumped back against her pillow, knowing that once again he'd slept downstairs. Kate closed her eyes, punched the duvet and sighed, suddenly remembering the phone call, the secrets and lies of the night before.

'This isn't getting you to work, Kate Duggan.' She took a deep breath. 'Get up, you have a new job to go to.' She threw back the duvet and launched herself out of bed. But as she did so, her stomach turned and the nervous nausea began.

It would be the first full-time job she'd taken since the accident just over a year before. Thirteen months since her whole world had fallen apart. Everything had been such a mess, most of her family had both blamed and needed her in equal measure. But then she'd met Rob. It was just a few weeks after the accident, a time when she'd really needed to be loved. He'd worked, provided for her and, at that moment in time, she'd been happy to let him. She hadn't thought about what he did for a living. How a personal trainer worked, or how often he'd end up spending days, if not weeks, working away from home. All she'd cared about was that someone actually loved her.

Was it any wonder they'd grown apart, just as quickly as they'd got together?

Flinging open the wardrobe door she scoured inside and without hesitation selected a black pencil skirt, new white blouse and high-heeled black patent leather shoes. Everything was easy to find. All the clothes were colour coded and set out in two distinct sections. There were tops and blouses on one rail and skirts, trousers and gym clothes on the other. Rob may have a problem sleeping with her, but that didn't mean she'd let her appearance or standards slip for the rest of the world to see.

She laid each item on the bed so she could check them carefully. There were to be no creases, no marks or loose seams. Appearance was everything, especially today. She just had to look perfect.

She scanned the perfume bottles on her dressing table. All stood in a row, all were in size order. All perfectly lined up without a millimetre to spare. She carefully selected the bottle of Vivienne Westwood's Boudoir and put it on the bed, beside her clothes. She liked everything to be there, just ready to put on. Satisfied with her choices, she padded through to the bathroom at the far side of the cottage.

Intense, bright, early morning sunshine bounced off the glistening white tiles, hurting her eyes. She turned down the blind and waited until she'd stopped squinting, before allowing the bathroom to come into focus. There was a splatter of toothpaste, which had imprinted itself across Rob's bathroom mirror. He'd left towels on the floor and a toilet that desperately needed attacking with bleach. These were all signs that told Kate that Rob was awake and had already been in the bathroom. She heard herself tut. They'd been together for just over a year and she'd repeatedly asked him to clean up after himself, but still it was always left like this. Even though he knew she hated it. Kate opened the cupboard, pulled on a pair of rubber gloves, and picked up the bleach.

Once she was satisfied that the bathroom was once again perfect, she began to take in her reflection in the mirror.

'I doubt I'd want to sleep with you either,' she mouthed as she splashed cold water onto her pale, freckled, scarred face. Her finger drew a line along the long red puckered scar that had been engraved into her jawline, a constant reminder of the accident and a day that had tormented her dreams every night since.

After all, it was a day she'd never been allowed to forget. The reminder was there every time she looked at herself, but according to her mother, she had been the lucky one: the one who'd walked away. A scar was nothing compared with what had happened to her twin sister, Eve, who'd been paralysed and hadn't walked since, or her poor brother, James, who'd been killed outright, and no matter how many times she'd tried to tell herself that it hadn't been her fault, the guilt still remained.

After taking a shower, she set to work to correct the disturbing image that stared back from the steamed-up mirror, beginning with the brushing of her long dyed auburn hair. It reminded her of a huge tangled bird's nest and the brush pulled as she dragged it repeatedly through the strands of hair, until they fell evenly down her back. She then turned her attention to her face and began applying the foundation that for the past year she trusted to hide her scar. Three thin coats, followed by a light dusting of face powder.

Once satisfied, she applied a smudge of eyeliner and a touch of clear lip gloss. 'Not too much, you don't want to look like a hussy, now do you?' she whispered, before smiling back at her reflection and, after dropping one damp towel into the wash basket and then wrapping a dry one around her body, she walked back across the landing and into her bedroom.

'Morning.' She heard Rob's deep husky voice before she saw him. It came from behind the open wardrobe door and she tried to determine what kind of mood he was in. She thought he sounded cheerful, not moody at all. Yet without seeing his face, she really couldn't tell.

'So, what's with sleeping downstairs, again?' she immediately demanded, and then cursed inwardly for jumping in so quickly. Her job in the police force had taught her that a person always looked down if they lied and she wished she'd waited until the wardrobe door had been closed before she'd asked. At least then she'd have been able to see if there had been any sign of lies or deceit in his eyes.

'Sorry, babes, fell asleep. You know, football on telly.' Rob smirked. The pine door of the wardrobe closed with a bang and he stood before her. He had a wide disarming smile that lit up his handsome face. His customary tracksuit bottoms hung loosely from his hips, allowing Kate full view of his perfect abs, and the dolphin tattoos that wrapped themselves around his equally huge and perfect biceps. In fact, every muscle on his body was toned to equal symmetry. Life had dealt him the Adonis card and his body really was his temple, and it was a tool he tended to use to his advantage, at every given opportunity.

'Stop admiring yourself, Rob. It's quite pathetic for a

twenty-something has-been.' She couldn't help herself. He'd hurt her, yet again, and this time she wouldn't back down.

He looked himself up and down in the mirror. 'Got to look my best, darling. No point being a personal trainer if the clients don't look up to me, now is there? Besides, one of us has to earn a proper wage, don't we?'

She resented his comments. 'It's not like I've never worked Rob, is it? I'd always worked before the accident.'

'Darling, you were just a PCSO.'

'Seriously, are you going to use that one? I might have been just a PCSO here in Yorkshire, Rob, but that was my choice. I had been a constable in the Metropolitan Police.'

'So, why swap from being a real copper to being a pretend special one?' He laughed. 'A special bobby, that's what you were, special.'

'Don't be an ass, Rob. There were no full-time posts to transfer to when I came back to Yorkshire. I came back to look after my grandmother, in case you've forgotten. I took what I could get.' She glared in his direction. He stood before the mirror, flexing his muscles, while admiring his physique.

'I know, baby. Why don't you arrest me for being an ass?' Again he turned and smirked. 'Oh, that's right, you were one of those coppers who couldn't arrest people, isn't that right?'

'Sod off, Rob. You have no idea what my job involved. No idea at all, so keep your opinions to yourself.' It was true, he didn't have any idea what she'd done. She'd never spoken of the times when she'd saved lives, or of when her own had been put in danger. She watched as he threw dirty clothes onto the floor, replacing them with clean ones out of the wardrobe.

'Rob, pick them up. The dirty basket is in the bathroom, and stop acting like I'm your mother, 'cos I'm not. I'm going to work and it's about time you learned to tidy up after yourself.'

7

'And what did you say your new job involved, baby?' He paused. 'Ah, that's right. You're off to play Inspector Clouseau. Really, Kate? What does your father think?' He picked up his shorts and threw them on the bed.

'Don't make fun, Rob. I'll be training to be a private investigator and, as for my father, don't you dare try to second guess what his opinion might be.' Kate was furious. Ever since she'd told him about her new chosen career, he'd made fun, belittled her decision and had constantly thrown at her how much her father had wanted her to follow in his footsteps and become a lawyer, just like James had been. She closed her eyes as the memory of her brother once again passed through her mind.

Would the pain ever diminish?

Kate opened her eyes, pulled the towel tightly around her, and looked across the room, down the passage and toward the stairs. She took in a deep breath, and silently thanked her grandmother for leaving the cottage to her, but then wondered if the gift had in fact been a curse. Was Rob only here for the free accommodation? Was that the reason he stayed? Or did he actually love her? There had been times when she'd thought he had, but today was not one of those days. She gritted her teeth and fixed his look with a glare. The 'football on telly' explanation wasn't washing with her. She'd heard the phone call and deep down she knew that there was something going on that he wasn't telling her.

Rob stepped towards her, his lips forming an exaggerated pout – he had the look of a scolded schoolboy – and reached out to snare her with his strong muscular arms, pulling her tightly into his bare chest.

'Let go of me, Rob. I'm trying to get ready.' Kate struggled against his all too familiar hold. 'I mean it. Let go.'

'Am I forgiven?' His lips momentarily brushed hers, as his hands travelled up and down the parts of her naked body that he could reach. The towel she'd been wrapped in dropped unceremoniously to the floor and landed in a heap at her feet, giving his hands the freedom to roam unhindered.

'Why, why would I forgive you, Rob?' Her serious expression crept into a smile. 'You're an asshole.' She began to laugh. After all, it was hard to stay cross whilst naked, especially with Rob.

'Am I, baby, am I forgiven?' He repeated the words, over and over, as he teased her mouth with the brushing of his. 'Please?'

Kate caught the strong scent of his aftershave – an earthy, musky, manly smell. His lips left hers momentarily and began to sear a path, kissing every part of her neck and chest, making her moan with desire. His lips once again captured hers; he was more demanding this time and his tongue sent shivers racing through her body as his fingers gently traced the curve of her spine. She closed her eyes as a sudden and overwhelming sensation took over her. It was a mixture of love and lust that engulfed her and she found it harder and harder to stay annoyed.

She felt his hands squeeze her gently, making her flick open her eyes and look deep into his. Melting into his arms, she still couldn't believe that someone like Rob loved her and the feelings she had right now were exactly the same as those she had experienced the first day she'd set eyes on him.

'Am I forgiven, baby?' His words were little more than a whisper, as Kate reluctantly nodded her forgiveness and lifted her lips back towards his.

But just as quickly as he'd pulled her to him, he released his grasp, a cheeky grin ripped across his face, and his hand grabbed his T-shirt from where it lay.

'Too late, kiddo, you should've forgiven me sooner.'

Kate's naked body landed on the bed, as Rob smirked, flashed a wink and strode out of the room.

The heavy footsteps on the stairs, the opening and closing of the fridge, followed by the slamming of the back door, all told Kate that he'd left for the day and he wasn't coming back.

'Bastard,' Kate shouted and in a gesture of frustration she scooped up one of her heels and hurled it towards the bedroom door. As the shoe rebounded, everything went into slow motion. She could see what was going to happen, but was powerless to prevent it. Before her eyes the black patent leather shoe caught the tall stemmed glass on the bedside unit and the remnants of the previous night's red wine splattered across a section of the cream shag pile carpet.

'Damn you,' she screamed. She grabbed at the fallen bath towel and dropped to her knees. She was still naked, but frantically used the towel to dab at the carpet, attempting in vain to get the stain to lift, as tears ran down her face.

The carpet would have to be professionally cleaned or replaced. She wouldn't allow anything to stay spoiled, not in this cottage.

Chapter Two

Kate was running late. She climbed into her old yellow Volkswagen Beetle. It was rusty and creaked, but the interior was spotless and Kate was loath to exchange it, even though, as with everything else, Rob made fun of it every chance he got. But to her, it was perfect. She loved it, and just like River Cottage, it had belonged to her grandmother.

There had been a time, after the accident, when she'd wondered if she'd ever drive again. She had fond memories of driving around North Yorkshire with her grandmother, and it was only the memory of that which had actually got her back in a car, driving. At first, she'd forced herself to take short journeys around the moors. She'd gone looking for and picking heather, even though she didn't need or want any. And on days when the sun had shone, she'd spent hours looking for the perfect picnic spot, and then sitting quietly to watch wildlife, all the time daring herself to get back in the car and to drive back home. Even now, on occasions, she'd begin sweating or feel nauseous and would have to keep stopping the car to sip water, or to wipe her hot, clammy hands on a small towel that she now kept in the door pocket for such an occasion.

Kate took note of the time and reversed out of the drive. She had just twenty minutes to get to Bedale. A quick calculation meant that she only just had enough time to get to work for her nine a.m. start. She cursed inwardly while repeatedly and anxiously keeping one eye on her watch, the other eye on the road. She drove carefully. She hated to be late and normally prided herself on her timekeeping, but the carpet had been stained and she'd had to at least try her best to repair the damage.

The road between Caldwick and Bedale was unbelievably clear, which was quite unusual for a Monday morning and the car gained momentum, snaking around the long isolated roads and past the low stone walls. It was April and the fresh spring morning air made the drive pleasant, and Kate smiled as she saw sheep, scattered through the fields, all with newborn lambs by their side. Kate found herself slowing the car down to a crawl while she watched a beautiful white swan cautiously herding its six young cygnets away from the road and into the safety of a nearby pond. The swan watched vigilantly as one after another of her babies jumped in with a splash, before making their way to the safety of her side. It reminded Kate of days before the accident, days when she, James and her sister Eve would run side by side, just as the cygnets did. Days when their mother had cared enough to shepherd them to safety. Days when they'd been a family group and the happier days she'd had before the isolation she felt following the accident. It had been as though she'd become invisible, as everyone had rushed to take care of her mother, father, and Eve.

Pulling into the town, she looked at the clock embedded in the church tower. It was just five minutes before nine o'clock and she felt her breathing begin to relax. She drove over the cobbles, past pedestrians and cyclists who were also making their way to work. A parking space appeared before her and she aimed for it, knowing that she had no time to spare.

'Noooooooooooo!' she screamed as her foot slammed down on the brake. She narrowly missed the silver BMW, which had swiftly slid in front of her and into the space that should have been hers.

'That was my space, you moron,' she shouted shakily through the open window of her car, which now stood in the middle of the cobbled road, with nowhere to go. She knew she'd overreacted and felt the need to apologise to the driver, but there was no time. She had to move the car, find another parking space and get herself to work.

It was exactly nine o'clock by the time she'd parked. Near misses were not good and for a moment, she just sat and waited for her breathing to calm and for her heart to stop palpitating heavily in her chest.

Memories of the accident flashed through her mind, the car that came from nowhere, the screech of brakes, the sound of metal upon metal and then the darkness.

Parker & Son was situated close to the church. A double fronted Victorian terraced house with no signage, it stood impressively between two similar properties. A wine bar stood to the right and to the left was what looked like a new bakery. It had no signage either, but the smell of fresh bread drifted out from the open door, making Kate's mouth water. Not only had she missed breakfast due to the wine spilling incident, but cleaning up after it had meant that she hadn't had time to make herself any lunch either.

Kate felt a tinge of excitement. She couldn't wait to see what lay beyond the shiny, jet-black front door and reached out for the polished brass door handle. Taking a deep breath, she checked her clothes one last time, flicked her hair back, straightened her skirt and with a look of confidence, stepped forward.

'Oh, hi, you must be Kate?' A woman stood up from behind the reception desk and smiled. 'I'm Gloria.'

Kate stepped forward and allowed the door to close behind her. Gloria fumbled with a packet of Hobnob biscuits, until they spilled out onto a small china plate. She then held out a hand to where Kate stood.

Gloria had a warm smile. She was elegant, looked around fifty years old and had soft, short, golden hair. She was a mixture of Mary Poppins and a younger version of her grandmother, which made Kate feel immediately comfortable.

'Sit down, honey. I'll put the kettle on.' Gloria walked to a small table that stood in the corner of the room. 'I bought the biscuits in your honour. Do you want some coffee?'

Kate nodded appreciatively. 'That'd be great, thank you.' She took a seat on the brown leather settee. 'What a lovely room,' Kate said as she looked around the reception and admired the deep skirting board and ornate coving. Half the room was overpowered by a huge traditional high-fronted mahogany reception desk, the other half taken up by the leather settee on which she sat.

'Mr Parker will be ready to speak to you in a minute; he was just taking a call.'

Kate sipped at the coffee. Her stomach grumbled nervously and she searched the walls for something to talk about.

'It's fine. I really don't mind waiting. It's nice to have a few moments to compose myself, especially after being late. I had a nightmare of a morning.' She began to explain. 'First, I had a spillage accident at home, last night's wine.' She pulled a face. 'And then, I was just about to pull into the space right outside the door, when some moron stole my parking space. I ended up having to park right down at the bottom of the high street.'

'Ah, I think that moron may have been me?' A deep assertive voice filled the room, just as a man's broad six-foot frame suddenly occupied the ornate doorway that stood between the reception and a hallway beyond. 'Ben Parker,' he said as he held out his hand to shake hers. Kate looked up and gasped as she took his hand and caught the deep density of his eyes. They were jet black with a sparkle that came from somewhere deep within. He released her hand and she glanced down to take in the expensive cut of his suit, which screamed money and her heart sank as she looked between Ben and the entrance, wondering how quickly she could make an exit. Shouting like a banshee had not been the impression she'd wanted to give her new boss, especially on her very first day.

'Ah, I see you and Ben have already met. Coffee, Ben?' Gloria asked completely ignoring Ben's comment and automatically picked up a third cup before Ben had the chance to reply.

Ben stood for a moment without speaking. Kate seemed nice and he was angry with himself for having taken the parking space, wishing instead that he'd played the gentleman and given up the space to her. At least then, they'd have got off to a better start and the atmosphere in the room would have been a little less edgy.

He looked her up and down. She was stunning and looked perfectly proportioned; she was beautifully dressed and her smile immediately caught his attention. She looked nervous, which was probably his fault, but her high cheekbones and expressive brown eyes held his attention for much longer than he'd intended. Even her clothes were beautiful; they were expensive and gave her a certain quality that he admired.

'Your coffee.' Gloria passed him the mug, smiled and glanced between him and Kate.

'Thanks.' He looked fondly in Gloria's direction, caught her eye and discreetly shook his head. He knew by the look on her face that Gloria would have loved to play matchmaker. He knew she wanted to see him happy again, but mixing business with pleasure would never be a good thing and Gloria knew it, giving him a sense of relief that at least this time she'd leave well alone. The last thing he needed right now was for Gloria to try and fix him, make him whole again, repair his damage, like everyone else had tried to do. It was as though the world didn't see you as a whole person, not unless you were attached to someone else. But the sudden death of his wife, Julia, had taken its toll and even though it had happened four years before, the thought of moving on had never crossed his mind. It was only recently that he'd realised that his life was empty and that he needed something more than work.

'Hobnob?' Gloria's voice broke through his thoughts and he took the biscuit from the plate, turning himself purposely back towards Kate's gaze. He once again held it for just a moment too long. His entrance had obviously shocked her and he was enjoying himself, watching her indecision.

'Kate. When you're ready, maybe you'd like to follow this moron through to the office,' he said with a cheeky smirk and a wink, as he turned and strode from the room. 'Mr Parker's waiting and unless you're the prime minister, you shouldn't keep him waiting for very long. He doesn't like it.'

Kate's head spun between the door that Ben had walked through and Gloria, who had picked up another Hobnob, taken a bite and then waved it frantically in the air, indicating to Kate that she should follow.

'Go on, William doesn't bite, honestly. No matter what Ben says.' Gloria continued to nibble at the biscuit, which she held in one hand, while she stirred her mug of coffee with the other.

'But ... I thought Ben was Mr Parker,' Kate questioned as she jumped up from the settee, straightened her clothes and stepped towards the door.

'He is dear, he's Mr Parker junior. The Mr Parker that you're about to meet, your boss, is his father.'

Kate felt the tension once again rise up in her chest; her hands felt hot and clammy and her heart began to beat rapidly. Again, she looked toward the exit.

Should she run now, or later?

She swallowed hard. She was determined not to fail. She caught her breath and pulled the door open, to find herself in a corridor where there were several closed doors and a staircase which rose up before her. Each new obstacle added to her already indecisive morning. And, as though things hadn't been bad enough, she now had two Mr Parkers to deal with. But she'd been in worse situations than this. Hadn't she? How bad could it really be?

She studied the doors. Which one would Ben have gone through? She began to play 'Eeny, meeny, miny, mo' in her head as a tall, slim, dark-haired man rushed out from one of the rooms, almost colliding with her in his haste to leave the building.

'Oh, hi there, how you doing?' He grinned. He seemed to pause and waited as Kate smiled back. She raised an eyebrow and once again she looked between the doors. The man pushed his over-sized glasses up his nose.

'Well, the idea of working here seemed so much more fun when the woman at the employment agency told me I had the job,' Kate said as she held out her hands. 'Where did he go?'

'Doesn't it always? And if you're looking for Mr Parker's office, it's in there.' His smile faded as he looked at his watch and pointed to a door.

'Thank you.' The man's face looked familiar, but Kate couldn't place him and looked over her shoulder to where he now raced through reception, before she nervously entered the room.

The office was bright and filled with light and in comparison to the reception was quite modern and airy. It had obviously been recently refurbished. The smell of fresh paint still lingered in the air and there was no sign of the traditional ornate decor anywhere. The desk was huge and impressive. It was curved, made of oak and behind it sat an older, more distinguished looking duplicate of Ben.

'Now then, Miss Duggan, please take a seat.'

Kate nodded and sat down in the tub chair that stood before his desk. She glanced across at Ben who was perched against a sideboard. She was hoping for reassurance, but his hands were clasped tightly together and although he smiled, his face gave nothing away.

'Welcome,' William Parker said as he ran a hand through his dark, peppered hair. The tiny speckles of grey were just starting to appear by his sideburns, making him look older and more mature than Ben and she guessed that he'd be around twenty-five years Ben's senior. He crossed his legs, to reveal shiny black shoes that could have been used as a mirror. Kate loved well-kept shoes and she made a decision that her new boss had to be nice. Why else would he take so much care about his appearance?

'Thank you so much and I'm so sorry that I was late this morning,' she announced. 'I really didn't mean to shout at your son.' Kate was nervous and tried to cover her tracks, just in case Ben had told him about the incident.

'Don't apologise for being feisty, we like feisty women, don't we, Ben?' He grinned, stood up and walked back and forth behind the desk, finally perching against the windowsill. His hands clasped together, matching Ben's mannerisms and they both studied her in a silence that seemed to go on forever.

Kate took note that Ben had purposely failed to answer his father's question, which made her wonder why, or how scary Mr Parker might really be after all?

'So, you want to be a private investigator?' he said, his words suddenly slicing through the silence, like a newly-sharpened knife.

'Yes, sir, I'd like that very much. The agency that

recommended me, well, they thought I'd be ideal for the job.' Her answer had been polite and it occurred to her that his words could have been either a statement or a question. 'You see, sir, I've always been interested in the law.'

'So I see. You're twenty-eight, is that right?'

'Yes, sir, I am.'

'And you worked for the Metropolitan Police. As a constable?'

'I did. Yes, sir.'

'My dear, my name's William, not sir, I don't like it ... and you're correct, the agency has always been excellent at sending us the right candidates. That's why we ask them to do it.'

He walked away from the window and to the front of the desk, perching on its edge, allowing Kate to look him up and down. Like Ben, his suit looked expensive. Even his haircut screamed money. 'I see you went to law school?'

Kate nodded. 'Yes, I did. I graduated with honours.'

Ben stepped forward, a file held in his hand. 'Father, Kate not only graduated with honours, her reports say that she was the perfect student.' He smiled and Kate saw that the sparkle was back in his eyes.

'So, why didn't you go into law? You could have become a solicitor.'

Kate shrugged. Closed her eyes for a moment and thought about her answer. 'You want the truth?' She looked at him for permission to continue. 'I guess I wanted to annoy my father.'

Both William and Ben looked at one another and smiled.

'Sound familiar, Ben?' William asked and gave Ben a knowing look. 'My son here used to do everything he could to annoy me too. Must be a generational thing.'

Ben walked back to lean against the sideboard. He shifted uncomfortably against it and looked down at the floor.

William studied the file. 'The scar on your face. It happened just over a year ago, am I right?' He tapped his pen on the file. 'There was a place on the application asking about your personal life and about anything that could affect your role. Did you not think this relevant?'

'No, I'm sorry. I didn't think it was.' She took in a deep breath. 'How did you find out about it? I don't normally tell anyone.' She looked between both William and Ben. The accident was personal and she hadn't written anything about it on the application form but now realised that she was going to have to explain. She looked down, purposely holding the scarred side of her face away from him, and held back the tears. She hated the scar and hiding it had become a habit since the accident; it was hideous and the fewer people that saw it, the better.

William coughed, drawing her attention back to where he sat. 'Of course we know, Kate. Don't be alarmed and don't take it personally. It's what we do. It didn't take Ben a moment to find out about your background.' He laughed. 'He is a private investigator, after all. Doing these checks are second nature to him. Once trained, it'll be second nature to you too.'

Ben cringed, caught her eye and mouthed 'sorry'. He liked the way she came across, appearing to be timid, cautious, yet with the flick of a switch, she'd turn feisty, and easily capable of standing her ground.

She intrigued him. He realised why she thought the accident was personal, he could understand her not wanting to talk about it in public and why she had omitted it on the application form. After all, he knew that her sister had been paralysed, her brother killed and out of curiosity, he half hoped his father would push her for just a few more answers.

Ben once again caught her gaze. She looked defenceless

and ready to run; her eyes held the light like mirrors and sparkled as though full of tears that didn't or couldn't fall. He smiled at her and her mouth curled up slightly at one side in a quirky, nervous half smile and then there was the scar, a scar that carved itself into her jawline. It was definitive, yet somehow added to her vulnerability, and for some reason, it made her even more beautiful.

He breathed in deeply and then closed his eyes. She wore a fragrance that reached its way across the office. It was fresh, musky and distinguished and he kept his eyes closed momentarily to enjoy the scent.

Rousing himself, he walked to the door and excused himself from the room. He then stood in the passageway with his back against the wall. His hands made fists and he felt angry with himself for looking at Kate that way. She was a work colleague after all, and he reprimanded himself for thinking otherwise. It had been the first time, since Julia had died, that he'd admired another woman. Or had thought of one in that way and, for a moment, he felt as though he'd betrayed her memory. Even though he knew he didn't need it, he looked up to the sky for forgiveness, before taking a deep breath, opening the door and walking back into the office, where Kate and his father were talking.

'My father, he's a barrister,' Kate was explaining. 'He wanted me to go into law once I'd qualified, just like my brother had done. But I didn't want to. I joined the Met police, went to live in London for a while and only came back to join the local force when my grandmother became ill. I came back to help look after her, until she died. By then, the only position available was as a PCSO, so I took it until something more permanent came along.' She looked across at Ben. 'I was considering joining my father's firm, doing as my father wished, then ...' She faltered. '... then there was the accident.

My sister Eve was paralysed and James, my brother, was killed. Everything changed.' She paused and swallowed hard. 'After the accident I simply couldn't follow my father's wishes. I couldn't step into James's shoes; it wouldn't have felt right. I couldn't comprehend the idea of doing the job that he'd done. It was all too painful. Besides, my father sold the company, went to York and took a position there within another firm.' Her voice drifted off; again her mind flashed back to the accident. She vividly remembered drifting in and out of consciousness. The pain that had soared through her and the memory of her brother's body, lying there.

Kate glanced around the room. She knew he'd be watching her mannerisms, watching how she handled herself under pressure. But it was easier to look around than at where William perched. He was still clasping his hands tightly together as though holding onto something for dear life. She waited for him to speak, but when he didn't she looked over to where Ben now sat, studying her every move.

'I'm sorry, I should have told the truth, you know, on the application form,' she said as she crossed her legs. 'It felt easier to omit the truth, than to try and explain. Yet here I am, trying to explain.' She felt stupid that Ben had so easily managed to find out so much about her.

'So, why did your father sell the law firm? Surely it would have been something to hang onto?' William suddenly asked.

The question had been fair but Kate struggled to answer. 'He ... he didn't want it any more.' She took in a breath and gritted her teeth. The last thing she wanted to do was to cry, not here, not today. 'He couldn't bear to drive these roads, or to walk into the office and to see James's desk empty. You see ...' She choked back the tears. '... James ... he ... he was his favourite, the only boy and my father didn't take losing him very well. He didn't even tell us about the sale. I was at the hospital a lot of the time, with my sister, and before we knew it, he'd sold everything and even though he only moved to York, it was far enough away for him not to have the daily memories that the company had given him.'

She looked around, battling her thoughts and was relieved when Gloria walked in with a tray of coffee and biscuits, carefully placing it on the desk next to where William still perched.

'There you go, I brought more coffee. Just give me a shout if you need anything else.' She glanced at where Kate sat. 'Now, don't you two go upsetting Kate. It's her first day and I quite like the idea of having another woman around the place.' She gave both Ben and William a stern look, before smiling at Kate and patting her on the shoulder. 'Be nice to her,' she said, before sweeping out of the room, allowing the door to slam shut behind her.

William picked up his mobile, checked the screen and then tossed it back on the desk. 'You'll be working with Ben for the first couple of weeks. I know you did surveillance work in the force, but you need to follow our way of doing things now. But, don't worry, you'll quickly learn the ropes. Ben will show you around the place, get you acquainted with the technology that we use and teach you as much as you need to know. The one thing we're strict on, Kate, is that we do things by the book. At Parker and Son we stay within the law. So, no breaking the rules.'

Kate looked him directly in the eye. 'Yes, sir. I'm pleased to hear that.'

'Good.' He looked at Ben. 'Maybe you could take Kate out with you on the next job. Let her show us what she can do and, Kate, my name is still William.' He smiled, but then stood up and Kate watched as he walked across the room, opened the door and once again, he smiled. 'I'll let Ben show you to your office. And Kate,' he paused and held out his hand to shake hers. 'Welcome to Parker and Son.'

Chapter Three

Kate stepped out of the bakery and into the daylight. It was uncharacteristically mild for the time of year and the heat of the sun warmed her face as she headed towards a small stone wall that stood near the church. She leaned against it and caught her breath. It was a shaded spot and she precariously balanced her mobile under her chin and phoned her twin, whilst attempting to take her chicken sandwich out of its paper bag.

The morning had gone so quickly. She'd sat with Ben, talking about surveillance, how they did it, what their parameters were and then, while Ben had responded to his many emails, she'd set to work, repositioning and organising her new desk and had taken great delight setting it up with items of stationery and a brand new laptop. The only annoying sound that had disturbed the past hour had been her stomach, which had growled continuously and, eventually, she'd excused herself for an early lunch.

'Hi, honey, how you doing today?' Kate asked as Eve answered her phone.

'I'm good, Kate. How are you?' Eve's tone was warm and just for a moment, Kate closed her eyes and listened to the loving sound of her voice.

'Well, other than missing you and Maxy, I'm fine.' Kate smiled and looked up the street, which was full of people, all going about their daily business. Some shopping, some couples all loved up, workers grabbing lunch.

Eve sighed. 'Do you really miss me, Kate?'

'Of course. I always miss you and Max. Give him a cuddle for me, oh, and one of those nice doggy treats that he loves.'

'Kate, if he had a treat every time you phoned, he'd be one

very fat Labrador, wouldn't you, Max? Come here, say hello to Kate and ask her if she'd like to come and visit us.' The sound of snuffles filled Kate's ear and she could imagine Eve sitting in her wheelchair, allowing the dog to lick the phone.

'I'm working today, Eve, remember, it's today that I started my new job.' She tried to sound excited in the hope that Eve would be excited too, even though she knew that by working she'd see less of her sister than before. A thought that neither of them liked.

'Oh yes, of course.' Eve sighed. 'We wondered why you hadn't called in earlier, didn't we, Max? How's it going?'

Kate took a small bite of the sandwich. She could hear the disappointment in Eve's voice and every instinct told her to drop everything and run to Eve's side, take Max, the black Labrador, out for a walk and ensure that Eve was okay. Just as she normally did.

'Look, Eve, do you need me to come? I could just about make it.' She looked up at the church clock, and quickly calculated that it would take her just under an hour to get there, nip Max out and get back. But she hesitated. If she did it this once, Eve would begin to expect it and she'd end up popping over every lunchtime, on a daily basis.

'No, don't be crazy. I'm fine.' Eve's voice trailed off and Kate wondered just how fine she really was.

'Has Zoe been in to see you today?' Zoe was Eve's carer. She called twice daily to ensure that Eve was washed, dressed and to make sure, Max, was walked.

'Yeah, of course she has. So, tell me all about it, how's the new job going?' Eve asked.

Kate sighed, and hoped that Eve wasn't sulking.

'Eve, it's really good,' Kate began. 'I'm loving it. The owner's a bit scary. He looks really strict, although I think he's more bark than bite. The lady, Gloria, who works in reception reminds me of Grandma, you'd love her, and then there's Ben ... He's amazing, Eve, he's the owner's son and a similar age to me. We get on really well already and get this ... we have to share an office. Well, to tell the truth, I'll be sharing with him and two others, but the other two guys are out most of the time, they work on surveillance.'

'What, four of you in one office?' Eve began to laugh. 'I can't see you enjoying that one, especially if the other three are messy. Do they have any idea you're a bit OCD?'

'Eve, I am not, I just like things to be clean and tidy, there is a difference.' She continued to nibble at the sandwich. 'There are two desks that are covered in heat circles, like the people who sit at them have never been introduced to a coaster. But, then there's Ben. His desk is tidy and it looks polished to within an inch of its life.'

'You like him, don't you?'

Kate stalled. 'What ... like who?'

'You like Ben, Kate, why else would you mention him repeatedly? Is he handsome, sexy, do you want to—'

'*Eve* ... enough.' She laughed. 'I don't want to anything. I'm with Rob.'

Eve groaned. 'Kate, you know I love you and I'm sorry to be so blunt, but I really wish you'd rethink the Rob situation. I mean, come on, what do you ever do together, you know, as a couple? In fact, do you actually get anything at all out of that relationship? Hey?' Eve paused and Kate could hear her fussing Max, giving her a few moments to think about what Eve had said. 'I know what Rob gets out of it,' Eve continued, 'he gets free board and lodging, an all-inclusive deal. That is, if and when he decides to come home.' The words struck a nerve. It was true. Rob did use the house as a hotel. Kate once again looked up at the clock and tried to ignore the truth in her sister's words.

'When Zoe came earlier, did she have time to walk Max?' Kate asked in an attempt to change the subject.

'Yes, of course she did and she'll be back later. Now, tell me more about you and Ben sharing this office.'

'There is no me and Ben.' Kate took another bite of the sandwich. 'Is Max okay? Did I hear him bark?'

'Yeah. He's okay. He's just run down the garden to terrorise next door's cat. Now, come on spill the beans. I can tell you like him, and to be honest, who'd blame you? Rob isn't very nice to you, Kate. And I'd hardly call him husband material, would you?'

'Wow, Eve, back off. What did Rob suddenly do wrong to you?'

'He's done nothing to me, but I love you, Kate, and I hate the way he treats you. Let's face it. Rob loves himself far more than he'll ever love anyone else. Ask him to leave, move on.'

Kate shook her head. To Eve, life was literally that simple. Before the accident she'd spent most of her evenings as one big opportunity to find another man. She used to have three different boyfriends at any one time. They'd come and go like buses, normally at Eve's request. If they were nice to her, they'd stay around for a week or two, but if not she wouldn't think twice before ending the relationship, and moving on. Kate smiled as she remembered the day that Eve had picked the house phone up to a guy saying, 'Hi, Eve, it's me …' which, of course, had sent Eve into a frenzy trying to guess who it was. After that, she'd always got her mum, James or Kate to answer the phone and find out who was calling.

'Eve, Rob loves me.' Kate tried to say it as convincingly as she could, but she still couldn't understand his sudden change in mood, the sleeping on the settee or the days and nights he spent away from home.

'Yeah, sure. Now … come on, humour a woman unable to get out much and dish the gossip. Just how *tidy* is this Ben?'

Kate laughed but didn't respond. She just thought about Ben. Everything about Ben was just a little more than tidy and it occurred to her that she wasn't just talking about his desk. 'He's tidy,' she finally said, before picking up her water and sipping from the bottle.

Kate nodded. She liked tidy.

'I knew it,' Eve said triumphantly. 'Lucky you, a new job and a tidy new man.' Kate could hear the despondency that had now crept into her voice. 'Kate, I've missed you today. I'd really love to see you.' Kate could tell she was brooding. 'Didn't we, Max? We missed Kate, didn't we?' The sound of Max whimpering broke Kate's heart. She'd bought him for Eve the year before. A black Labrador of a year old, who'd been unruly at first. But, Kate had friends in the right places and she'd happily paid one of her former colleagues, a police handler, to have Max expertly trained. And now, he could retrieve, go find the remote control, the telephone or even collect the newspaper from the specially designed post box.

'I know you do, hun, but I had to take a job. Firstly, I didn't want to starve and second, I really couldn't bear watching daytime television any longer.' Kate looked back across at Parker & Son, her mind drifting to Ben and what he'd be doing inside.

'What would I do without daytime television?' Eve said softly and Kate once again closed her eyes and thought of how boring and lonely Eve's daily life really must be.

'Okay, okay, I'll pop over after work. We can take Max for a walk together, but I can't stay long. I need to talk to Rob, you're right, things are not good.'

Eve's bungalow was on her way home, which meant that Kate could easily call in after work without going too far out of her way. Besides, she liked spending time with Eve, even though that meant she quite often neglected Rob. But Rob worked away and more often than not he didn't come home till late. He didn't really need her. Yet, he'd made it very clear that he didn't like Kate being at Eve's beck and call either.

Kate pushed the last of her sandwich into her mouth, took a gulp of the water, screwed up the paper bag, threw it in the bin and then turned to look up at the church clock.

'Okay, Eve, I've got to get back to work now or I could be employed and dismissed all in the same day. I'll see you later. Love you.'

Eve put the phone down and began to stroke Max. She was happy. She'd wanted Kate to come over and was really pleased that her plan had worked. She knew that she'd gently manipulated her sister, and almost hated herself for doing so, but sometimes she got so lonely and spending time with Kate always cheered her up. Kate would be here just after five and already Eve was hoping she'd stay until at least six or seven.

Maybe it was a twin thing, but Kate was the only one who understood her. She was the only person who knew what she had been through. She'd been there during and after the accident. She'd slept beside her at the hospital, refusing to leave, and had held her hand through all the indignity of being poked, prodded and jabbed by the doctors and nurses. The endless invasion of catheters, enemas and drugs had gone on for months. And each invasion had eventually taken away every inch of dignity that she'd previously had. She'd recoiled from all around her, from everyone except for Kate.

She remembered the weeks after James had died, the way that everyone had mourned him. Of course, at first everyone was sympathetic that she and Kate had been hurt, but they hadn't died, not like he had, they'd survived, so that was okay.

But both her life and Kate's, as they'd known it, had been

29

lost too and Eve knew that her life would never be the same again. She'd lost the ability to walk, yet no one really seemed to care, except Kate, who'd been continuously apologetic for not having been crippled too.

After a while it had become normal to act withdrawn. She'd enjoyed the attention that Kate had given and had continued to keep up the act long after her release from hospital. Besides, their relationship was better now, they were closer and it was different to how it had been as children.

She laughed, remembering the identical dresses that their mother would buy. The matching shoes, hair ribbons and toys. As toddlers and teenagers everyone had expected them to be identical. Do identical things and wear identical clothes. But they'd both rebelled and had gone out of their way not to wear or do anything remotely similar. They led very individual lives. They'd had their own friends, their own clothes and their own hobbies.

Kate had been the geeky one that had studied continuously. She'd read books and spent time with her equally geeky friends. She'd been the perfect student. The one that father had expected would go to law school. The one he'd expected to succeed and, in his eyes, the one, along with her brother, who would take over the family firm.

Eve hadn't cared. She'd been the wild child. She'd had no intention of becoming a lawyer. She'd worked hard as a beautician and she'd played hard at being wild, beautiful and free and the last thing she'd ever wanted was to become their father's pet. Oh no, she'd been more than happy for James to fill that role.

After the accident their father had become difficult. No one could speak to him and both he and their mother had treated Kate as though the accident had been her fault. Their son had been killed and both of their daughters scarred or injured for life, but in their eyes perhaps Kate had suffered the least, so she bore the brunt of their pain and sadness. And if she were honest, Eve had been pleased when her mother and father had moved to the other side of York. It had given both her and Kate some peace, without their constant invasion of looks and questions.

Eve stroked the black Labrador. 'Kate's coming later, Max. Are you excited she's coming?'

Chapter Four

Kate walked back into the office, and headed straight for the room she now shared with Ben. In her absence he'd moved the desks around and into a more uniform pattern. A filing cabinet now stood to the side of her desk and a bright pink chair stood behind it.

'Great, you're back. We have a client.' He pointed to a file.

'Really, that's excellent.' Kate felt her stomach churn; the thought of going on a job filled her with nerves and excitement all at once.

'We've watched this person of interest before,' he said as he flicked through the pages. 'Nothing came of it last time, and, to be honest, I'm not sure we'll turn anything up this time either. But it'll be a nice starting point for you.'

Kate sat and waited until Ben looked up from the file. He pulled out a picture and passed it to her. It was of a casually dressed man; he looked to be of a medium build and seemed fairly good-looking. Kate noticed that his eyebrows were neatly trimmed, as was his short black hair.

'This … this is our person of interest?' She moved in her seat. 'Okay.' Kate nodded. 'Who is he?' She fiddled mindlessly with the pens and pencils on her desk with one hand, while holding the picture in the other. 'I mean, do you want to fill me in on his story, especially if we're going to be following him?'

Ben laughed. 'Of course. This is Luca Bellandini. He's a librarian. Obviously Italian. His employer thinks he's up to something, and they're probably right.' His voice was calm, yet sounded bitter. 'Budget permitting, we keep him under surveillance and look for clues. They've suspected he's been up to something for a while and I've been spending time in the library on and off over the past few months. I sit there and pretend to read and watch what he does. I keep notes on everything, including what time he seems to take toilet breaks and who he speaks to. It's all in the file. Here.'

Kate flicked through the folder that Ben had passed her, before once again picking up the photograph. She held it up to the light. 'What on earth can he get up to in a library?'

Ben shook his head. 'You'd be amazed.'

'So, what do we do next? Do we just keep watching, or do we take a new approach?' Kate was genuinely interested; she couldn't work out what it was about the photograph, but something niggled her. He was just too familiar.

'What we do is go to the library tomorrow. Pretend to look up information, read and study. All we do is watch what he does. Under no circumstances do you do anything other than watch and make notes on how he behaves, who he talks to and how well he seems to know them. I'll be interested in comparing our notes at the end of the day, see what similarities we get.'

'Comparing notes. Won't we be together?'

Ben shook his head and picked up his coffee. 'Not all the time. I'll probably pitch my spot at the other side of the library. I might come over at some point and chat to you. But we'll act as though we've met in there by chance. If he goes out, just let him go. I don't want you following him, not yet, nor do I want you taking any risks. Surveillance has to be learnt. Even if you have done it before, you still need to learn how we do it.' Ben walked around the office and then sat back in his chair, making Kate wonder if he ever sat still for more than a moment or two.

'His boss says he's been acting suspiciously again. His mannerisms seem to have changed and he isn't as tolerant as normal, and they think he could be getting mixed up in the family business again.'

'The family?'

'The Bellandini family, they're notorious in these parts, always wheeling and dealing in something and always in and out of jail.'

'What do they mean by he's less tolerant?' Kate studied the picture again.

'Well, let's put it this way, his employer says he has a bit of a temper and the last time they saw his girlfriend, she was wearing really heavy make-up. Could have been covering bruises, if you know what I mean?' Ben cringed.

'He hit her?'

Ben shrugged. 'They don't know. Either he hit her or she'd walked into a very heavy door. To be honest, his many girlfriends are not their main concern, but the possibility that he might be dealing drugs in the library is.'

He tapped on the keyboard, read something that interested him on the screen and then looked back towards where Kate sat shaking her head.

'And you're happy to leave me alone with him, are you?'

Ben shook his head. 'Not really, but you'll only be alone for short periods, I won't be far away.'

'Good, because I'd probably kick his arse for being a woman beater.' She looked directly into Ben's eyes, which sparkled back at her, like shiny pieces of black onyx. They captivated her. Kate inhaled and caught her breath, before looking down and turning her face away.

'And that is exactly what you don't do.'

Kate glared. She knew he was right, but she couldn't bear the thought of a man hitting a woman. However, kicking Luca Bellandini's arse and blowing their cover would be the last thing she'd want to do. Even if he deserved it. 'Okay, tell me again, what do you want me to do?' She picked up a notepad and began scribbling across the page.

'It's easy. All you have to do is sit there. I'll be at the other end of the library, which means we'll get a visual from both ends of the building. All we'll be doing is observing him, nothing else. If he starts disappearing up the Home and Garden aisle on a regular basis, maybe you could walk past and look for a book, just don't do it every time, it'd become obvious what you were doing. Write down what you see. If he sits at the reception and eats wine gums, write that down too.' His voice was gentle and Kate watched him as he continued to sip his freshly made coffee. She saw his gaze fall upon her scar and she purposely turned her face away from his view. The scar was something no one spoke of, no one ever mentioned and yet she knew that Ben kept looking and she held her breath, knowing that at some point he'd mention it.

'Okay, spend this afternoon getting up to speed on the file and we'll start first thing in the morning, let's say 9.30 a.m. Be the easiest challenge you've ever had. It doesn't get any simpler.' He smiled, turned back to his laptop and began tapping on the keys.

Kate grinned. She knew she hadn't been employed to dust the desks, but going on an assignment on day two was more than she'd expected. She began to laugh nervously.

'Simple, you say.' She smirked. 'What happened to the training your father talked about, what happened to my bloody induction?' she teased and held her face square to his. 'And there was me, thinking that your dad was the scary one.'

Chapter Five

'You're here. I've made tea.' Eve smiled and held her arms out to hug Kate, before wheeling herself into the kitchen. 'I've also made a quiche,' she said as she pulled it from the oven. 'Freshly baked, I made it myself, and a salad to go with it.'

Kate held herself back, and fussed Max who sat patiently sniffing the air. She desperately wanted to rush forward and help her sister with the hot oven, but resisted and watched through half-closed eyes until the quiche was safely placed on a wooden board that had been positioned on a low table.

She breathed in appreciatively. 'Wow. That smells good. I'm starving.' She took a step towards the dining room and looked in to see that Eve had already laid the table with a salad, pretty napkins, and two plates.

'Here, do you want me to carry that?' she asked lurching forward, but then cursed as she saw the look on Eve's face. Kate drew in a deep breath. It broke her heart to see Eve in a wheelchair and every time she thought of that night, of their birthday, she kicked herself so hard for insisting that James drove them into town. If only they'd taken a taxi, or the bus, everything would have been so very different. But she'd wanted to arrive in style. The thought of catching a bus for the first time in years had been unthinkable. If only she hadn't been such a snob, Eve would not be confined to a wheelchair, James would still be alive and a lawyer in their father's firm and she ... what would she be doing? Would she still be in the police force? Would she have met Rob?

'I'm fine. I can manage, Kate. I just have to get myself organised.' Eve placed the quiche on a lap tray, balanced the bean bag base over her legs and wheeled herself into the dining room. 'After dinner, I'm going to do your nails for you. About time I got back into practise with the acrylics, it's been too long and you, my darling sister, are to be my guinea pig.'

Kate looked across and noticed the table that Eve had set up with an array of nail polishes, acrylic pots, brushes and a UV lamp. 'Oh, Eve. I can't stay long. I need to get home for a bath. It's been an odd day and I start a new assignment tomorrow.' She sat down at the table.

Eve looked disappointed and sighed. 'But it won't take long, I promise. I need to get back into practise, I'm thinking of setting a little salon up here. I thought I could convert the garage.'

It was obvious that Eve had been thinking about her future, which was a positive step in the right direction for her, so Kate relented. 'Okay, okay. Hey, Maxy.' The Labrador rested his chin on her knee and Kate stroked him gently, as a pair of huge sorrowful eyes stared up at her.

'See, Max wants you to stay.' Eve smirked and cut into the quiche.

Kate laughed. 'Of course he wants me to stay, don't you, Max? I always give you lovely treats, don't I? It's called cupboard love, isn't it?' Once again Kate fussed Max before pointing to his bed. 'Go on. Off you go while we eat.' Kate watched as he slunk off to the soft bean bag, where he rested his chin on the floor.

'So, what's all this about?' Kate pointed to the nail bar.

Eve's eyes pleaded with Kate's. 'I'm lonely, Kate. No one comes to visit any more, not since the accident.' She picked up the salad bowl and dished some onto her plate. 'All my friends used to come, at first. But now, well, they stay away. I don't think they know what to say to me. That's why I have to do something. I'm going to open the nail salon. It's one of my skills I can do sat down, then maybe, just maybe, my old customers and friends will start coming back.'

The accident had happened on their twenty-seventh birthday. She and Eve had been to their parents' for supper, but had organised a big celebration with friends in town later that evening. The evening meal had taken longer than usual, with their mother making a fuss. James had been wanting to get off to his girlfriend's, but Kate had begged him to wait, to give them a lift and to save them the expense of a taxi or the shame of going on the bus. He'd urged them to hurry so many times, but they'd taken clothes to change into and, as usual, had been fussing over their appearance, applying more make-up, and checking their hair, which in turn had made James even later for his date.

They'd only been in the car a few minutes, when the nightmare began. There was the screech of brakes, the sound of metal upon metal and then the spinning as the car had left the road, turning over and over to land in a water-filled ditch. Kate remembered the air bags that had covered all the windows like huge white clouds and a mist that blocked the light from outside, giving her a feeling of being hidden within. And then there had been the water, cold icy water that began to creep in through the doors.

She remembered the piercing scream that had left her brother's lips and the sobs that had come from Eve, before the mist had closed in and for a while she'd taken pleasure in the darkness, but another piercing scream had made her open her eyes.

She was on a grass verge, with Eve lying beside her. Eve looked grey and terrified, her eyes pleading for help, but the road was deserted. Kate remembered trying to sit up, to look for their saviour, for the person who must have pulled them from the car, but they were alone. Where was James? It was then that she looked down into the depths of the ditch; she could see the car and knew that James must still been inside and she scrambled down the verge to get to him. It was then that she saw him. Lying on his side, his pale, grey face below the surface of the water, and she'd known immediately that he was gone. Her brother was dead.

Another scream had brought her thoughts back to Eve. Her hands were in spasm and Kate was terrified that she was about to lose Eve too. She had leaned into the car, located her bag, which had escaped the water, and had grabbed at her phone to call for help.

Then, she'd scrambled back to where Eve lay on the grass. Confusion surrounded her. She clearly remembered being inside the car, so how had they got to be high up on the verge? Had she pulled Eve from the car? Or had someone else saved them?

It was only then, like a flash of lightning, that a severe pain tore through her, a pain that seared through the left side of her face like a scythe slashing its way through corn. Her hand lifted up to her chin. Blood poured from the wound. Fear and terror hit her. Her brother was dead, Eve was screaming, louder and louder, and a piercing noise that came from within her own body sounded like it had come from elsewhere and had lasted forever.

Then from nowhere, there had been sirens: ambulances, police and paramedics.

Bedlam had begun.

'Kate, do you want some salad?' Eve's voice brought her back to reality. She looked up, stared at her sister, then stood up and hugged her. A tear dropped down her cheek; no one knew how many times she'd prayed that it had been her instead of Eve and that, if she could, she'd happily take Eve's place. Was any of it really her fault? Had she dragged her out of the car, causing her injuries? Surely, she couldn't have, could she? But if not, how had they got out and why did her heart break every time she looked at Eve, or thought about James?

Chapter Six

Kate sank into her candlelit bath, held her hands up and admired her newly polished nails. Her whole body ached and the heat of the water soon began to relax her. It was already eight o'clock, and after two hours of being at Eve's, she'd crawled into the cottage, up the stairs and straight into the bathroom.

She loved the times when she had the cottage to herself. It was pure luxury and Kate found great pleasure in the peace and solitude. She had such poignant memories of her grandmother here and when Rob had rung to say he wouldn't be home till late, she'd been annoyed at first, but now she didn't care. Sipping a glass of Summer Red wine, she eased back against the bath pillow. The bath was huge, double ended and meant for two, meaning that it was far too big for one little person; she couldn't touch the bottom and she had to press her feet against each side of the bath to stop from slipping too far down and drowning.

Her eyes closed as Kate thought about her day. She loved working again, and loved being around Ben. They'd spent most of the day chatting, and talking about the different aspects of running the business side of investigating. The budgets, the cost per hour, and the continuous reportage. Ben had explained how he'd once been asked to trace a woman, had been told that she was in danger, only to find out in the nick of time that the man he was working for had been her former husband. She was of an ethnic background and he'd had every intention of killing her, as and when he found her. But Ben had realised the mistake and ever since, every aspect of a job had been thoroughly checked prior to taking it on. And even though she knew he'd only been doing his job, telling her all she needed to know and was only being friendly, trying to make her feel part of the team, she was sure he'd enjoyed his day too. For the first time in over a year, she felt vibrant and alive. She'd forgotten how it felt, but knew that it was a feeling that she wanted to continue.

'You okay, baby?' Kate jumped as Rob's voice broke into her dreams and thoughts. She'd dozed off and hadn't heard him come into the cottage, never mind the bathroom. Quickly she began moving the bubbles around trying to regain the warmth of the water that had now turned cold. A shiver travelled through her body.

'Mmmmm, I'm fine,' she replied sleepily. 'Just tired, it's been a really long day.'

Swallowing hard, she looked up at Rob. He was kneeling beside the bath. His huge dolphin-tattooed biceps were stretching the T-shirt material to bursting point and his dark eyes were sparkling in the candlelight. Kate stared into their depths. She loved him so much, but after the way he'd treated her that morning, he barely deserved it. She closed her eyes for a second and thought of how he used her. All she was to him was a housekeeper. The woman who continuously cleaned up after him, picked up after him and served his food. Why did she keep doing it? He was an adult and capable of doing it all for himself, but ... she shook her head. Was she grateful to him? Was she just happy that someone had taken on the girl with the ugly, scarred face?

Her stomach tightened in anticipation as she noticed Rob's eyes travel appreciatively up and down her naked body. Did she want him to touch her, and if he did, would he drop her unceremoniously, like he had earlier?

'Are you cold, baby? You look cold. Let's see if I can warm you up?' His voice came over husky and sexy as Kate felt his hand begin to sweep down the inside of her thigh.

'That's nice,' she managed to whisper as his lips came toward her. She wanted their relationship back to the way it used to be and found herself responding hungrily, and melting into the familiarity of his kiss. She knew every movement off by heart, every touch of his hand, every flick of his tongue. The past few days of uncertainty were forgotten, as she lifted herself up and onto her knees. She reached towards him impatiently and began tearing at his T-shirt, dragging it rapidly over his head.

'You like that, baby?'

He teased her with his tongue, and in one swift skilled movement he lifted her from the bath and laid her down on the bathroom floor.

'You know I do,' Kate moaned. Her hands moved over him, returning his touch, just as he'd taught her on so many occasions before.

His lips came down heavily towards hers, but quickly moved to her neck. His hands worked fervently and before she knew it, he'd pushed himself deep inside her.

Kate winced. But his mouth expertly fell upon her, and his hands pushed hers high above her head as she began to relax as his rhythm built. They moved from floor to bed; the lovemaking was turbulent, wild. Yet still, there was something missing.

Kate looked over to where Rob now slept with a natural rise and fall of his chest. His perfectly bronzed face looked happy and peaceful. But a tear dropped down her face. She'd thought his presence would make her happy, thought their lovemaking would make everything right, but instead of happy she felt an extraordinary emptiness. A void that she knew needed filling, but had no idea how to do it.

They'd just made love, but it hadn't been how it used to be and, if she were perfectly honest with herself, she knew it was more having sex than making love and wasn't sure that Rob was aware of the difference. In her heart she knew that the distance between them had just widened and she had no idea how she could ever bridge the gap. Or even if she wanted to.

Chapter Seven

If Kate had thought that watching daytime television had been boring, then maybe she should have tried sitting in a library for hours on end, watching Luca Bellandini, who stamped books and made polite conversation with small children and numerous women who all looked to be over the age of fifty.

He was currently seated behind the counter checking books that had been returned that morning. Basically, he was doing his job. Nothing suggested to Kate that he was doing anything wrong and from what she could tell, he hadn't even been in the bathroom for more than a few moments at a time.

She'd tried her best to look busy and had even dragged her old rucksack out of the loft and had filled it with her old pencil case, chocolate bars and cartons of juice. All her stationery was now laid out a little too neatly on the table before her. Her eyes glanced over the perfect line of products. To her, the rows were normal, but she knew that others thought it to be strange and she purposely made the decision to move the highlighter and ruler into skewed positions, and then stared at them, before quickly straightening the items back to where they'd previously been.

She'd taken her seat at 9.30 that morning and had looked around periodically, but still hadn't spotted Ben. Maybe he'd got to the library first, and sat himself in an alcove. The thought that he could be watching her while she was watching Luca Bellandini made her bristle with excitement and Kate shifted uncomfortably in her seat. She'd stared at the same page of the reference book for over an hour and peered over to where Luca Bellandini now stood, and had to make a conscious effort to turn the page over each and every time he looked in her direction, or make notes on her pad. It was all she could do to try and look relaxed, while deep inside, her stomach turned in circles.

A writers' group of six women walked in and sat at the table next to hers. They were all chatting about a new writers' scheme and who would be the next J K Rowling. One woman, a thin lady with short blonde hair, kept mentioning biscuits and another talked constantly about a new publishing deal that she may or may not have.

Kate listened in, hoping to learn something about what they did, and wondered how anyone ever managed to write a whole book. She smiled. Maybe one day she'd try and write, especially if this job didn't work out. After all, she knew all about the law; maybe she could write crime.

It couldn't be that hard, could it?

'Are you studying law?' The enquiring voice of Ben Parker came from behind her, making Kate catch her breath. She stared at her books. The sound of his voice made her begin to tremble inside and her eye began to twitch all by itself. She hadn't realised he was here. She'd thought that she was alone and she'd thought he'd keep a distance. It made her worry that she'd done something wrong.

He was supposed to be sitting at another table.

'Act naturally,' he whispered sitting down across from her. Ben opened his book and pretended to read. 'Do we have anything yet?' he said as he glanced over to where the six writers sat, all nudging each other and smiling simultaneously, as Ben removed his brown leather jacket making himself comfortable for what looked to be an extended stay.

'Not really, he doesn't seem to do anything wrong,' she whispered nervously. 'What are you doing here? Shouldn't you go over there somewhere, at the other side of the room?'

She indicated tables beyond the reception desk, and smiled, just as Luca Bellandini glanced across.

'Well ...' His lips were pursed and mischievous. '... the truth is; I was missing you. I just couldn't wait a moment longer before coming over here to see you.' He smiled as he picked up one of her pens and began scribbling notes down on a pad.

Her heart skipped a beat. He was far too charming for her liking. His mannerisms were effortless, sexy and compelling, and his eyes sparkled with mischief.

'You ... you're not serious?' she quizzed, wriggled in her seat and dropped her pen on the floor. Ben's presence made her nervous and she looked around to check how many people were watching their interaction.

'No, I'm not serious, Kate.' Ben looked into her face; she was so open, yet closed all at the same time and he liked the way she switched from feisty to naïve, without notice. He thought he'd met every kind of woman that there was, as over the past four years every one of his friends had introduced him to almost every available woman in Yorkshire, yet Kate was unique and none of the others were quite like her. He knew he'd unnerved her and tried to change the subject. 'Look, I thought you'd need to get some lunch, or a comfort break. I'll wait here and watch our person of interest until you get back.'

He looked over his shoulder and watched Luca as he rummaged under the desk, nodded to a young man and then disappeared to the other end of the library. To the end where he was supposed to be sitting.

He mentally kicked himself, stood up and stretched. Just long enough to see Bellandini take something from his pocket and place it down on a bookshelf, only for the other man to walk behind him and pick it up.

'Oh. Right, of course, I should have guessed.' She stumbled on her words and then paused as she looked around the room. 'Actually, I could use some food. It hadn't occurred to me how hungry I was until you mentioned it,' she rambled. Once again she felt as though she'd been dismissed and quickly packed her pens one at a time into their correct part of the rucksack, before adding the notepad into the back pocket.

Her stomach growled and she felt stupid. After all, she should have realised that Ben would watch Bellandini while she got lunch. Even though she'd worked undercover in the Met, it had all been very different. There you had a big team, lots of people to cover the job, but at Parker & Son there was just a few of them. All the work had to be shared and she really hadn't thought about how their daily routine would work. She laughed and thought of all the many episodes of *Magnum, P.I, Miss Marple* and *Poirot* that she'd watched, realising that it had never occurred to her that none of them had ever taken a bathroom break. Or had they?

Her eyes looked down at the book that Ben was reading.

'Your book,' she whispered, while laughing nervously, carefully pointing towards it. 'You might kind of want to turn it round. It's upside down.'

Kate picked up the rucksack, just as her mobile bleeped. She'd forgotten to silence it and quickly grabbed it from the bag. Rob's name appeared on the screen and she immediately read the message.

Don't wait up. Not sure when I'll be home.

Kate glared at the text. How dare he. She was angry with Rob and threw the phone back into her bag, making the writing group all turn around and stare.

'Sorry,' she whispered, realising how loud the noise must have been and how much attention she'd just drawn to herself.

But she was annoyed. There had been no 'good morning', no 'love you', and not even a kiss at the end of the message. He often worked late, she knew that. But up until a few months ago, he'd always made a point of speaking to her during the day and if he did have to send a text, it would be more than just a few words and he'd always put kisses at the end. She felt tears spring into her eyes.

'Hey, I know your private life is none of my business, but … well, are you okay?' Ben questioned in a soft whisper, his eyes never leaving the book that he continued to flick through.

Kate glared and grabbed at the rucksack. 'I'm fine and you're right, my private life is none of your damn business.' This was not the place to talk about it and right now she was far too angry with Rob to share her emotions with her intriguing, gorgeous, new colleague.

She closed her eyes for just a moment. It wasn't Ben's fault. 'Look, I'm sorry. I shouldn't have snapped. I'll go and get lunch.'

Chapter Eight

'Are you still here?' Kate smiled jokingly as she approached Ben. It was just after two o'clock and he was still sitting at the table, pretending to read his book.

'Of course I am. You could at least try and look pleased to see me. I thought it'd be a good idea to hang around and give you some support. Besides, what was it you wanted ... oh yes, a bloody induction,' Ben whispered, making Kate chuckle.

He turned on the smile. His whole face lit up and his eyes once again sparkled with mischief. Anyone watching would be convinced that he was flirting with her and Kate wondered if the circumstances had been different, would he have flirted with her for real or was it just a compelling act that he'd mastered perfectly?

She looked away.

Ben had already stacked some of his books up on the table and smiled hopefully in her direction, as Kate glanced over to where Bellandini sat before his computer, tapping away on the keyboard.

'Here, pretend to look at this book.' Ben moved the reference book around for her to look at as she took a seat. He stood up and sat beside her, whispering, 'He's been behind the counter for the majority of the time. He did, however, disappear for just over ten minutes. A room at the back of the library, at least three people went in and out of there during that time and I really want to know what he did in that room.'

Kate inhaled. Ben's deep musky scent overpowered her senses as she closed her eyes in a vain attempt to stop herself looking directly at him. Her bag dropped noisily from her knee and caught the table leg making Bellandini once again look up from behind his counter.

The writers' group seemed to have disappeared from the table beside them and in the time that they'd chatted, the whole room had practically emptied.

A rotund elderly female assistant had appeared in the library and now sat beside Bellandini, but, Kate noticed, they didn't appear to talk at all, which for colleagues she found odd. Their body language screamed at each other and they sat as far apart as they possibly could, and she quickly wrote the detail in her notebook.

So, what was Bellandini up to?

Kate looked back at Ben. He smiled at her and she took note that he really was a good-looking man, and with a great body too. Kate felt uncomfortable. She was staring and it suddenly occurred to her that she shouldn't be admiring her boss's son in that way, and she forced herself to make a conscious effort to appear engrossed in her books, while at the same time looking around the library in a desperate attempt to ignore her growing attraction to Ben.

An hour later Ben stood up, bid her goodbye and left.

Kate spent the next hour looking at a book she'd found on spinal injury. It covered most of Eve's problems, but a T4 Incomplete was different for Eve than most other sufferers. There were so many things that Eve could do that were described as impossible, and Kate found it difficult to understand why; her mind drifted.

The monotony of the day caught up with her.

'Have you finished with these?' The sound of Bellandini's Italian accent made her jump. He'd disturbed her thoughts and Kate saw his hand land on the pile of books that she'd already dug through.

'Yes, thank you,' she said politely. She'd hoped for the

whole day that he'd make conversation or do something that might incriminate himself, but now that he stood before her, she had no idea what to say to him.

'You're studying medicine?' he queried.

Kate watched him leaf through the books that were all piled up in size order. Large books at the bottom, smaller books to the top; a perfect tower, all perfectly stacked.

'Oh, err, yes, my sister, she has a spinal injury. I'd like to help her.' She stumbled over the words, wondering what to say next. 'She was in an accident, you see.'

'Have you tried *Spinal Cord Medicine* by ... Wait a minute.' He suddenly disappeared.

Bellandini returned with a large book. 'Ah yes, Vernon Lin. It's got loads of information about spinal problems in it, covers everything from surgical procedures to rehabilitation.' His Italian accent was strong and Kate enjoyed listening to the rhythmic tone.

He stood back and Kate suddenly felt guilty. She knew it was her job to spy, but Luca was nice. And she suddenly wondered what a drug dealer would really look like or how he would act. All he'd done all day was run around, clearing up after people and helping them. His knowledge of the library was extensive, which to her meant that he'd worked here for years, honing his craft.

'Thank you,' she said sincerely as she accepted the book from him and laid it on the table before her. 'I'm Kate,' she announced, holding her hand out toward him.

'Luca.' He shook her hand and smiled. 'Just shout if you need any more help. I'll be over there.' He pointed to the reception, smiled again and walked away.

The last hour passed quickly and Kate shuffled in her seat as the lights flashed on and off in the library. It was the normal signal to all in there that it was five thirty and that the library was about to close. Kate gathered up all her pens and pads, carefully putting the pens neatly into the rucksack where she'd kept them for the past four years. The pads were all closed and placed in size order.

If everything had a place, you always knew where to find it.

She took a final look at the book she'd been studying, before returning it to the reception desk. She then walked down to the foyer where the large coffee shop tempted her to sit down for a moment, buy a drink and sip at the liquid served in the Styrofoam cup. She hated the cups, they tainted the coffee with the taste of plastic, but the warmth of the drink was at least a little comforting.

She watched as people filed past her. They were leaving the building, going home for the night and she wanted to go too, but what was there to go home to? Rob wouldn't be there; he'd said so on the text. She finished her coffee and walked towards the door. The sky had turned dull and the air chilly. It was as though the weather was about to change and the rain would pour. But right now she had to call Ben and give him an update on the day. She grabbed her phone out of her rucksack, just as it began to ring.

'Darling, is that you?' The sound of her mother's voice cut deep, as her mind went into overdrive.

'Mother,' she cringed. 'Are you okay?'

Her mother only called when she wanted something. Kate always dreaded speaking to her on the phone, knowing that something nasty or cruel was about to be said. Her mother was practically the world record holder for backhanded compliments and even though she'd probably be mortified if she thought she'd offended anyone, the words seemed to fall out of her mouth at a constant rate.

'I'm fine, darling. Where are you?' The words and tone of her mother's voice hit her like a thunderbolt. Her mother asking where she was could only mean one thing. Kate sat on the stairs. She put her head in her hands and pulled frantically at her long auburn hair.

'I'm at work,' Kate responded. 'Where are you?'

'I'm outside your house, darling.'

Kate screamed silently. The cottage would be like a bomb site. Rob would have been home for lunch, there would be dirty dishes all over the kitchen, and he would have showered, used the toilet and changed out of numerous sets of sweaty jogging pants, leaving his dirty ones all over the floor. Not to mention the red wine stain that still marred her bedroom carpet.

Why? Why? Why was her mother standing outside River Cottage? Kate knew that she'd be checking how dirty the windowsills were. They were probably filthy and covered in dust that would have blown across from the fields. They certainly hadn't been cleaned for at least a week or two, which would give her mother a whole raft of ammunition to use against her.

'Mother, I'm working. I'm at the library in Bedale. I'm sure I mentioned my new job.' Kate made a huge attempt to sound calm and cheerful, as deep down she began to suck in deep breaths of air to stop her heart from pounding so quickly. It hammered in her chest in an attempt to escape as she stood up from the stairs and grabbed at the bannister.

'Darling, I've been standing outside this tiny little cottage for the last twenty minutes. I thought you'd be here.' The words were said in a cold, insulting and patronising tone. Kate's worst nightmare was true. Elizabeth Duggan was here, in Caldwick, outside her home, calling it 'tiny'.

Kate mentally worked out it would take ten, maybe fifteen minutes to get back to the cottage, if she hurried and left immediately. The roads should be quieter now as it was almost six o'clock.

One more deep breath and Kate looked back over her

shoulder and waved a goodbye to Luca Bellandini, who was just walking down the stairs and toward the door.

Her eyes closed involuntarily. If only her mother hadn't phoned. She'd have had a great opportunity to thank him for finding the book. But instead she had to watch Luca disappear out the door, while she rushed off to entertain her mother. Who was, no doubt, huffing and puffing with her finger hovering over the windowsills, which would have already been tutted at and now she'd be sneering at the hanging baskets or pulling the dead heads off the rhododendrons.

'Mother, had … had you said you were coming to visit?' she said as politely as she could, while racing toward her car at a million miles an hour. She was positive that her mother hadn't mentioned it. And she'd have definitely remembered an event so big and so very unbearable.

'Coooooey.' The voice of Mrs Winters came like a blessing from God and Kate heard a muffled sound as her mother momentarily put a hand over the phone, 'Isn't it Kate's mum? Oh, it's lovely to see you again. How are you, dear?'

Mrs Winters was Kate's eighty-five-year-old neighbour and the exchange of words told Kate that her mother was being hugged and hounded into her house for coffee and cake. No one ever emerged from Mrs Winters' within an hour; sometimes it took two before they escaped. This would give Kate ample time to get home and sort out the mess. She might even get time to wipe the windowsills in the hope that they hadn't already been finger swiped. But not before she stopped off at the village shop and bought some much needed wine that she would be desperate for later.

Chapter Nine

'You can't drink this one you know.' The shop assistant laughed as he held up the bottle of bleach. He punched the prices into the vintage till and put the bleach in the carrier bag, along with the two bottles of red wine that had been in Kate's basket.

'Well, no shit Sherlock,' Kate snapped, unsure if he'd been serious or joking. She was tired and grumpy. Mother was waiting and the 'I'm not coming home' text from Rob had been niggling in the back of her mind all day. She needed to phone Ben, it would have been expected that she'd update him on what had happened after he'd left. She glanced down at her watch.

Looking up at the cute shop assistant, she immediately felt sorry. She really shouldn't have snapped. She'd used this shop for years, and she felt a wave of embarrassment take over her as she noticed the look of shock and dismay on his face.

Kate watched as he looked back toward the cash register, hurriedly tapped in the last of her purchases and shuffled back and forth from one foot to the other behind his counter. He paused, looked up, pushed back his unkempt hair and hitched his glasses up higher on his nose. The black plastic rims were far too big for his narrow face and slipped down his nose again and again as he spoke. He reminded her of Clark Kent, with his glasses, dark hair and thick black eyebrows. He was a similar age to her, a little geeky, and she suspected that one good hair cut would leave him fresh faced and really quite gorgeous underneath.

'Look, I'm so very sorry. I didn't mean to snap. I'm having a really bad day.'

'No, no, it's me that should be sorry,' he said ironically,

looking down at a Sherlock Holmes book that was next to the till. 'I didn't mean anything by it. I was just trying to be amusing. You know, funny ha ha. It always tends to backfire with me.' He rambled on nervously without stopping. 'Some people can get away with it, you know, telling jokes, being funny, they always get everyone laughing, but I can't. People always take me the wrong way. I can't ever tell jokes. I always mess them up, or forget the punchline before I get there.' He stopped abruptly, realising that he'd spoken without taking a breath, and began to shuffle newspapers into neat and tidy piles.

'Okay, let's both be sorry! My day has been rubbish. Nothing's gone right, and now my mother has turned up to visit,' she tried to explain as she flicked open her black leather purse. The lack of cash meant that once again she had no choice but to pay with her already maxed out credit card.

'Are you reading that book?' She indicated the Sherlock Holmes novel as she pulled the card from her purse.

'Yes. I like mysteries. I read lots of crime fiction. I've joined a book club and this is the one they've chosen to read this time, although I must say, I've read it before, but for the sake of the group, I'm reading it again. I like to try and solve the mystery before the author reveals it.'

Kate smirked.

'The author always tries to lead you down a different trail, lets you think it's someone else. It always ends up being the person that's the most hidden in the words, and then they bring him or her out at the last minute. When you know what to look for, it becomes so obvious.' He smiled with pride.

Kate thought back to the Sherlock Holmes book that she'd read in English literature at least fifteen years before. It hadn't been her favourite subject and it occurred to her that she really hadn't been very good at literature back then, and she was positive that she wouldn't like it any better now.

'Wow, super sleuth,' Kate mocked and immediately wished she hadn't. She was supposedly well educated, but really did manage to open her mouth at the most inopportune moments. Once again she'd managed to offend the young man before her.

His defensive wall sprang up and he hitched up his glasses, took a handkerchief from his pocket and blew his nose. For the second time he rearranged the newspapers. He was obviously irritated and looked impatiently up and down as though waiting for another customer to enter the shop.

'I am so sorry,' Kate said as sincerely as she could. She looked down at her feet, waiting for a response that didn't come. 'I'm a private investigator,' she suddenly announced, in the hope that he'd be impressed. 'It's a new job and I started yesterday. You see, I love crime too.' She looked at him directly, hoping that he'd smile. When he didn't, she continued, 'Could I ask your name?'

He shook his head. 'You're not a very good investigator, are you?' he said quite firmly. He wagged his finger at her before turning away from her and tidying up the tins of beans. Each tin was faced forward. All in neat, tidy rows. Kate smiled in approval.

'You see, I know all about you.' He concentrated on the beans. 'You're Kate Duggan, you're twenty-eight and you live in River Cottage on Clover Lane. You live with your fiancé, who's never home, you don't have pets and you began working at Parker and Son yesterday morning,' he concluded as Kate stepped back.

'Oh my goodness. How do you know all of that?' she asked nervously, her hands twisting the handles of the carrier bag until one broke.

Handing her another carrier bag, he laughed with amusement and waited while she re-packed the shopping. The wine was placed in one bag, the bleach in another.

Kate shuffled nervously. How did he know so much about her? Could he have followed her, stalked her? Was he one of those people who'd have hundreds of secret photos of someone pinned all over their wall?

'That's easy,' he said with a laugh.

He'd obviously unnerved her and he liked it. She shouldn't have been so unkind to him in the first place. It was now his turn to be the clever one, the one with the answers.

'Well,' he began, 'you've just paid by card, and your name is on the card. It says here that you have your Sunday paper delivered to River Cottage on Clover Lane. You wear an engagement ring, but have only bought wine. You looked at the pet treats and smiled, but didn't buy any.' He paused and smiled. 'And you bumped into me in the corridor at Parker and Son yesterday morning. I opened the door to William's office for you. I work there too.' Again, he looked over his shoulder. 'And I work here to help my parents out, when Ben doesn't need me.' He smiled smugly.

It was Kate's turn to laugh now. He really was quite the detective, which in contrast to being a psycho stalker, was quite a relief. He'd also completely outsmarted her and she knew it.

'Of course, that was you? I thought you looked familiar, but didn't recognise you, and I'm so sorry. So, you're right, I'm not a very good investigator, am I?' She laughed again and sighed at the same time. 'I have a lot to learn and do you know what? You still didn't tell me your name.'

Kate watched as his hand went up to his chest, tapping on a large white plastic badge that hung from his shirt, the word 'Eric' clearly marked upon it.

Eric winked. 'It's true. You do still have a lot to learn. Don't you?'

Chapter Ten

Kate drove home to River Cottage, walked to the back of the house and let herself in.

It was half past six and she breathed in a deep sigh of relief that her mother wasn't standing on the drive. She must be still in Mrs Winters' house, with no chance of escape until she'd drunk at least three cups of tea.

Kate's stomach turned and her whole body began to tremble. The thought that her mother was in the house next door made her feel nauseous and she glanced around the house, summing up what needed to be done first, and began to tidy. As always, Rob had left the house in a mess after his lunchtime visit. Dirty dishes were quickly thrown in the dishwasher. The clothes that Rob had dropped all over the floor between showers were tossed in the washing machine and the bathroom was once again attacked with copious amounts of bleach and hot water.

Kate felt a shiver go through her, and she walked into the lounge. The April nights could turn chilly and she decided to light the wood-burning stove, along with the scented candles that surrounded the room. She closed her eyes to take in the aroma. The cottage had a warm and homely feel, so why did she feel so cold inside with dread? Why since the accident did spending time with her mother fill her with an overwhelming sense of anxiety that had never been there before? Kate shook her head. She was sure that her mother blamed her for the accident, but then again, why would that be a surprise? No one could blame her more than she did herself.

Kate walked up the stairs and into the bedroom where the wine had been spilled and stared at the carpet, wishing she'd called someone in to clean it. She sighed. There was nothing she could do about it now and she dragged a rug in from the second bedroom, tossing it over the stain.

'It'll have to do,' she announced to herself, 'because like it or not, she's here.' She knew that her time was up as she heard her mother's traditional three taps on the glass, followed by the sound of the back door opening and banging to a close.

Swallowing hard, Kate attempted to stay calm. Her stomach still turned and she checked herself in the mirror to ensure the foundation still covered her scar, before walking down the stairs to be met by the sight of the ever perfect Elizabeth Duggan, who had turned away and was rubbing a finger along the hallway shelf, checking for dust.

'Hello, Mother,' Kate said as sincerely as she could, but not before taking note of the huge suitcase that stood at Elizabeth Duggan's feet. Kate sighed. The suitcase could only mean one thing. She was staying and not only was she staying, but judging by the size of the case, she'd be staying for an awful long time.

'Kate, only fish walk around with their mouths open,' her mother said as she tapped her daughter under the chin. 'Now give your mother a hug.'

What Kate really wanted to do was correct her on the fact that fish would never walk but swim, but she decided against it knowing that the lecture that would follow really wouldn't be worth the trouble. Instead, she bit her tongue, hugged her mother and apologised.

'Sorry, Mother.'

'Now then, dear, let me look at you.'

Kate watched as her mother stood back, placed a hand on each of her hips and looked her up and down with a determined gaze.

'Katie, darling, you've had your hair cut,' her mother

stated as Kate waited for the insult that would follow. She felt herself being spun around while her mother took a better look. 'Never mind, darling, it will grow.'

There it was. The insult. If nothing else, her mother was very predictable.

Kate felt as though she'd been complimented, and then slapped in the face with a wet sock. She had no idea how her mother had the talent to say something that sounded like praise, only to turn it on its head and slap her sideways with the next comment.

'Coffee?' Kate asked as she walked into the kitchen. She suddenly felt the need to do something with her hands and clicked on the kettle before once again picking up the antibacterial spray and squirting it at the side.

'No, thank you, dear, I had a cup of herbal tea with Mrs Winters. I like to watch the calories you know.' She tapped her perfectly flat stomach as though proving a point before adding, 'You probably should start watching the calories too, Katie, dear. You may be slim now, but you are almost thirty and like it or not, the pounds will start to add up quickly.'

Elizabeth Duggan promptly turned around and walked around the house as though checking its suitability for her stay. Her nose was in the air as she swept her hand along all flat surfaces as she went, which included the top of the fridge freezer that stood in the space below the stairs. She walked into the living room and stopped at a sideboard, where a picture of James stood in an oak frame. 'There he is, my beautiful boy.' Her finger touched the picture and she stared at it for an eternity, before turning away and looking around the lounge.

'You've changed the carpet, darling,' she said after she'd inspected the room. 'I'm sure you had your reasons. Did it look nice in the shop?'

'Yes, it did, and what's more, Mother, it looks nice in my front bloody room too,' she growled. Her mother ignored her comment and walked back towards the suitcase that stood by the back door. Kate bit her lip and hoped for just one moment that her mother would pick it up, leave and go and stay anywhere other than River Cottage.

'Darling, get that no good boyfriend of yours to bring that up for me. I think I'll go up and take a shower. You know, freshen up before dinner.'

Kate slammed her fist down on the kitchen worktop as her mother turned and stamped up the stairs.

'Oh, and don't bother trying to cook tonight, dear. We'll go to that nice pub in Bedale. Give Eve a call, let her know I'm here and invite her to come out with us, will you?' She spoke with an air of authority and Kate shook her head in disbelief. She'd been brought up to respect her parents, to answer yes and no in all the right places. But sometimes she really felt the need to answer back. Tell her mother exactly what she thought of all the backhanded comments and the way that they seemed to reel off her tongue with ease.

Kate followed her, swiftly hauling the case up the stairs behind her. Rob had said he might not be home, which meant that if they waited for him, the suitcase could be standing at the bottom of the stairs for hours. Besides, her mother taking a shower was perfect. At least if she were upstairs, the comments would stop. She'd only been in the house for ten minutes and up to now she had insulted her hair, her figure, her carpet, her tiny cottage, her cooking and her boyfriend. Kate frowned as the case hit the top step. Not only did she need to speak to Ben and give him an update on the day, she needed speak to her father, form a plan and get her mother back to York ... fast.

Kate walked down to the kitchen and made herself coffee. No matter what her mother thought, she didn't need to lose weight and she added extra sugar to her mug just to prove a point. The aroma of coffee filled the small kitchen as Kate moved around flapping her arms up and down like a spoilt child hoping that the smell would drift up the stairs and into the bathroom, where her mother was probably examining the shower for its suitability before she used it.

Kate glanced up the stairs just as the shower burst into life and she used the opportunity to leave the cottage and walk back towards the shop. The two bottles of wine that stood on the kitchen worktop suddenly didn't seem nearly enough. She needed more and had a sudden urge to drink till unconsciousness, or at least until her mother had gone home.

Kate pulled her phone from her bag and flicked through her address book until she found Ben's number. She paused. She wanted to give him an update about the day, but most of all she just wanted to hear a friendly voice.

'Hi, it's Kate.' She kept walking towards the shop as she spoke. 'I ... I just thought I should let you know that Bellandini actually came over and spoke to me.' She heard Ben gasp.

'Did he really? Wow, that's great. Did he say anything, chat you up maybe or offer you drugs?'

Kate shook her head. 'No, don't be daft. He wouldn't advertise the drugs, would he? And why on earth would he chat me up?' She laughed, but her bottom lip began to tremble and she tried to pull as much air into her lungs as she could.

'Kate, he's a red-blooded male, and you, you're a gorgeous woman, why wouldn't he?' She could hear Ben walking from room to room, as doors slammed behind him.

Kate blushed at the compliment, but stayed silent.

'Kate, are you okay?'

Again, she nodded without speaking and stared at the

pavement on which she walked, carefully ensuring that as she stepped forward, her foot stood central on each slab and that she didn't step on the lines. It was something she'd done since childhood, something else she couldn't explain.

'Kate, answer me.' She could hear the panic in Ben's voice and wished she were sitting in the office, drinking coffee with him and Gloria, with people she'd only met the day before, but already thought of as friends.

'I ... I'm okay.' She sighed.

'Kate, you're not okay. I'm here if you need me. Do you want to tell me what's wrong? I mean, I fully understand if you tell me to mind my own business.' The sound of a laugh left his throat. 'Actually, isn't that exactly what you told me to do earlier?'

Kate laughed. 'Yeah, right. Sorry about that.' She paused; was it right to tell him her troubles? She turned the corner of the street and smiled at a man who walked past with his dog. 'Look, earlier, you were right. My fiancé, Rob, he's acting like a dick, and I could cope with that on its own, he's always a dick, but now my mother's turned up and by the look of the suitcase she just dragged in behind her, she's staying for weeks.' An involuntary sob left her throat. 'I think she blames me for my brother's death and, to be honest, if I were her, I'd blame me too. Most of the time she hates me and, if truth be told, after all that's happened, I'm not much fond of her either. The thought of her staying here, in my home, is unbearable.'

'Ah, I see. Well, I can't say that I've ever had that problem, but I understand that it must be difficult.'

Kate heard what sounded like Ben locking a door. 'Look, I'm sorry, you don't need to hear this. I'd best go. I ... I should probably phone my father. I need to persuade him to come and get her.' She pulled her long auburn hair over her shoulder, deliberately twisting it as she went.

Ben had gone quiet. He couldn't possibly understand. He had a caring and wonderful father, he probably had the perfect mother, the perfect family and the perfect wife. 'I'm sorry, I really shouldn't have said anything.' She held back the tears.

She heard Ben's car start up and the phone switch to hands free. 'Kate, you sound upset. Do you need me to come and get you? Where are you?'

Kate looked up to the sky. The clouds were swirling, all grey and moody. She was now around ten minutes' walk from home and felt sure it would rain. The thought of someone turning up to drive her home was appealing. She shook her head. 'No, Ben. Don't come.' She held onto a lamp post, closed her eyes and imagined those deep, dark eyes, the way they sparkled when they caught the light, how his mouth would turn up at one corner in a half smile, and the way the smile lines on his face said everything, without saying anything at all. 'But, Ben, thank you.' She opened her eyes and saw Eric coming out of the shop. 'I'll see you in the morning.' She pressed the red button without waiting for a response, and rushed towards the shop.

'Please don't say you're closed, Eric. I need wine. Lots of wine.'

Kate hid in the front room with the phone in her hand and whispered to her sister.

'Eve, she's practically moved in. Says she's going to stay here in Yorkshire until she sorts things out with Dad, which of course could take forever, because as always, he's away on business. Oh, and get this, apparently we're all going out for dinner. She's in the bedroom at the moment and I can hear the hairdryer, so I suspect that food could happen anytime between seven and nine. I'll phone you back with a time. It all depends on how long it takes her to look perfect again.' Kate had to think on her feet. 'Eve, what do I do? Things between me and Rob aren't right. She'd have a field day if she found out. Just think of all the backhanded comments she'd come out with then and she acted all strange when she looked at the picture of James, you know, the one on the sideboard.' Kate opened the door slightly and listened to make sure the hairdryer was still on. 'Eve, can she stay with you?'

Eve went silent.

It would be fair to say that Elizabeth Duggan had never been the most natural parent in the world and the thought of her staying for longer than an hour would be even more of a nightmare for her than it was for Kate.

It had been because of Elizabeth Duggan that Eve had first left home They'd never really got on and at just nineteen years old, she'd rented a small flat above the beautician shop in which she worked and then she'd bought a small terraced house in Caldwick. She'd bought one property after the other, renovating and selling each property in turn, with the help of one boyfriend after the other and, at one point, Kate had wondered if she'd asked for their capability as a plumber or electrician before she'd dated them.

But then their grandmother had died, she'd been left some money and had put a deposit on a large town house in York. It had been a house that Eve had loved. But then the accident had happened and Eve had been given two choices: she could buy the bungalow she now lived in, and agree to carers, or go back to live with their parents. Which would never happen.

Eve began to chortle. 'I've got an idea; you come here and stay with me. You could leave Mother there with Rob. They hate each other so much that when we call back in a few days, they'll have killed each other during a duel at dawn.'

* * *

It was true. Her mother and Rob did hate each other and Kate wasn't sure which one would kill the other first. She thought for a moment, allowing herself a sly smile. Maybe it wouldn't be such a bad idea. Besides, even though Eve was demanding at times, Kate loved staying with her. At least once a week they would have a girly night in, with DVDs, chocolate, popcorn and wine, not to mention the hair colouring and beauty nights that they'd happily add into the equation. But, of course, now their mother had arrived these nights would come to a halt, everything would be controlled and any thought of having any twin fun would be on hold until she took herself back to York.

'You will come out for dinner, Eve, won't you?' Kate asked, still wishing that she could simply sink into a bath and ignore the world. 'Please. I simply can't stand the thought of a night alone with her. What would we talk about?'

'Okay, I'll come, but under one condition,' she added quickly. 'She stays with you, Kate. After all, she's already moved into a bedroom at yours. It'd be silly and quite rude to move her out now, wouldn't it?'

Kate sighed. 'Fine, she can stay. But if she's still here at the weekend, she's coming to yours. Do we have a deal?'

Chapter Eleven

Eve put the phone down and then pulled herself out of her chair to stand, holding onto the worktop for support as she shuffled her way around the units. She had around an hour before Kate arrived and she slowly but surely managed to move her feet, inch by inch, until she stood before the bread mixture that she'd left next to the stove to rise.

Removing the cling film, she punched the dough down, before turning it out onto the worktop before her. She loved to stand up and knead bread. It was insignificant exercise for some, but for her, it was a full body work out that took all her energy to do. It reduced the aches and pains of sitting all day and replaced them with the different, but good, aches and pains of standing. She looked down at the wheelchair, knowing that she'd most probably always need it, but prayed for the day that she didn't.

She began to pummel the dough and found herself picking it up and throwing it down at the worktop at speed. But then, her legs suddenly gave way. She grabbed at the kitchen unit and breathed in deeply, as she looked around to where the chair stood. It was just a little too far away for her to reach and Eve allowed herself to drop to the floor, and then watched in horror as the bread dough dropped off the worktop and onto the floor beside her.

Eve squealed, which alerted Max, who bounced into the kitchen, looking undecided as to what he'd jump on first, her or the dough. Time on the floor meant playtime and Max ran to where Eve sat and licked at her face, fully intent on making the most of the unexpected fun and interaction.

'Oh, Max. What would I do without you?' She tickled him and watched as he playfully rolled on his back, while his head switched from side to side, and his tongue lolled out. For a moment, Eve stopped tickling, but a short, sharp bark brought her attention back to where Max patiently rolled. 'Oh, Maxy, Mother can't stay here, can she? You wouldn't like her staying here, spoiling our fun, would you?'

Eve dreaded the thought. If her mother stayed, she'd be sure to interfere. She'd find out that she could stand and would insist that she go for more physiotherapy sessions. But that wasn't the plan. Eve was determined to do things at her own speed. To her, every time she stood up was a miracle. Every time she took a single step, she held her breath – still unable to believe that she could stand at all. And before anyone found out, she had to be sure that she'd be able to walk without failure.

She sighed; the thought that her mother might leave Kate's and turn up to stay would have a dramatic effect on her daily routine. The exercises would have to stop and the muscle and stamina that had taken so long for her to build up would be gone.

Eve thought back to how independent she used to be and how easily she'd got used to the fuss that Kate had bestowed upon her. She hadn't minded Kate at all. She loved to be with her and had always loved being one of an identical pair. Even though deep down, their personalities had been totally opposite and, on most occasions, they'd done their best to look and act differently, people would always compare one twin directly to the other. Like peas in a pod, and she'd enjoyed watching their reaction as she and Kate had walked down the street. But then, suddenly in flash, she'd become different; her whole world had changed, her brother had died and she'd never be one part of an identical pair again. She cursed inwardly that she'd ended up in the wheelchair. She was now someone people looked down to, pitied and spoke over. She resented the chair and everything about it, and was determined that it wouldn't define her.

So why, when the sensations had returned in her feet, why had she made a decision to hide that fact from everyone? Over the past months, her legs had got a little stronger. She could at least stand now, even though little insignificant steps were all that she could manage and she knew deep down that Kate would be more than delighted. So why hadn't she told her?

Chapter Twelve

Kate and Eve sat in the corner of the Fox and Hounds and chatted aimlessly about anything and everything they could.

Not long after they'd arrived, Mother had begun chatting to an older lady who was sitting alone on the table next to theirs. Apparently she was also a member of the Women's Institute and both she and their mother had already begun to swap notes on everything from how to wrap gifts, to new recipes for cupcakes.

'How's Max?' Kate asked as she lovingly held onto Eve's hand. 'Has he caused you any trouble today?'

'Oh, he's fine. Zoe came and walked him earlier. He went over the quarry and rolled in fox poo, so he ended up with an impromptu hose down in the back garden, along with a dousing of tomato ketchup, which apparently gets rid of the smell.' She screwed up her nose and looked over Kate's shoulder to where their mother sat. 'What's Mum really doing here, Kate? Do you think she's fallen out with Dad again? I mean, it's not like she wanted to see us, is it? She's barely spoken to either of us all evening. In fact, I'd say she's done everything she can to avoid speaking to us at all.'

Kate shook her head. 'Oh, I don't know, sis, seems neither of us really exist since James died. It's as though she turns up and goes through the motions. Speaks to us when she has to. She uses my house as a hotel rather than yours purely because it used to be our grandmother's and she still feels that she has a right to be there, and, as you say, all of this happens when she falls out with Dad.'

Eve once again looked over Kate's shoulder and toward the crowd of people that stood around the bar.

'Who do you keep looking at?' Kate asked as she turned to look.

'There, the guy in the jeans. The one with the glasses. He's waved at me a couple of times. I'm suspecting he's someone that knows you. Albeit, if he does know you, I need to know who he is, he's really cute.'

Kate laughed as her eyes searched the crowd. 'Who?'

Being twins, they'd soon got used to people waving at them who they didn't know. It was a reaction they'd encountered their whole life, and normally meant that a friend of one had waved at the other twin or vice versa.

'The really cute guy.' Eve emphasised the word cute and waved back to the man. 'You are going to introduce me, Kate, aren't you?' Her face lit up with a smile.

Kate looked, just as Eric glanced over his shoulder. His eyes quickly went between her and Eve. And they both laughed at the confusion that crossed his face.

'Eric, we meet again.' Kate stood up to greet him as he walked tentatively towards her. It had only been a couple of hours since she'd been back to the shop to buy wine and now, once again he was here.

Eric pushed his glasses up his nose. 'Oh my word, I feel like I'm stalking you. Honestly, I'm not. I always come in here. I live alone you see. The food's normally quite good here and I don't really like to cook for myself and, if I'm honest, I don't like the telly either,' Eric rambled, then knocked back the remnants of his drink. 'I'll be off home now, you know, leave you to it.'

Kate sighed. It was a small town and this was the nearest pub to where they both lived. Besides, she noticed the way he seemed to be looking at Eve and she at him.

Both blushed.

'Eric, seriously, please sit down.' She indicated a chair at their table. 'I'd like you to meet my twin sister. Eric, this is Eve.'

Chapter Thirteen

Kate munched on her second packet of crisps as she walked from the car park and into the library. She was determined that she didn't need a diet, not at her age, no matter what her mother thought or how many times the night before she'd mentioned how many calories there were in a single plate of fish and chips.

Eve and Eric had chatted non-stop and Kate had excused herself early, leaving Mother to drive Eve home. The cottage had been peaceful when she'd arrived back. It was the one place in the world where she normally felt happy. The memories and the good times she'd shared there with her grandmother seeped out of every brick and Kate sank into her bed with a deep sigh, before drifting off into a long, peaceful sleep.

But morning had come around far too quickly and Kate once again found herself in the library, which was currently full of children. Each child wore a matching green jumper and grey trousers or skirt. A local school had obviously organised a trip to encourage them to read books and every child ran up and down the aisles, pulling one book off the shelf after the other, leaving discarded books all over the low tables or the floor. Bellandini, to his credit, smiled and picked them up, putting each one back in its correct position on the shelf.

It was now just before lunch and her mobile flashed for what seemed like the hundredth time and Kate wondered how long she'd get away with ignoring her own mother. Leaving her bags where she could see them, she walked into the foyer and pressed the answer key.

'Finally, Katie.' Her mother sighed. Her irritation clearly

came through in her voice. 'I've been trying to get hold of you all morning. It was quite rude of you to leave me to babysit your sister and her love life last night, and by the time I got back to the cottage, you'd disappeared off to bed.' Her mother paused but didn't slow down long enough for Kate to answer, give explanation or apologise. 'Your mousetraps, dear, where are they?' she demanded. 'I've found a dropping under the kitchen cupboard.'

Kate held the phone away from her ear and stared at the handset in disbelief.

'Mother, what the hell are you doing under my bloody kitchen units?' she snapped with annoyance as it occurred to her that not only had her mother had to get the kick boards off to look under there, she'd also have needed a screwdriver to remove them.

'Darling, I'm just cleaning and it's a good job I am. One dropping could lead to an infestation. There's no wonder Robert stays out most evenings, especially if you don't clean properly. Now, where are those mousetraps?'

'Mother!' Katie snapped. 'For goodness' sake. Why don't you bugger off and annoy Eve for a few days?'

Kate felt like a petulant child and pressed the off button on the phone. She really didn't want to argue with her mother. She didn't need to be accused of having mice and found her mother's constant insults just too difficult to live with.

It now occurred to her why, after university, she'd left Yorkshire in the first place. She'd happily moved her life to London to join the Met Police. If her grandmother hadn't taken ill and subsequently died, she'd probably still be there, and the accident might never have happened. She closed her eyes and wondered if she should phone her father. She'd resisted calling the night before in the hope that their mother would see sense and go home. But she was getting desperate and thought that if she asked nicely, maybe, just maybe he would come to Caldwick and take her mother home.

Kate went back to her table and glanced around the library. While she'd been on the phone, Bellandini had disappeared and so had the group of school children.

Chapter Fourteen

Ben knelt by the gravestone, carefully emptied the stale water from the flowerpot and walked the short distance to where the water tap hung from a pipe. Using a cloth, he cleaned the pot, filled it with fresh water and then carried it back to the grave, where his wife and unborn child both lay.

Julia Parker, taken too soon, along with her unborn child.

Ben wiped his eyes. 'I miss you so much.' He pulled the flowers from their carrier bag. 'I still find it so unbelievable that you're gone. I miss chatting to you, the way we'd talk about nothing and laugh about the ridiculous.' He paused and flicked at the cellophane that wrapped the flowers. 'I miss the silly things, like arguing about the right way to pronounce scone or bath, you in your southern way, me typically northern, and the way we'd laugh about it till we cried.'

He thought of his wife. She'd always wanted the best for them both, had created a home, a life with a child. Yet, in one day, the meningitis had overtaken her whole body and she'd been taken from him, along with the child he'd never had the privilege to hold.

He glanced up at the sky. Clouds had formed and between them he could see diamond shapes that gave the hope of sunshine, but then he felt the tiny raindrops that began to fall on his face. He closed his eyes and for the first time in years, he prayed.

He thought of Kate. Of how he enjoyed the time he'd spent with her. Was it wrong for him to laugh, to be happy or to enjoy time with another woman? He felt the guilt that he'd always felt since Julia had died, but somehow it didn't tear through his heart, not like it once had.

He'd spent the past four years throwing himself into his work. He'd left the police force, joined the family business and had sold his house. He couldn't bear to live in the home he'd shared with Julia. It had been the one where the nursery had been, all decorated, ready for their child. He thought back to Kate, to how she'd told him about her father selling the family business and how she hadn't felt able to take her brother's job, to sit in his seat or to even work in his office. He nodded. He knew how she felt. He turned his attention back to the grave.

'Hey, you'd think I'd get better at this.' He fiddled with the paper that packed the flowers. 'But I don't. I never know what I'm supposed to say. Except that I miss you. But I guess that'd be a bit obvious.' He searched around in the carrier bag by his side. 'And you'd kind of think I'd get better at remembering the stuff, you know, like the scissors.' He pulled the cellophane open and allowed the flowers to drop all over the grass. 'I forget everything when it comes to visiting, don't I?' He picked up a single flower and lifted it to his face. 'And do you know what's worse? I miss your nagging. I miss you telling me to get my shit in order and yeah, yeah, I miss you bossing me around.'

The flowers were placed one by one in the vase, then Ben stood up. He pulled a tissue from his pocket and blew his nose. 'That was the last thing I said to you wasn't it, stop nagging me, I'll do it.' A tear dropped down his cheek. 'God, Julia, I wish you were here to nag me now. I hate how torn I feel.' Ben walked away from the grave, placed the cellophane and carrier bag in the bin and then walked back to the gravestone.

'But that's the question, isn't it? How do I feel? It's what everyone asks and I have no idea what to tell them.' He paused. 'What I should say is that I'm suffocating inside, and sometimes there are days when I can't breathe at all. I

77

feel as though someone placed a vice on my heart and every so often, they squeeze it just a little bit more. That's what I should say, but, of course, I don't. I just say that I'm fine, which I'm not, but it's the British thing to do, isn't it?' Ben looked up, and then took in a shallow, stilted breath.

He glanced around the graveyard, at the other people, crouched by headstones. It was so peaceful, yet so disturbing all at once. Was this it? Was this all there was in the end?

'Julia. I feel sorry for saying this, but I need someone to be there for me. I need someone to boss me around, to tell me when I'm out of order and, yes, to tell me that they love me,' he whispered, as though fearful of saying the words out loud. 'Is it so wrong that I need this? Is it so wrong that I want to live again? Would you mind too much?' He gulped and lifted his fingers to his lips, kissed them and placed the fingers to the top of the stone.

'Take care of our baby, Julia. I loved you both so very much.'

Chapter Fifteen

Kate ran through the library, looking up and down each aisle as she went. The library had two floors and she wondered whether or not to take her search downstairs to where the literary section was, along with the coffee shop that openly encouraged people to read the books while enjoying lunch.

She took the stairs, two at a time. The coffee shop was busy and she quickly queued up at the counter and bought coffee in a Styrofoam cup, while glancing around. She walked across the shop, and took a seat near the window just a little too soon. If she'd waited and looked for a few more minutes, she'd have noticed that in one corner sat Luca Bellandini and with him the most beautiful woman that Kate had ever seen. And now she was sitting too far away to hear what they were saying.

Kate pulled the phone from her bag, cursed her mother for calling about mousetraps that she didn't need and began to text Ben.

Bellandini is in the coffee shop with a woman. She's beautiful and, for some reason, I think I recognise her. Kate x

To Kate's horror, she realised that she'd put a kiss at the end of her text and had pressed Send too quickly. She now watched the phone, wondering what Ben must have thought, and waited for him to reply.

Are you far enough away to speak to me? x

Kate smiled like a schoolgirl. Ben had put a kiss too and she wriggled in her chair, not knowing what to do. If she phoned Ben, would Bellandini hear her? The coffee shop was busy and Kate judged that at least twenty people sat between her and the person of interest. She picked up her phone and called Ben.

'Hey,' she whispered.

'Hey, to you too,' Ben replied. 'Okay. Let me do the talking. Stay where you are and just watch. You say you recognise her? Yes or no?'

'Yes, but—'

'Shhhhh ... don't say too much.'

Kate closed her eyes for a second, imagining Ben sitting at his desk talking to her.

'Without moving, do you think you could take a photograph without them seeing you?'

'Maybe.'

'Okay. Phone me back when you've done it.' The phone went silent and for a moment, Kate felt sad that the reassuring voice of Ben was gone. She turned her attention back to Bellandini and the woman, and even though she was looking longingly at him, their conversation seemed strained. She looked anxious and kept glancing around her, making Kate wary of using the camera. She had to wait, had to ensure she wouldn't be seen. She sipped at her coffee.

Kate watched. Bellandini and the woman were now deep in conversation. Kate flicked the phone screen to the camera and pretended to take a selfie. She looked down at the screen, only to realise she'd taken a perfect picture of the woman's very expensive Louboutin shoes, which stood out a mile against the cheap, torn brown leather brogues that Bellandini wore. She tutted at herself, and once again switched the camera on.

'Are you finished with that?' a waitress asked as she pointed to the coffee cup, making Kate jump. Kate shook her head in annoyance, before lifting the phone to her ear. This time she went through the scenario of pretending to be on the phone, while taking the picture. 'Got it,' she whispered as she looked back down at the phone, quickly clicking on the screen to send the picture to Ben.

Then Kate phoned him.

'Great picture, well done. Did they see you?' Ben asked. His voice had gone soft, and husky.

'Of course not,' Kate said, all the time watching Luca Bellandini, who gazed into the woman's eyes. He was obviously smitten with the woman's perfect face. He didn't look away. Not even when she reached into her bag, took out a small parcel and passed it to him under the table.

Kate fiddled with the phone, stood up and walked away from the table, just far enough to create a distance. She began to browse the books, glancing over at them to watch what was happening. 'I've seen her before, but I can't place her. It will come to me, no one is that sickeningly beautiful,' Kate whispered back to Ben who'd gone silent on the other end of the phone.

'I know who she is,' he announced. 'The woman you're looking at is Isobel Reed.'

Kate picked another book up and pretended to read the back cover. 'I know that name.' Her voice was still a faint whisper and she smiled, realising that even though Ben was back at the office, he was whispering too.

'She's the widow of a drug dealer who was shot on his own doorstep two years ago. Her face was all over the papers,' Ben explained, just as Bellandini stood up from the table and without a second look, walked away from the woman, leaving her to drink her coffee, alone.

Chapter Sixteen

'Okay, this is our next person of interest,' Ben said as Kate entered the reception of Parker & Son, where both he and Gloria sat. Kate noticed a photograph in his hand and held out hers to take it from him. 'She's called Isobel Reed and it appears that she's following in her husband's footsteps.'

Kate looked up and caught his eye. He held her gaze as his eyes searched hers and he gave her a smile. 'You okay?' he mouthed as Gloria got up to go back behind the reception.

Kate smiled, nodded and blushed at the same time. She thought back to the previous night's phone call, the way she'd wanted to hear his voice, yet now she wished she hadn't said quite so much.

He continued. 'Every law enforcement agency in the country has tried to catch her out since her husband was shot on his own doorstep. What's more, and I have the information in the file, there's a couple hundred grand' reward that goes to the first person to bring Isobel Reed and the gang to justice. And, thanks to you, Kate, we may just have found a way to earn it.' His eyes were fixed on her reaction.

'Isn't that a big reward for the police to cough up?' Kate looked back at the photograph, 'I've never heard of a reward that big.'

Ben shook his head, 'It's not the police. It's a private donor, clouded in mystery.'

'But, who the hell has money like that?' Kate questioned and looked at Ben for answers.

'Well.' He shrugged his shoulders, 'whoever it is has more money than sense and obviously has a huge reason to want them off the streets.'

Kate shook her head. 'Could it be anything to do with the husband getting killed? I think I remember the shooting.'

'It was on the local news, and that's probably where you've seen her before. She was on the front page of all the tabloids, you know, grieving widow and all that.'

Kate finally put the photograph down, removed her coat, and folded it in a neat pile, placing it carefully on top of her bag. She sat down next to Ben and once again, she picked up the picture. Isobel Reed was the most beautiful woman she'd ever seen, but Ben was right, she had seen her in the papers.

Ben pulled other pictures from a file and passed them to Kate. 'So, as far as we know, she's dealing drugs. I think you said that she passed something to Luca, so he's either taking them or dealing them, which explains why his boss is suspicious. People on drugs act differently, moody, and they lie. As far as Isobel is concerned, she's not the kind of dealer that stands on a street corner, oh no.' Ben shook his finger in the air and then pointed upward. 'Word has it that she's a high-class dealer. She's right at the top of the food chain, the one that brings them into the country and sells them directly to the dealers. Which again is probably what you saw her doing with Bellandini and why there's such a bounty on her head.' Ben caught Kate's eye.

'So how does she get them into the country?' Kate tried to focus and studied the photos.

Ben laughed. 'Well, if we knew that, we wouldn't have any reason to stake out her house for the next few days, would we?' His eyes sparkled with amusement. Kate knew that he was making fun of her and slapped his arm with the photographs, before turning to where Gloria stood behind reception, her normal mugs of coffee held out in her hand.

'So, what happens next?' Kate was eager to start. She'd worked on drug raids in the Met, had loved the adrenalin rush, the speed of the take and the way that the officers all knew exactly where the other would be at any one time.

'We sit, we watch and we do nothing unless we have some evidence. Once we get the evidence, we pass the information onto the police and at the same time, we collect the reward.'

Kate felt disappointed. 'What, no storming the house, searching or arrests?'

Ben shook his head. 'Sorry, we leave that to the authorities. We have no power to arrest them.' He raised his eyebrows as though looking for her approval.

'Okay, fine. The authorities get the arrest. So, until then, are we to work together, or am I watching the house alone?'

Ben sipped at his coffee. 'You won't be alone. I can't promise that it'll be me that's with you the whole time, but I will try to be there as much as possible.'

'Thank you,' she said gratefully as she leaned forward to take a thick blue file from his hand. She liked the thought of working with Ben, even though the idea of being locked in the back of a van with him for hours both scared her and excited her in equal quantities.

'You'll need to do some research.' He closed his eyes as though waiting for a bad dream to pass and Kate wondered what was going through his mind. 'I had her followed this time last year,' he continued, 'but we couldn't prove anything substantial. She appears to be a serial adulteress as well as a drug dealer. I think the two have gone hand in hand and it was quite apparent that the Louboutin shoes were not being bought from her widow's pension. But other than that, we found nothing.'

'She's so young to be a widow. Did they ever find out who shot him?' Her hand accidently brushed against Ben's leg, sending electric shocks up her arm.

'It was a deal that had probably gone wrong. Nothing was ever proven, the killer never caught.' Ben got up and began to dig in a filing cabinet. 'I have a file on his death in here somewhere.'

Kate stood too and looked over his shoulder into the filing cabinet. The files looked neat, tidy and in order. She approved.

'Ah, here it is,' Ben said as he pulled the file out and placed it on the reception desk before both Kate and Gloria. 'Take this into our office and start looking through it. I'll be back in a bit. I have things to do.'

Kate spun round on her heel as Ben walked toward the door. 'But, wait, where are you going?' Kate noticed his smile and backtracked. 'Not that it really matters. I mean, it doesn't matter at all,' she rambled, 'I just wondered if it was something to do with the case, you know, so I'd know what to do, next time.'

Kate saw the amusement in Ben's face. 'Well, first, I was going to the bathroom. You can observe if you like, but I doubt you'd really want to. But after that, I have to go to the bank, and pay in the wages.' He shook his head and pulled a face.

Kate was still blushing when she sat down at her desk. The file was huge, at least a hundred pages, and she quickly realised that some of the notes went back for more than two years. Kate had been engrossed in the pages for over an hour when the door opened.

'The drug they believe she sold was MCAT, just like her husband. It's got many names and you need to know them all and what they look like,' Ben said as he rushed in and back out of their office, making Kate look up from the file. 'Give me a shout when you're done. I'll be out back dressing the van.'

Kate worked on the case for the rest of the day. The file had been read and the photographs collated. She'd pinned selections of photographs to a dry wipe board and by the time she'd finished, Kate knew where Isobel's hairdresser was, her beautician and her gynaecologist. She'd studied MCAT on the internet and had found numerous forums giving her other names that it was known as; Mephedrone and meow meow were the two most common. She knew what it looked like and that dealers tended to sell the drug to teenagers under the idea of it being a 'legal high', but the side effects were dangerous and the drug was highly addictive.

There was a knock at the door and Gloria walked in, coffee in one hand, sandwich in the other. 'Here, I thought you'd need this. You haven't moved all day.' She looked up at the evidence board that Kate had created. There were perfectly positioned photographs, all laminated, and typed sheets of information, again all in rows down one side of the board. 'Gosh, you have been busy.'

'It's what I used to do in the force. They always gave me the job of organising the evidence board, knowing that my OCD would ensure that it was all in nice neat rows.'

Gloria walked over to the board and tapped one of the pictures. 'Is this what they sell?' The photograph showed two types of drug: one a small coloured tablet, the other an ampule of fluid with a syringe by its side.

Kate nodded. 'It is. They sell it in two forms. Dependent on who is buying. It can cause fits, hallucinations and panic attacks,' she said as Gloria studied her board. 'It's also a type of anaesthetic. Did you know Ketamine can actually stop you from breathing?'

'Where do the kids get the money, that's what I would like to know,' Gloria said, shaking her head as she turned to where Kate sat reading the information that she brought up on the computer screen.

'They're selling the tablet form really cheap; just a few quid would get them some. Most kids have access to that sort of money these days, by way of pocket money.' Kate tapped on the keyboard. 'Look,' she pointed to the screen.

'Closely related to amphetamines, like speed and ecstasy,' Gloria read out loud. 'It's renowned for being a dirty drug; it can be mixed with just about anything.' She shook her head. 'What does that mean?'

'It means that the kids don't even know what they are taking. We had a case in the Met where the drugs were mixed with both soap powder and rat poison. Kids were dropping like flies. It's disgusting.'

'One unnecessary death is one too many,' Ben snapped as he walked into the office. 'People have no idea how death of the young affects others.' The words were just a little too personal and Kate wondered who Ben had lost and looked towards Gloria, hoping for answers. But Gloria had looked away.

'Right,' he said as he dropped a small box on the desk. 'Let's move on.'

Kate noticed Gloria dab at her eyes before excusing herself, leaving the office to return to the sanctuary of her reception.

'Van keys, there are three sets to the vans that you'll find out the back. Each van comes back here at night where they are then dressed and ready for the next day.'

'What do you mean dressed?' Kate pouted as she picked up each set of keys one by one and placed them in a row on the desk.

'We need to be inconspicuous.' He walked over to the window. 'Out there are the vans.' He pointed into the yard at the back. 'We have various sizes and various signs. All are magnetic and easy to fix to the side. One day it could be dressed as a plumber's van with ladders and plastic piping on the roof. Another day it could be TV licensing and another it could be double glazing or window cleaning. We park in different places daily and the surveillance team stay in the back. The driver takes you to the site and then gets out of the cab and walks away. It kind of gives the appearance that they've left for the day.'

'Ah, okay. They did this in the Met, but I didn't really have anything to do with it. We were the legs on the street, so to speak.' She paused. 'Just a thought, if they are working vans, wouldn't they park on people's drives?'

'Not necessarily, lots of workmen park on roads so as not to block drives. Sometimes, they even park and get into other vans, especially if they're going into town to work. Saves them paying double for parking.'

'Next you're going to tell me that there's a toilet, bed, kitchen and sofa in the back.' Kate was joking but the look on Ben's face told her that she may actually find that at least some of her list would be found in each van. Her mind went into overdrive and she had the urge to run down to the yard, look inside each van and check the cleanliness of any potential toilets.

'There's also camera equipment in there. It's simple to use. Just point and shoot. Shall we go down and take a look?'

Chapter Seventeen

Kate sat in the back of the van with Ben. Most of it was filled with computers and screens, a couple of chairs and a curtained area in the far corner. She'd been watching him pick up and show her one object after the other for the past two hours. There was one transmitter that sent out a signal, and a receiver where the signal came back to. Everything she looked at was new to her, and she did her best to study each piece of equipment. But even with detailed explanations on how and when she should use each item, she doubted that she'd ever remember what she'd been told and made notes in a small book, all in code language that only she'd understand, just in case it ever got lost or landed in the wrong hands.

A dry wipe board was attached to the back door of the van and Ben drew a map on it. 'These are the areas where you'll be parked. Either here, or here.' He drew two crosses on the map of the road. 'I'll get Patrick to position the van carefully. No one should suspect that the van is anything more than a tradesman doing a job. There's video surveillance fitted in the grill of the van, in the back of the wing mirrors and in the back door. Always check who is near the back door through the cameras before opening it. No one gets in unless you know them. If you need to get out for any reason, use common sense, maybe wear a high-vis jacket, or a hard hat. Make yourself look like a plumber, a builder or a TV licensing inspector.' He looked her up and down. 'And, above all else, do not put yourself in danger. Understood?'

'Yes, sir. Understood.' She turned and once again studied the map. 'Won't you be with me?' Kate's bottom lip began to tremble. She knew that all she was really doing was sitting in the back of a van and waiting to get the right pictures, but she feared the new technology and desperately hoped that Ben would be with her.

'Sorry, not tomorrow, I have an appointment in London. I can't miss it.' Ben placed a hand on her shoulder and stared deep into her eyes. He saw her doubts, her confusion and her fear. 'You'll be fine. I'm sending Don out with you, he's a good guy. You'll like him. Patrick will be driving and he'll come back for you, either when you call for a pick up, or at a time discussed prior to the drop off. You'll never be on surveillance for longer than five or six hours. If you get a problem, call. Patrick won't ever be far away and will be back with you within minutes.'

'But, I don't know Patrick or Don.'

'Kate, I'm sorry. I can't be there.' His voice was stern and he immediately regretted it. He knew it was daunting to begin a new job and he knew he'd promised Kate that he'd train her, look after her and show her the ropes, but he couldn't miss the appointment. The meeting with a marketing team. It had been planned for weeks and if the marketing and adverts were well placed, who knew how much more work they'd bring in through the door. Besides, his father was breathing down his neck, insisting he do more promoting of the business, more sales and Parker & Son needed the revenue if they were to grow during the next year. It had been a job he'd been putting off. Julia had been working on a marketing campaign before her death. Posters, adverts, and a new website. But that was four years ago and he knew that if he were to ever honour her memory, it was time to move on, time to pick up the reins and time to turn her work into something for the future. Ben sighed. Just thinking of Julia hurt, and the thought of seeing her posters and adverts again played on his mind, especially today, the anniversary of her loss.

'Ben, are you okay?'

Ben's eyes were fixed on the dials; his face showed signs of distress and Kate wondered what was going through his mind.

'Yeah, I'm fine.' But Kate could tell that 'fine' was far from how he was really feeling. There was either something about this case that was bothering him or something more personal that was going through his mind.

'Are you sure?'

'I said I'm fine,' he snapped, closed his eyes and turned away.

Kate sat back in her chair, held her breath and waited until Ben spoke again.

'So shall I go over the camera functions again?' Ben eventually asked, changing the subject. He picked up the camera and flicked on two separate switches. A panel with over thirty buttons was fixed into a board behind the driver's seat, each one having a different use or purpose.

Half an hour later Kate finally felt that she had a grasp of the equipment.

'It's amazing, I knew these kind of vans existed, but I never had any idea just how much went on in one.' She indicated the van as she climbed out and inspected it from the outside.

Ben laughed. 'Luckily it does look like a normal van, and it's probably a good thing that Joe public doesn't have a clue what technology we really have.'

Kate smirked. 'We really are spies, aren't we?'

Ben locked the van. 'Of course we are, this is what gaining intelligence means. This is spying, it's what we do, albeit as my father said, it's important that we always stay within the law.'

Kate laughed nervously.

'And this,' he said, handing her a mobile phone and charger, 'it looks like a normal phone. Keep it charged and keep it with you.'

'What do you mean by looks like?' Kate asked as she turned the phone over and over in her hand.

'Have a play with it sometime. It has some interesting apps and features. Most importantly, it has an emergency code which Gloria will give you and if you ever need assistance fast, key it in. We will be able to find you really quickly, as the tracking device would tell us exactly where you are. All our operatives have one. Now, go on. Get off home. Tomorrow is going to be a long day. Be here for seven o'clock. That way you'll have the van parked before anyone else is around.' He rocked backwards and forwards, from one foot to the other. It was obvious that he had something on his mind. 'And Kate, be careful,' he finally said. 'I'll see if Eric's available too. I'll give him a call, get him to come and help you.'

Kate walked to the front of the building, where her trusty yellow Beetle was parked, and climbed in.

She looked at her watch; her dreaded mother would be waiting and after the earlier phone call about the mousetrap, she knew that she'd have to go home and face her. Unless of course, her putting the phone down on her had sent her into a spin, and maybe, just maybe, she'd get home and Mother would have gone to Eve's, just as she'd suggested – or even better, back to York and her father.

'Kate?' Ben shouted, just as she was about to drive off.

'Yes,' she answered, carefully lowering her window to look up at him. He looked tired and washed out. The day had obviously taken its toll and he stood looking down at the ground. His crisp white shirt was undone at the collar, his tie had long since been abandoned and his hands dug deep down in his trouser pockets.

'I ... I owe you an apology,' he blurted out as he looked up and toward her car. She could see pain in his gaze and Kate wondered what she should do. She knew he was hurting, but didn't know why. If this was a girlfriend of hers she'd be offering her a hug. But Ben was not a girl or a close friend, he was her colleague. There was a difference and she had no idea how to handle a situation like this.

'What are you apologising for?' She turned off the engine and climbed out of the car.

'Earlier. I shouldn't have snapped at you.'

'Listen, it's fine. You must have had a reason.' She paused and wondered what to do next.

'It's hard to explain.' He finally looked at her. 'I lost my wife, she died.' Again he paused. 'It was four years ago ... four years ago today ... meningitis.' He looked down and appeared to be studying his shoes. 'She was pregnant ... I lost them both.'

Kate's mind exploded. She'd known something was wrong, known that something had been on his mind, and it had occurred to her that Ben had lost someone, but had had no idea that it was something as huge or as life changing as this.

'Oh my goodness.' She felt awkward and searched her mind for all the platitudes she'd been given after her brother had died, but knew how useless they were.

'Look, do you ... do you want to go get a drink?' she asked. It was all she could think to say. Kate found herself also looking at the ground. She was nervous of his answer and had no idea why she'd suggested it, except that she really didn't want to go home and he didn't look like he wanted to go home either. Besides, Ben looked as though he needed both a drink and a friend, and not for the first time that week, she needed both too.

Kate looked up and into Ben's eyes. They sparkled back at her, full of tears that wouldn't fall. A gentle smile crossed his lips and gone was the anger and frustration from earlier. In its place was a tired, but peaceful expression.

'Do you know what? I could murder a drink. Where would you like to go?' Ben said as he held out an arm, indicating that she should lead the way.

Kate thought for a moment. 'Well, we could drive all the way into Richmond, there are great cocktail bars there, but then, we could always pop into Vino's.' She pointed to the wine bar next door and laughed. 'Think it's a bit closer, don't you agree?'

Chapter Eighteen

Kate led the way into Vino's. It was beautifully decorated in a traditional style, with the lively hustle and bustle of a town centre bar. It was still early, yet couples sat in small booths that lined one side of the room, while others stood at the bar clinking glasses as they enjoyed the end of another working day. Candles flickered with a luminosity that gave the whole bar a genuine feeling of warmth. Kate led the way through the crowd. She looked back to where Ben followed; he caught her eye and smiled.

A fair-haired waiter spotted Ben, obviously recognising him and he immediately ushered them away from the crowd and into a private booth near the back of the bar. He passed a wine list to Ben, but Ben shook his head. 'Bottle of Rioja, please, the nice oaky one that you do,' he said as he held an arm out to Kate. 'Rioja, is that okay with you?' he asked, indicating that she should take a seat. Ben stayed standing up and began emptying his pockets of his phone, keys and wallet, which were all dropped in a heap onto the table, before returning his attention to Kate, who nodded at the thought of a good wine.

'So, how are you enjoying being at Parker and Son's?'

Before she could answer the waiter returned with a bottle and two glasses. 'Do you want to taste the wine, sir?' he asked.

'No, I'm sure it will be fine. Thank you.' Ben took the wine from the waiter, and checked the label.

'Well,' Kate said, answering his question. 'On my first day I was a little scared of the boss. But now, I'm more scared of his son.'

Ben smiled. 'Scary, am I?' He poured the wine and passed her a glass.

'Thank you.' She lifted her glass to tap against his, lifted it to her lips and drank a huge slurp of the wine. 'That is so good and so very needed tonight.' It was delicious. 'I hope my car is safe where I'm parked, as this is too good to just have the one glass.' She looked to Ben for reassurance. 'I'll get a taxi.'

Ben nodded and flashed an appreciative, dazzling smile. Kate caught her breath. For some strange reason she felt more alive than she had for months, and she sat back, allowing Ben to refill her glass.

As the evening began to draw in, the soft candlelight created an even warmer ambience within the room. The conversation was effortless. The self-assured confidence that Ben had shown in the office had now disappeared. He now came over as very gentle, calm and just a little vulnerable, making Kate feel comfortable and relaxed. She sipped at the wine, allowing it to trickle down her throat with a warmth that only came with a good red. She held the glass with one hand, whilst using the other to hide the left side of her face from Ben's view.

'Don't let it define you,' Ben suddenly said as he lifted his hand to hers and pulled it slowly away from her face.

'But it's ugly.' Kate immediately lifted her hand back to cover her scar and in response Ben shook his head.

'Don't do that. You don't need to hide it, it isn't ugly.' He took hold of her hand, and once again pulled it away from her face. Her fingertips were on fire, pins and needles rushed through them and she simply stared at their conjoined hands and enjoyed the warmth that now spread from her fingertips to her arm, moving upward with the intensity of an erupting volcano. Kate gasped.

Ben released her hand. 'I'm so sorry.' It was as though he'd suddenly realised what he was doing, making Kate lift her hand away. She massaged her fingers with the other hand as though trying to take away the burn.

'The scar, the accident and everything else that happened that day, it was the worst day of my life.' Her hand once again lifted to her face. It was as though if she hid it, it wasn't there. 'I feel so guilty. I think it was all my fault. My brother, James, he died and poor Eve, she'll be in a wheelchair for the rest of her life.'

'Who says it was your fault?'

Kate sighed. 'No one. I just know they all blame me. You see, it was me that insisted James drove us, I insisted that he take us into town, even though I knew he'd be rushing. He was late you see; he was going on a date. Yet still, I insisted. And Eve, I think I pulled her from the car, moving her was what would have paralysed her.'

'What do you mean, you think?'

'I don't remember. I remember the crash, the airbags and then I think I must have blocked the next few moments out. I really can't remember anything until I was on the grass, with Eve. But no one else was there, so it must have been me. I must have pulled her out of the car and if I did, why didn't I get James out too?'

'You couldn't have possibly known what would happen, Kate.'

'My parents, they've never said as much, but if I were them, I'd blame me.' She paused. 'My father doesn't say much, but my mother, she's just acted odd and been awful to be around since the accident, and right now, she's staying at my house. She and Father will have argued, and because my cottage used to belong to her mother, my grandmother, she sees it as her right to turn up and stay whenever she likes.' Kate closed her eyes and thought of her mother who would now be stomping up and down the kitchen, waiting for her to arrive. 'What if she never went home? I'd be distraught if that happened. I couldn't bear it.'

'Kate, you wouldn't be you without your history. You

can't turn back time. God only knows that if you could, you would have done it by now.' He once again picked up her hand. 'But, Kate, there is a time when it becomes harder to stay in the past than to move forward. Trust me. I know.'

Kate raised her eyebrows. He was talking about his wife, about her death and about that of his child and for a moment she wondered what his wife had been like.

'One day everything is normal,' he continued, 'then the next day, everything changes in a heartbeat, everything you know has gone or has changed and there's nothing you can do about it.'

Kate was all too aware that what he was saying was true. His eyes once again sparkled with tears and Kate knew that he was hurting inside, but also realised that he wouldn't allow the tears to fall.

'Could I ask you a really personal question?' Ben asked.

'Of course,' Kate answered just a little too quickly. Placing her wine back down on the table she looked down and away from Ben's eyes. She could sense that Ben was thinking before speaking. This could only mean that he wasn't sure of the question he was about to ask. His hand gripped tightly onto hers, sending sparks flying up her fingers.

'Kate, do you love your boyfriend?'

'W-w-why would you ask that?' Kate was shocked.

Ben stared into her eyes. 'Do you?'

Kate thought of the day that Rob had come into her life. A chance meeting at the hospital after a visit with Eve. Rob's car had been parked next to hers in the car park. He'd been so charming, so caring and she'd felt an excitement that she hadn't felt since before the accident. But then he'd changed and she had no idea why. She stared into space. The question should have been an easy one to answer, so why couldn't she? Kate stared at the table and just to prove to herself that all was not bad, she tried to come up with a recent good time. There had to be something he'd done or said that would have made her happy.

She looked up at Ben, and a tear slipped down her face.

'Kate, you are unhappy. I saw the way you reacted in the library, when he sent you that text. You deserve more.'

Kate stared at their hands. They were still held together. His thumb gently moved back and forth over hers in a slow rhythmic movement.

Ben was right. She did deserve more. But who would want her? Who would ever fancy her, looking like this? She wiped away her tears; there was no point in crying, not any more.

'How about you, Ben?' she asked. 'Don't you deserve more?'

Ben released her hand. He picked up his drink and sipped at the wine, then held a hand up to the waiter, who promptly delivered another bottle of red to the table.

'I know I need to move on, Kate. I loved my wife, so much. We were having a baby. We were going to be a family and then suddenly, it was all gone. It's taken me four years to realise that she isn't coming back.' He leaned back in his chair, his hands now clasped tightly around his glass, and Kate wondered if he'd continue.

'I know you said it was meningitis. But … what happened?' she finally asked.

'I don't know. I'd been working away and when I got home, she was there, on the floor. I rang the ambulance, but it was all too late. One day we were happy, we were looking forward to being a family, and the next, everything changed, my whole world ended and I was left alone, with nothing.'

'I don't know what to say,' Kate said sadly. She picked up the bottle of wine and began to refill the glasses. She needed something to concentrate on other than Ben's shaking voice and hands. The volcanic sparkle in his eyes had turned to a deep and profound sadness.

'Don't say anything. You're the first person other than my immediate family that I've spoken to about it for years. If I'm honest, it's a bit of a relief to say it out loud.' He looked into the depths of his glass.

'Does this place serve food? I'm sure they do and I'm starving,' Kate said, changing the subject. 'Let me find that waiter.'

'It's eight o'clock,' someone shouted across the bar. The words made Kate look at her watch. She knew that her mother would be waiting and stamping her feet all around the cottage, ready to throw her another insult the moment she walked through the door. But she'd been so happy, chatting to Ben, they'd both been laughing about nothing in particular and, for just a few hours, their problems had been pushed to one side. The wine had flowed, the food had been served and Ben had continued to hold her hand.

'Look, I'm so sorry, I really have to go. I guess I have to face my mother, that's if she didn't bugger off to Eve's like I told her to,' she said as she stood up abruptly and began to dig in her bag for some money.

Ben shook his head and placed his hand over hers. 'Don't, it's on me.'

Kate looked up and into his eyes, 'Oh, okay. I'll see you in the morning then and … thank you.'

'Actually, I'll get you a taxi.' Ben jumped to his feet, but it was Kate's turn to shake her head.

'It's fine. There's a taxi rank just up the road. I'll tell them to send you the bill.' She laughed, winked, grabbed her bag and began to walk away.

'Seven o'clock in the morning. Don't be late.' Ben tapped his watch face.

Kate turned as she reached the door. Through the crowd she could see Ben was still standing, watching her leave; his imploring eyes had followed her out. It was then that she realised that he needed her friendship and company so much more than her mother did.

A split second later she found herself sitting back at the table with Ben, indicating to the barman for another bottle of wine.

'I thought you had to go?'

'Well,' Kate replied, 'I do, but I have a choice. I could go home, face Mother and be in trouble for being late. Or I could stay here with you for another hour and still get in trouble for being late. So, I choose to stay here.' She paused. 'That's if you want me to?'

She knew she was testing the water. Knew she was treading on dangerous ground. But Ben flashed her a smile, and poured the wine. Which told her everything she needed to know.

Chapter Nineteen

Isobel fastened her diamond belcher chain and gazed over her appearance in the tall full-length mirror. She wore a long white dress with inlaid diamante jewels that dropped into a deep cowl to reveal her flawless, bare back.

'Are you ready for your guests, my darling?' Giancarlo asked as he moved behind her, seductively and repeatedly kissing the back of her neck. His six-foot frame towered over her petite body as she slowly turned, allowing her lips to meet his.

'Absolutely. I love dinner parties,' she replied, giggling playfully as she picked up her bracelet and held it out to him. 'Would you fasten this for me, Giancarlo, my love?'

'Of course I will. Now, who is attending tonight?' His voice was strong and his accent held a soft Italian note. Isobel breathed in deeply; his aftershave was subtle but rich. It was the smell of money, a scent that she particularly liked.

'Oh, the usual suspects will be here: Roberto, Colin, Martin, Simon and Jason, Luca and your lovely wife, Elena. That makes nine of us in total.' Isobel turned to preen at herself in the mirror. 'I'm still never sure why Elena always comes. You know I like to be the centre of attention?' She pouted as she spoke in the hope that Giancarlo would notice.

'Well, my darling, because it balances the room. You wouldn't want to be the only woman, would you? Besides, Elena is jealous of you. Inviting her hopefully allays any suspicions she may have and it makes her happy.' His hands rested on her shoulders and she felt the firm squeeze of his fingers.

'Maybe I should take another lover then, you know, to balance my side of the room.' Isobel liked Giancarlo's company, but since her husband's death, and unbeknown to Giancarlo, she'd been known to enjoy the company of many men. She got a thrill from the chase, of seeing how many men she could lure, but the chase had become boring. She needed a new game, a new challenge and she thought about Roberto. She'd already seduced Giancarlo's nephew, Luca, but he was too easy, a puppy dog with an insatiable attitude to please. His other nephew, Roberto, he was new blood. And if she wished, she knew that she could use him to make Giancarlo jealous. She looked over her shoulder to where he stood, and saw the anger in his face.

'My dear, you will take another lover at your peril.' He turned and walked towards the bed. 'No one touches what is mine, you know that. Not without paying dearly.'

Isobel sighed. Why shouldn't she have some fun? He had Elena to go home to, who did she have? Her life over the past two years had been hell and she didn't see why she should be the only one to suffer. Her own marriage had been ruined, her husband killed on their own doorstep and now she was determined to have some fun.

She thought through her options. She'd make her intentions known early and steal Roberto away from the dinner on the pretence of showing him her new gym; the equipment had arrived a few days before and still sparkled with a newness that she knew Roberto would love.

She looked across at Giancarlo. She'd loved him so much, she'd given him her heart, but he didn't seem to love her back. If he did, he'd have left Elena by now, but every night he went home to her, and much to her disapproval, Giancarlo always brought her to the dinner parties. Isobel knew that it was time for her to move on, but worried about what Giancarlo had meant by 'at her peril'. Surely he wouldn't do anything? Not when he pushed Elena in her face every day. Maybe being with another man in front of him would teach him a lesson. Besides, she'd been intending to seduce Roberto for the past year, whether Giancarlo liked it or not.

Was it time to end it? To start again? After all, why keep the relationship going? Why didn't she take up with Roberto or Luca on a more permanent basis? Or was she staying for the drug money? Selling the drugs was the only thing that still kept her near to Giancarlo. But did she want to still be near him? That was the question. She didn't take the drugs herself, she didn't need the income, not anymore, so why not leave this life completely? Find herself a good man, with a real job? She nodded to herself, knowing that it would be the right thing to do. After all, drugs had been such a huge part of her life. Her husband had been a dealer, and Giancarlo his boss. From the first moment they'd met, Giancarlo had immediately chased her. He'd made his intentions known. But she'd been a faithful wife, madly in love with her husband, and it had only been after Scott's sudden death that she'd allowed Giancarlo to finally seduce her.

Giancarlo stretched out on the bed. Isobel watched as he lay against the pillow, lifting his hands behind his head, his eyes looking her up and down in a possessive and demanding way. He was a businessman, a man who always got his own way and Isobel had often wondered how far he'd really go. Word had it that he really did kill to get what he wanted and she considered the fact that he could have been responsible for Scott's death. Could he have wanted her enough to remove his only competition? And if he'd done that to Scott, would he do it again?

She flashed a smile at Giancarlo. For now she had to keep him sweet and as she walked towards him, she slipped off her diamante shoes and locked the door. Her bare feet sank luxuriously into the plush cream carpet as she walked toward him lifting her dress, and with a wiggle of her fingers, she allowed her underwear to drop unceremoniously to the floor. She knew the response that Giancarlo would give and he didn't disappoint. He grabbed her hand and pulled her roughly down and onto the bed.

'Shush, the caterers are downstairs. They'll hear.'

Giancarlo laughed. 'The caterers are staff, Isobel. They're paid staff.' He paused, his lips travelling down her neck. 'You can do what you like in your own bedroom, can't you?' Again, his voice was strong and demanding and not for the first time that day, Isobel melted into his arms.

Chapter Twenty

Darkness outside had dropped and Isobel paraded herself up and down the dining room, her hand constantly touching and rearranging. Table centres and candlesticks had to be central, equally spaced and the silver cutlery had to be perfectly polished. A speck of dust caught her eye on a side plate and she wafted it away with her finger and tutted.

'Waiter, the plates. These are dirty, besides I prefer the ones with the gold edge. Change them for me.' She spoke with authority and watched as a young waiter scurried around the room, collecting side plates and removing them from the table.

'And tell that girl, the young one, to come and check the cutlery. I've already repositioned three knives. I shouldn't have to, that's why I pay you.' She walked over to the antique sideboard, picked up a decanter and poured a large brandy into a crystal glass. 'My guests will be here in ten minutes, people, you need to hurry. Is the soup ready?'

'Yes, madam, it's all ready to go.' A shout came through from the next room and Isobel pulled a face.

'Then it's ready too early. Make sure it doesn't split.' She once again tutted and walked out of the room and into the hallway where she paced up and down, waiting for the men. They were always prompt, always wearing dinner suits and always ready to do business, which was why she entertained them. Their purchases would make her money and, above everything else, she liked to be rich.

'Ah, there you are, my darlings,' she said as she opened the door to Simon, Jason and Martin. 'Did you all travel together? How very sensible. Simon, you look amazing, I love the waistcoat, is it new?' She kissed each of them on the cheek, and then stepped back, allowing them to enter in turn. 'We have champagne and canapes in the library,' she said as another two cars pulled into the driveway. 'If you'd like to go through, I'll join you in a moment.'

The guests all stood around the library chatting and drinking champagne. The soft lighting complemented the carved oak bookcases, which stretched from floor to ceiling, full of books that Isobel had never read. This room had been Scott's, a room where he'd come to do business, and had been the room where he'd been sitting just moments before answering the door to his death.

'Why is he late?' Giancarlo whispered to Isobel. He stood, beautifully dressed in his tuxedo, with glass in hand, and Elena by his side.

Isobel once again counted the guests. There was still one to arrive. She once again checked her watch, and noted that Roberto was already ten minutes late. 'I have no idea, he's normally so punctual.' A waiter appeared at the door; he looked worried and beckoned to Isobel, who reluctantly left Giancarlo's side and walked across to where the waiter stood.

'What is it?'

'It's the soup, Mrs Reed. I'm so sorry but if we don't serve it soon, it'll split and Chef is pacing around in the kitchen with steam coming out of his ears. He said for me to say that if you don't go to the dining room soon, he'd be having to make a new one.' It was obvious that the young waiter had been sent to relay the message, like a lamb to the slaughter. He didn't know quite what to say and for a moment Isobel felt sorry for him. His whole body trembled with fear of what she'd say next. She thought for a moment before speaking.

'Tell Chef that we'll be seated immediately.' She smiled

apologetically at the waiter and then turned back to the library.

'Gentlemen and Elena, would you care to follow me to the dining room. It appears that the soup will wait for no man, not even for Roberto.'

A grumbling went around the room. 'We should wait,' Martin said as he stepped forward, placing his glass on a silver tray. 'I'm not happy about eating and doing business, not until he gets here.' He paused and looked at his watch. 'Something must be wrong. What if he's been arrested, what if he's talked, or called the police?'

'We could all be sitting ducks,' Colin added.

'Hold your nerve. He wouldn't rat us out,' Giancarlo said confidently. 'He's my nephew, he knows how this family runs.'

'Do you think he would?' Luca asked nervously, moving to glance out of the window at the driveway. 'You know, rat us out? He wouldn't, would he?'

Simon stood up. 'Well I, for one, don't like it. The rule is, we are all prompt. That way, we know we are all safe.' He paused and looked apologetically at Isobel. 'Forgive me, Isobel, but I'm not waiting for the police to turn up. It's time I left.' He pulled on the lapels of his tux and walked towards the door.

Suddenly there was the sound of a gunshot. Plaster and wood chippings dropped down from the ceiling. Both women screamed and everyone, even the toughest of the men, ducked down to the floor. All except Giancarlo, who stood with a gun in his hand that pointed upwards. A large hole had now appeared in the ornate coving and dust fell like snowflakes.

'Giancarlo, for God's sake, my ceiling,' Isobel screamed.

'Shut up. I'll repair it. Now, the lady said that we should take our places at the table,' he growled. 'Would anyone else like to object?'

Chapter Twenty-One

Kate wriggled on the small camp chair. She looked at the monitors, and even though it was daylight, Don's six-foot frame filled every spare millimetre of space and the inside of the van still felt dark.

He was squashed into an equally small camp chair.

'You okay?' he asked as he lifted his hand up to the dial, pressed a number of buttons and then gripped his stomach. 'Thai curry last night. Could have been a bit on the spicy side.'

Kate wished that the window could be opened. The fresh air would be welcomed by her head, which still pounded from the night before and she now wished that she'd stopped drinking after the first bottle of wine.

'I'm fine,' she replied, but continued to take in deep breaths in the hope that her oxygen-filled lungs would somehow help the feeling of nausea that took over her mind. Turning her attention back to the surveillance screen, she watched as the odd bird or two flew into the frame. It had been the same monotony ever since Patrick had driven them to their position, climbed out of the driver's seat and walked off. Her legs and bottom had gone numb, not to mention her bladder that now screamed out to go to the toilet.

'What do we do about toilet breaks?' she asked, hopeful that Patrick would come and relieve her.

Don pointed to the corner where a curtain hung from a rail. 'Behind there. Ben had the curtain put up for you. Thought you'd want a bit of privacy.' He chuckled. 'Think I might need to use it myself in a bit.'

Kate recoiled. She couldn't bear the thought of going to the toilet in the corner of a van. Especially behind a limp curtain that hung from the roof on what looked like a less than secure rail. She wasn't sure which was worse, going to the toilet herself or the thought that Don might go and she'd have to listen.

They'd begun the stake out at Honeysuckle House at eight o'clock, yet it was still before noon and the lack of anything to watch on the monitors had given her far too many opportunities to drink juice and think about the night before. She and Ben had sat chatting effortlessly for hours, while sipping wine in the candlelight. They'd laughed, joked and shared far too much information that only a bottle of wine or three could help release. Her head pounded and her eyes grew heavy. Going out on a work night was definitely not the right thing to do and she made a mental note not to do it too often.

Her mind then drifted back to Rob.

Once again he hadn't come home until after midnight, giving her mother ample ammunition to throw at her over breakfast. Not to mention the snide, cutting comments about her own night out and the single mouse dropping that her mother had found, which instantly meant that her home was a health hazard.

'It's a wonder the cottage isn't totally infested,' she'd said as she'd chewed on her toast. 'You really need to clean once in a while, Katie dear, there's no excuse. If you don't have time, make time. But then again if you go to the pub every night after work drinking wine, there's really no wonder that you don't have time to clean, dear, is there?'

'Mother, give it a rest. I've been to the bar once for God's sake. I've only worked there for three bloody days. It's hardly a habit.'

'Well, I've never been spoken to so badly in my life,' her mother had thrown back at her as she'd stamped up the stairs, making Kate feel guilty for snapping. She normally tried not to retaliate where her mother was concerned, but the constant jibes made it difficult to stay quiet. She knew that her house was perfectly clean. She also knew that no one else other than her mother would turn up and pull the kick boards off the cupboards to check behind them. And what's more, she seriously doubted that there were any mouse droppings at all. It was probably just her mother trying to be significant. It was something she'd done on a regular basis since James had died. Besides, Kate knew that she was completely over the top when it came to cleaning and she sure as hell wasn't going to chastise herself for not pulling the kick boards off more often.

Her attention shifted back to Isobel's home, Honeysuckle House, and she longed to go for a walk, look around and see for herself what kind of house Isobel Reed really lived in. She still hadn't emerged, which wasn't surprising as it had begun pouring down with rain and by the looks of the dark, grey clouds in the sky, it wasn't going to stop any time soon.

'Don, I'm going to go and have a look around,' Kate said as she stood up and turned towards the back doors of the van.

'But what if you're seen?'

'Don, I've done this before. I do know what I'm doing. I'm going to walk around, try and see if anything is happening. Give Patrick a call and get him to come back. There's a lane round the back of the house. Meet me there in twenty minutes with the van.'

Don once again looked as though he was grabbing at his growling stomach.

Ben had said she could leave the van so long as she was dressed appropriately, and she grabbed a hi-vis vest and rucksack, before jumping out of the back doors. She stretched her aching legs and was pleased to get the opportunity to do something other than sit in a small chair.

She looked around the street and took notice of the houses that stood along the road. They looked different from the sepia picture she'd been used to watching on the surveillance screen.

All the houses were exclusive, all stood on the edge of the National Park, and all were totally individual. Each house was worth at least a million and had long tree-lined drives. Each property had between six and eight bedrooms and would have hallways bigger than most people's front room. It was hard to believe that these houses were less than a couple of miles from Caldwick, where her own cottage stood.

'Why would anyone want to sell drugs if they lived here?' Kate mumbled to herself as she admired the property. 'Or, here's a thought, are the drugs the reason they get to live in a house like this?'

The rain had slowed down to an annoying drizzle. Kate pulled the hood up on her jacket and began to walk casually along the street, clipboard in hand.

Honeysuckle House was not the biggest in Ugathwaite, but it was by no means the smallest either. It stood back impressively in its own grounds. Huge oak and cherry trees stood close to the building giving the upstairs dormer windows a degree of privacy. Albeit very nice for the occupants to have the privacy they wanted, it didn't help a private investigator who wanted to spy on their every movement. An extension branched out from the rear of the house with glass doors all along its length. It looked like the pool house but without getting closer, Kate couldn't be sure.

Kate edged her way around the property. She needed to get a better look at the house. There were so many bushes and trees she could easily keep herself from being seen. Ben had told her that the village name of Ugathwaite was the Viking word for Owl Meadow. Kate looked up into the vast copse of trees and could easily imagine why the area would have been given this name.

A silver Mercedes with blacked out windows drove past her. It pulled up on the drive of Honeysuckle House and Kate quickly took off her hi-vis vest and hid it in her rucksack. She didn't want to be seen. She crouched behind a bush to get a better look as the driver climbed out and walked toward the door. Taking out her mini binoculars, she watched as a huge bald-headed man dressed in a tight leather jacket and jeans stood banging at the door. His jacket almost burst at the seams as his muscles made a desperate attempt to escape from the restrictive leather. He pulled a mobile from his pocket and she could see that his hands and fingers were covered in tattoos. He made a call, but received no answer and walked around the back of the house pushing the mobile into a pocket as he went. Putting the binoculars down, Kate took out her mobile and clicked a couple of pictures, hoping that one of them would catch his face and give them an identity.

Looking down at the phone she flicked through the pictures 'Stupid,' she said out loud; both pictures had caught a perfect image of the back of his head. She needed to get closer, and she began sneaking along the edge of the bushes that lined the drive. She peered toward the house in an attempt to get a better view. She thought back to the surveillance cameras on the van, maybe they would have caught a picture of the man.

'What the—' A hand went over her mouth, dragging her rapidly to the floor. She attempted to scream as she grabbed at her attacker and struggled to breathe. His muddy hand was clasped tight over her mouth and a frenzied panic immediately took over her body.

'Shush,' the man's voice whispered. 'You're going to get us both killed.'

Kate managed to spin around as the attacker's hand slowly let go of her. He looked down at her, and his black plastic-rimmed glasses amplified his terrified wide eyes. A finger was held up to his lips, demanding her silence. They heard the sound of a car door slamming and the sound of the engine as the car drove off.

'Sherlock, what the hell?' Kate growled as she remembered that Ben had said he'd send Eric to help. What he hadn't said was that he could be lurking in the bushes ready to pounce. Breathing in huge gasps of air, Kate took a moment to get over her shock, before looking down at the mud that was now smeared all over her jeans. She brushed furiously at the mess. 'Eric, look at my jeans, they're ruined.' Anxiety rose inside, her hands were making the dirt worse and the more she rubbed, the more she panicked.

She looked over to where Eric was still crouching down behind the huge laurel bush, his face as white as a ghost, with mud all over his clothes.

'Th-there was a m-man,' he stuttered, pointing towards the house. 'He had a gun.'

Kate ducked back down, the mud and dirt suddenly becoming secondary to the thought of being shot. 'What man? Are you sure?' she asked as she peeped over the bush.

'He was this big.' Eric held his arms out to prove a point. 'He wore a brown leather jacket, nearly burst out of it, he had knuckles the size of ... oh, Kate, I swear, if he'd seen us, he'd have shot us.'

Kate looked up at the sky. 'It's okay, Eric. He's gone. His car just drove away. I presume he was in it.' Eric was physically shaking and she had no idea how to tell him that all she'd seen was in fact a mobile phone and not a gun.

'Thank God,' Eric said as he almost curled up in a ball and hugged his own legs.

'Eric, are you okay?'

He nodded. 'Her husband got shot here you know, well there actually.' He pointed to the door.

Kate decided to keep him talking. She had no idea what else to do. His face had gone beyond the initial pale colour and had turned to ashen grey and she wondered how long it would take her to go and get help. But if she did so, it would blow their cover and she decided it would be better to just sit it out, until Eric's colour returned. They were a long way from the van, which had now moved and was being driven to the pick-up point on the back lane.

'What did you actually see?'

'The man, the gun, oh … I don't know. I was so afraid. I hid behind here,' he said, pointing to the large thick laurel bush that would have been equal to the size of a mini. 'Then I heard footsteps.' Eric took a deep breath. 'I … I … I thought he was coming after me.'

Kate closed her eyes. Last night she'd been so pleased to call herself a private investigator. She'd enjoyed her time with Ben and had begun to feel as though being part of a team would be a huge benefit to her confidence and to her lifestyle. But today couldn't be more different. It couldn't get any worse, unless of course Eric was right and she could have been shot. Other than that, she was sitting on the ground, in the rain, covered in mud, with Eric quivering like a jelly.

Eric peered out from behind the bush. 'Are you sure he's gone?'

'Eric, I don't think he had a gun. I mean, I saw him with a phone but not a gun, and his car went a while ago. Come on, I think we should get back to the van.' Kate nodded sympathetically. Eric might look like Clark Kent, but he certainly wasn't planning on being a superhero any time soon. He sat up quickly, suddenly very embarrassed.

'Oh my g-goodness, I am s-so s-sorry,' he began to stutter as he hurriedly jumped up, then remembered the attacker and looked all around to assure himself that he really had gone. He pulled a tissue from his pocket and began to wipe his brow. Without realising it he smeared more and more mud across his face. 'I was so scared. What if he'd seen me hiding? He could have easily walked over and if he had got a gun, he could have shot me.' He shook his head looking around him. 'I'm too young to die, Kate. I'm much too young. Besides, I only just met Eve. She's lovely, by the way.'

Kate liked the way he mentioned Eve and tried her best to reassure him. 'Eric, he's gone. He drove away, don't worry.' She was desperate not to smile. He needed support, not her pity, and even though she was initially amused by the mud that he'd continued to smear across his face, she did her best not to burst into laughter. She then remembered the mud that still covered her own hands and clothes and the amusement fell from her face. Standing up she pulled a wad of tissues from her rucksack and wiped her own hands, before attacking her jeans. The word 'ruined' crossed her mind for a second time, as the mud seemed to rub in rather than rub off. She tried to keep calm even though every part of her mind screamed to be clean.

Kate and Eric separated and walked carefully toward where the van would now be parked. Kate knew it was important not to attract too much attention and made sure that no one was watching, before knocking lightly on the back doors.

Chapter Twenty-Two

'I swear that if there wasn't a couple hundred grand up for grabs, I'd say we were wasting our time,' Kate said as they jumped out of the van, took in a deep breath of fresh air and entered Parker & Son by the back door. 'Everything is so closed down around there, the trees don't help, nothing can be seen from the road and most of the property's windows are at the back.'

Eric still looked embarrassed and he sheepishly followed Kate into their office.

'So, what do you think?' Kate questioned as she gratefully took a steaming mug of hot coffee from the tray that Gloria brought in and passed one to Eric. He stood leaning against Ben's desk, with his back to her, studying the dry wipe board on the wall before him.

'Did Don go home?' Eric asked as his eyes quickly processed the information before him.

Kate pulled a face. 'Well, if he didn't, I don't think it'll be long before he does. The Thai curry he'd had last night hadn't agreed with him. He didn't look too well in the van and I saw him make a mad dash for the bathroom the minute we got back.' She sat down in the pink chair that was behind her desk, pulled a pad and a pen from her drawer and looked up at the evidence board.

'So, how do we get inside the house? Maybe I could knock on the door, pretend my car has broken down and see if she'd let me use her phone?' Kate questioned as she tried not to look down at her jeans; the whole muddy appearance made her feel hot and nauseous and she made a mental note to carry a spare set of clean clothes in the boot of her Beetle at all times, or to leave some in a cupboard at the office. She really needed a bath and more than anything she needed to repair her mud-smeared face with fresh make-up. 'Have a think while I clean myself up,' she said and quickly made an escape for the ladies' to sort herself out.

She looked at her reflection in the mirror. If she had a choice, she'd go home, shower and change, but William Parker had insisted they come straight back to the office and process all the information while it was all still fresh in their minds, and if Kate had learnt anything in the past few days, it was that no one disobeyed William. Kate looked at her reflection. Her make-up wasn't as damaged as she'd thought and a quick repair saw her smiling back at herself, before quickly heading back to her desk.

'Kate, you said you want to go in. Why would you want to do that? It could be so dangerous. Especially after we almost got shot by a man with huge knuckles,' Eric asked as Kate sat down at her desk, her face and hands now mud-free. 'They were big,' he told her, holding out his shaking hands towards her. He picked up the coffee mug again, holding onto it like his life depended on it.

Kate shook her head. 'Well, you're right, he did have huge knuckles, I'll give him that.' Kate laughed nervously. 'But to be honest, Eric, if a guy like him wanted to do some damage, I doubt he'd need a gun.'

Eric shook his head. 'I'd rather not find out what his muscles or his gun can do, thanks.'

'Eric, as I said before, I really don't think he had a gun, I saw him walking around the house, and I did see a mobile phone, but I didn't see a gun. Honestly.'

They both pulled faces and sipped their coffee. The relief that they'd both got away unscathed caused them to start giggling.

Composing herself, Kate pinned the surveillance pictures onto the noticeboard, wishing Ben was in the office with her.

The pictures were blurred and only showed the man from the back. Kate shrugged and shook her head, as the door opened and William walked in.

'How's it going?' he asked as he too stood in front of the evidence board, his hands clasped behind his back while he studied it.

Kate sighed. 'I took some pictures, but they're too distant. Sorry.' She hadn't wanted to admit to him that she'd made a rookie mistake.

'Maybe I can enlarge them or something, try and see his reflection in the windows or door?' She sat down at Don's desk and fiddled with the keyboard then clicked on print.

'Damn it,' she cursed. 'I still can't see a face or what's in his hand.'

'No you can't,' William said as he pointed to the print. 'But you can see that Isobel Reed is hiding behind the edge of an upstairs curtain. Well done. At least we know she's definitely at home.'

'But we're not there anymore.' Kate was puzzled and she picked up the print and squinted to see Isobel's hiding place.

'No, you're not. But the other team are. Patrick took a second van across, so don't worry. She's still under surveillance. If there is something going on, we'll find out about it.' William leaned back and smiled. 'Now, did someone mention coffee?'

Kate laughed. 'Sure, I'll go make you some.'

'How did you get those?' Kate quizzed as she returned to the office with a cup of coffee for William to see Eric flicking through the diary pages of Isobel's life on his computer screen.

'Ben got me to hack into her computer and we managed to retrieve her electronic diary. While in her garden I picked up her Wi-Fi and IP address and hacked in. I then sent the information back to the office. It's easy; remind me to teach you how to do it.' His attention turned back to the screen. 'Having these pages gives us access to everything she does.'

'Wouldn't her Wi-Fi need passwords?'

Eric tapped his temple with a pencil. 'My dear, you're talking to a pro hacker.'

Kate laughed. Eric was a little bit geeky, and she smiled in admiration that he really did know what he was doing. She paid attention to how he studied and analysed every piece of information on the pages, cautiously cataloguing every clue, carefully working out its relevance.

Eric began drawing a timetable on the left-hand side of the board with one hand, while the other persistently pushed his glasses back up his nose. Reading from his notes, he began to fill in the timetable.

'We know what days of the week she has set appointments: hairdressers', beautician, etc. But what we need to do is to look at the gaps.' He indicated towards the board as he began filling in day by day what appointments she had. These left clear blocks of time when she had no visible plans. 'These are the times that Isobel would have the opportunity to go out. We also look for codes, you know multiple numbers, stars, repeated words. She could use these symbols to remind her of things that she didn't want to write down,' he said smugly as he looked at Kate with a 'why didn't you think of that' look on his face.

Kate sat with her chin in her hands. 'Of course,' she said, nodding in agreement. 'So, what else did you see or do while rummaging around her bedding plants?'

'I saw that she had a visitor.'

Kate jumped up. 'Really? Who was it?'

'Well, I don't know who he was. But he had been there overnight and he wore brown leather brogues. I could see them through the glass in her hallway.'

'Did you get a photograph?' William asked.

'Sure, but I took it on my phone,' Eric replied as he tossed the phone across the desk. 'I'd only just arrived and hadn't got all my gear organised. I only just avoided being seen.'

'So?' Kate questioned as she looked at the photograph over William's shoulder. 'How do you know he'd been there all night?'

Eric laughed and pushed his glasses back up his nose. 'That's easy. His shoes. It was raining and had been for some time and so if he'd been out within an hour of my seeing them, there would have been signs of dampness on the leather or mud on the heels.'

Kate looked at him in amazement. 'Eric, that's very clever.'

Eric shrugged. 'It's not, it's easy. You just have to look for the clues. The shoes were dry, there was no mud. So, I assume that the shoes had not been outside that morning. Seeing as it was still early and not many people go visiting before eight o'clock in the morning, I'd assume he'd stayed the night.'

Kate suddenly jumped up from her chair. 'The brogues, Luca Bellandini wore brogues exactly like that, I saw them, in the library. Actually, I got a photograph, entirely by accident, and they had a tiny tear in them, right on the top. Sorry, I have a thing about shoes.' She picked up her mobile and flicked through the pictures.

'The brogues I saw did have a slight tear,' Eric said and grinned at Kate.

'This means that it was most probably him that stayed the night, which means we solved a part of the case. The shoes were Luca's. So he's definitely involved.'

William nodded. 'Not necessarily. Just because he may or may not have stayed the night does not make him a drug dealer. I'm afraid you need more proof than that,' he said as the door opened and Ben marched into the office.

Ben looked Kate up and down. 'Are you okay?' His eyes searched hers and she nodded. 'You're not hurt, are you?'

Eric coughed. 'Hi, Ben. I'm okay too, even though I almost got shot. But, hey, thanks for asking.' He smiled and Kate noticed that William quickly vacated Don's chair and patted Ben's shoulder before leaving the room.

'Right, fill me in on everything that's happened,' Ben said to Eric and Kate.

Ben sat at his desk and gave them his full attention, while both Kate and Eric told him what had happened that morning.

'So, you've solved one tiny part of the jigsaw,' he said when they had finished. 'But not all of it. Now we need to fit all the other parts together, preferably without getting ourselves killed.' He studied the dry wipe board, trying to fill in the gaps.

'What we suspect is that Luca Bellandini is having an affair with Isobel Reed. It was him that led us to Isobel in the first place, so this confirms a connection. But if Isobel is supplying drugs to dealers, we need to find out who those dealers are and whether Luca Bellandini is definitely one of them. Once we've done that, we not only need to find out how she's getting the drugs into the country, but who her main supplier is. Then and only then can we claim the couple hundred grand reward. So we've still lots of work to do.'

Kate thought about what Ben had said. He was right. Even her own messy life was one big jigsaw. She had a huge, caring, loving heart that had been torn apart. One piece of her heart would be missing for each part of her life that had been broken: the death of her brother, the scar on her face, her poor sister Eve, her relationship with her parents, and the loss of her grandmother, the only person other than Eve who'd truly understood her.

Everything and everyone had changed. Even Rob was different and she had no idea why. But she was determined to find out and piece by piece, she intended to mend her broken life.

Chapter Twenty-Three

Kate was still furious. The night before had been a nightmare. Her mother had insisted that she should be home in time for dinner and had then promptly announced that she was going out, which would have been exactly what Kate would have wished for, if she'd not had some cock and bull story from Rob as to why he was going to be late, again. She'd vaguely heard him come in. It had been gone midnight before he'd entered the bedroom and had slept so close to the edge of the bed that at one point Kate had worried that he might fall out. She'd lain awake for hours, desperate to talk, desperate to ask him what on earth was going on. But she hadn't thought that the middle of the night in a small cottage, with your mother in the next room, was the right time to discuss anything.

She pulled her car into a parking space in front of the office. Tears of frustration had filled her eyes and she sat, dabbing them and taking a moment to compose herself, before getting out of the car, where the aroma from the bakery next door stopped her in her tracks.

She walked in and eyed the pastries, cakes and scones that smelt as though they'd all come straight from the oven, before choosing a selection of pink and chocolate iced doughnuts.

'That should cheer us all up,' she thought as she carefully took the box from the assistant and walked out of the shop and in through the front door of Parker & Son.

Her eyes were immediately drawn to the brown leather settee, where Ben was sitting. He was laughing with a very young, slim, dark-haired woman, who may as well have been sitting on his knee. Her hand rested close to his leg, making Kate's head spin around, looking for Gloria, who for once, was not in reception.

'I ... I brought doughnuts.' Was all she could think to say as she hurried past. 'Shall I put them in the kitchen?'

'That's great,' she heard him shout behind her. She stood for a moment, her back to the kitchen door. She turned and dropped the doughnuts on the side and felt a huge rush of disappointment. After spending the night before with Rob, who had made it more than clear that he was only in their bed because her mother was in the next room, she'd barely slept, and for some reason, she'd been looking forward to seeing Ben. She'd been hoping for some reassurance from him and had felt a surge of jealousy fly through her, for which she immediately berated herself. He was young, free and single. He had every right to sit with whomever he wanted, but it had been the last thing she'd expected to see, especially at the office, and the sight had more than disturbed her.

Kate rushed from the kitchen to the office, slammed the door behind her and stomped over to her desk. Eric looked puzzled. He was standing at the evidence board filling in more information on the chart.

'How do you fancy a haircut?' he asked as he glanced across, making Kate's hands immediately fly up to her hair. She pulled a compact from her bag and checked her appearance. Her auburn hair was poker straight as normal and hung loosely around her shoulders.

'Why, what's wrong with my hair?'

'Ohhhhh, touchy, calm down, calm down,' Eric joked. 'I've gone through the diary. Isobel is due to have her hair cut later this morning and Gloria has secured you an appointment, right at the same time, in the same salon, but with a different stylist, of course.'

'Oh?' Kate picked up the ruler that had been haphazardly

thrown on her desk, lined it up with the keyboard, then shook her head, opened the drawer and dropped it inside.

Eric was laughing. 'Of course, Parker and Son will pay for the haircut and you, my dear, will be in the right place at the right time. Women tell their hairdressers everything, so what better way to listen in on her conversation? Ingenious, isn't it?'

'Who's the damn woman in reception? she's draped all over Ben.'

Eric spun around on the spot. 'Ohhhhhhh, that's what the attitude is all about. Would one of us be jealous?' His finger waved up and down in the air, before pushing his glasses back up his nose.

Kate shook her head. 'Don't be ridiculous. She looks like she's about twelve. Not the type I'd have thought Ben would be into. Anyway, none of my business.' She looked back at the door. The woman was obviously much older than twelve, but still looked far too young in comparison to Ben. 'I brought doughnuts, for everyone, that's all. Her being here took me by surprise. I didn't count on extra guests when I bought them.' She sat down and picked up the telephone, held it to her ear and then placed it back down. 'Does this thing ever ring?' she asked in a vain attempt to change the subject.

'So, you and Rob, you're all lovey dovey again, are you?' Eve's sarcastic tone came down the line. 'Since when?' Kate could imagine her sitting in the wheelchair pulling faces at the phone.

Kate sat in her car, counting to ten. She'd arrived at the hairdressers' early, parked her car and had decided to phone Eve to catch up on the gossip. She looked at her watch; it was almost time for her appointment.

'We didn't exactly fall out, Eve. He's been late home once

or twice and stayed on the settee for a few nights. That's all,' she answered defensively as she glanced in the rear-view mirror. She really didn't want to admit that her relationship with Rob was still feeling precarious. To admit it would make it more real and if Eve found out, then her mother would be the next person to know and an onslaught from Mother was the last thing she needed.

It was obvious that Eve knew something was wrong. After all, they were twins and Eve had always been able to tell when she was hiding something.

Kate closed her eyes, leaned back against the car's headrest and allowed the April sun to warm her face. She knew how self-centred Rob could be. Just about everything he'd ever done had been for himself. There had been so many occasions when she'd been suspicious of his motives, wondered what the reasons were behind his actions and why he'd disappeared for days and sometimes weeks at a time, without any real explanation.

'Maybe he's putting on a show for Mother's sake, you know, coming home, sleeping in your bed, playing happy families?'

Kate knew that Eve was angry, she could hear it in her voice, and knew that she was digging deep to get a reaction. It was a reaction that Kate couldn't give away. Not yet, not at this point.

'Maybe he just loves me, Eve.' Kate rummaged in her handbag and pulled out one of the chocolate bars she'd tossed in there that morning. 'Have you ever thought of that?' she said, opening the foil packet and nibbling at the edge of the bar. 'Anyhow, have you spoken to Mother yet?' she asked to change the subject.

'Yes, she says she's staying for around a week, maybe longer.'

Kate knew that having her mother in her home for another whole week would drive her insane. She could imagine that by the end of it one of them could end up dead and buried under the patio and, at this moment in time, Kate had no idea which one of them it would be.

She wondered if she really should try and phone her father. He used to take her feelings into consideration, but that was before. If Mother was driving both her and Eve mad, surely he'd come over and take her home? But then again, if her parents were fighting too, he'd probably be happy that her mother stayed away.

'Eve, please let her stay with you,' Kate begged as her sister went quiet and sulked. Kate knew that Eve had a problem with it, but couldn't understand why. Other than Max, Eve lived by herself, she always complained of being lonely and what's more she had a spare room with an en suite. Unlike Kate's cottage that only had two small bedrooms, paper thin walls and one bathroom between them.

Kate thought about Rob. She had to consider their relationship. Had to decide what to do, but had no idea how to do it, especially with her mother watching their every move.

'Okay, okay, she can stay here. I'll ask her later, make out it was my idea, but only if she's staying after the weekend. I could ask her to come here on either Sunday or Monday, say I need help with something,' Eve relented and took in a deep breath. The last thing she wanted was anyone staying at the bungalow. It would mean disturbing her routine and the thought of her daily physio being interrupted brought her out in a sweat. She couldn't allow her mother to know her secret; no one could know she could stand, not until she was sure that she could do it without falling.

'I don't really want her here, Kate, but for your sake I will. I think things are much worse between her and Dad than you think though. I've never seen her like this before.'

'Eve. Why would you say that? They've always fought, you know that. His job is high profile. It's harder for him now, working for another firm rather than working for himself, he's always under pressure and some days it gets too much for both of them, especially since James died.'

'She cried, Kate. I don't think I've ever seen her cry before. She said she was scared, scared of the future, said she had nothing left and she sobbed for hours. I think she's having a nervous breakdown, or something. Some of the things she came out with were really weird, it's like Dad can't do anything right, and you know how much she adores him. And she talks about James as though he's still alive. It was freaky, Kate. I don't think she's grieved properly, you know, with everything going on, and I think it's all catching up with her now.'

'I didn't know. I just thought she was being horrid and still blaming me for the accident.'

'Kate, what if she does something, you know, something stupid?' Eve's voice broke and for a moment she thought that she too would end up in tears. For their mother to move back to Caldwick, to where her worst nightmares had happened, even if it was just for a few weeks, must mean that things were either really bad between her and Father or she really was going through a breakdown. She'd hated the idea of their mother living with her, she needed to keep up her exercises if she wanted to walk again. But she had no choice, Mother needed someone to look after her. And with Kate and Rob's relationship being so difficult at the moment, they needed time to sort their life out. Which meant that looking after Mother was going to have to be down to her.

Isobel stared at her reflection in the mirror as Marcus lifted her hair and fastened the black vinyl cape behind her neck.

'And how's the lovely Isobel today?' His voice was

effeminate, soft, fluffy and friendly with a slight Scottish tone. He was as thin as a sapling tree and his flower covered jeans gave him an almost animated look. His hands went up and down as he pulled his fingers rapidly through Isobel's long blonde hair. 'Would you like a tea? You take it black, darling, don't you? I'll get Miranda to make you one. Now, what are we doing today?'

Isobel smiled. Marcus barely took breath. 'Oh, I'm good, Marcus. And, yes, tea would be lovely,' she responded. 'I'd like it tidying up, just a little off the length. And straighten it for me too. I'm going to my therapist later; I like to look nice.'

'Oh, I know exactly what you mean, my darling. How is your therapist, still networking?'

Isobel smiled and nodded. 'He is. He's thinking of getting a new Porsche.' She began to giggle like a schoolgirl. 'Bright red with a cream interior, what do you think?'

'My dear, I think it sounds perfect. Will you be buying one too?'

Isobel nodded. 'I thought I might. I might name her the Red Lady.'

'What will your neighbours say when it's delivered?' His arms once again waved around and he used his hands to pretend he was driving a car. 'Can you imagine it?'

'Oh, I don't worry about the neighbours. I'll have it delivered at midnight, so the neighbours don't see it, and preferably on a night when it isn't raining. I don't want it to get wet.'

Kate watched the exchange. Her own hair had already been washed and trimmed, while her hairdresser had chatted relentlessly about a holiday she'd just come home from, making Kate feel quite appreciative when she turned the hairdryer on and her annoying voice blended into the background. Kate's eyes were fixed on Isobel's mirror. She began wishing that lip reading had been one of her talents and did her best to pick up on as many words as she could. While Isobel sat calmly, her hairdresser waved his arms around, occasionally blocking the view of Isobel's lips.

It was obvious that Marcus had heard all of the tales before. The expression on his face was one of boredom. He didn't look overly impressed or surprised. But he did manage to smile politely in all the right places and continually repeated sentences that hadn't needed repeating, making Kate look twice each time he did it.

Kate noted that he'd used a water spray to damp down Isobel's hair, even going over to the bowl for a drenching seemed to be too good for the ever so perfect Isobel and Kate was disappointed that she didn't get to see her with a towel wrapped around her head, mascara down her face and smudges of foundation missing from her gorgeous face. Marcus began to use the comb to pick up tiny strands of hair, snipping away as he went. It was more than obvious that her hair wasn't really being cut. Just titivated, played with and styled in a way that obviously made Isobel feel better. An easy hour's work for an overpaid stylist.

'Yes, it will be next week. I'll give you an update as soon as I can.' Isobel looked pleased with herself and Kate wished she'd heard the beginning of this sentence. But with a hairdryer blasting in her ear, it had been impossible. Isobel had walked behind her and toward the desk just as Fiona began pulling strands of her hair with the straighteners, giving them a twist and allowing the hair to fall in soft curls around her face, making it impossible for her to turn and look where Isobel had gone. She had to think quickly and grabbed at her mobile phone.

'Fiona, do you mind if I just call my mother back? I just had a text. It's really important,' she said, putting the phone to her ear. She walked to the area near reception, pretended to make a call and listened as Isobel paid Marcus for the haircut she hadn't needed.

'There you go, Marcus, darling. Book me in again, my normal day and time.'

'Oh, nice hair,' Eric said as Kate walked back into the office, having entered the building via the back door. After her embarrassing encounter that morning, the last thing she needed was to walk in on Ben entertaining another friend in reception.

'Thanks, where's Ben? Out to lunch with her?' She looked through the door and toward reception, but all she could hear was the sound of Gloria on the telephone.

'Well, wow, we really are jealous, aren't we?'

'Don't be ridiculous,' Kate threw back as she went to the kitchen and picked out one of the doughnuts she'd bought earlier that morning, and began stuffing it into her mouth. The icing was soft and sticky and she grabbed for a piece of kitchen roll to wipe her lips.

Eric had followed her and was now laughing. 'Okay, I'll stop being ridiculous, but, from where I'm standing, you look just a little too concerned with the fact that Ben may or may not have a friend.'

'I am not concerned.'

'Yes you are, otherwise you'd have already told me all about what happened with Isobel by now.'

'Give me a chance. I was just about to tell you,' she lied and moved out of the kitchen, doughnut and kitchen roll still in hand, and walked over to their shared office. 'I didn't really learn that much. It's obvious that money means everything to her and she has a personal trainer that goes over most days, but other than that she didn't really say anything.'

Eric laughed. 'Ah well, at least you got a haircut out of it. Now, tell me exactly what she did say.'

Kate shrugged her shoulders wondering whether it had been worth it. 'Well, she mentioned a red Porsche with cream seats. Her therapist is buying one and she's thinking of doing the same and calling it the Red Lady. Said she'd have it delivered at midnight so the neighbours didn't see. She also hoped it wouldn't be raining, she didn't want it to get wet.' She paused. 'Oh, and something was happening next week and she'd update him as soon as she could. Sorry, I missed the beginning of the sentence, blooming hairdryer blasting in my ear. Is any of this relevant?'

'Yes, of course it's relevant.' He began scribbling on the board, just as Ben walked into the office.

'Hey. Nice hair.' Ben tipped his head to one side, taking in the view. 'Okay, Eric, what have we got?' Ben watched intently as Eric completed the board.

'There's a shipment coming in next week, could be in a red car, boat or aeroplane. The leader of the organisation is taking one delivery, Isobel the other. I'd say it's a cream substance or drug. Possibly the MCAT mixed with a cream or white powder, which normally means soap powder. Whichever it is, it's coming in at midnight, under cover of darkness, so the authorities don't pick up on it. Oh, and she didn't want it getting wet, which I'd take a guess at and say that she's bringing it in by sea. So by deduction, I'd guess we're looking for a boat.'

Kate looked between both Eric and Ben. 'Wait a minute, how the hell did you get all that from what I just said?'

Ben turned his back on Kate. He wanted to look at her, but couldn't stop himself from staring. She looked amazing and the last thing he wanted to do was make her or himself feel uncomfortable, especially in front of Eric. The haircut had added just a few curls to her long auburn hair, which now framed her face beautifully. She'd obviously altered her make-up and the stronger, darker eyeliner made her eyes stand out.

'Okay, Eric. That's great. Anything else?' He tried to concentrate on the board, listen to what Eric was saying, but closed his eyes for a second. He needed to focus on the job, concentrate on the clues and, more than anything, he needed to bring this case to a close. It was fast beginning to cost more money than it would be worth, especially if they didn't bring Isobel Reed in. 'Do you think she'll take delivery at the house? Or will it be elsewhere?' He tried to think.

'Oh, yes, she also mentioned the name Red Lady, you may want to dig around and see if there's anything relevant about the name.' Eric gave Ben a knowing look. 'As I said, my money would be on it being a boat.'

Ben quickly turned to his computer. 'Red Lady, I'll take a look.'

'And, Ben, the back lane,' Eric said quickly, making Ben look up from his computer. 'We should take a van to the other end, watch it from both sides. It's a second point of entry, easy to come and go without being seen.'

'So, if we take the van on the back lane, who gets to go in the van on the front?' Kate asked as Ben noticed her move from her chair to stand at his side.

Eric jumped down from where he sat on the desk, joined them both at the board and put a hand to his chest. He stood before her posing with his best sad face. 'I think that would be me,' he said before breaking into a laugh. Kate couldn't stop herself and began to laugh with him, just as Eric's glasses uncontrollably slipped down his nose and once again he pushed them back.

Pulling up just short of Owl Lane, Kate jumped out of the

van as instructed, wandered along the street and carefully planned her next move. She could see Honeysuckle House and made her way around the side, looking for a vantage point, a place where she could leave a remote camera where it would best serve its purpose, a place where they could see exactly who was coming and going.

She crouched down and pretended to tie her shoelace. She scanned the terrain and moved her position slightly to the left, where she placed the camera as far under an ivy bush as she could. It was close to the drive, but looked directly toward the back garden and faced the back door. Anyone coming or going would be seen. It was a good position, which made her smile as she dusted down her knees.

Standing up, she turned and began walking toward the back lane. Ben would be there, waiting for her. She happily bounded around the corner and saw the van, but a familiar noise made her stop in her tracks. Keeping herself hidden, she looked back along the road to see Rob's truck turn the corner and pull into Isobel's drive.

'Okay, calm down. Are you sure?' Ben asked as he pulled her into the van, sat her down and passed her a bottle of water.

'Of course I'm sure. It was definitely him. I knew the sound of that truck before I actually saw it pull up on the drive. I mean, what the hell is he doing here?' Disbelief turned into frustration and she looked up, staring intently at the surveillance screen that was still showing no movement. She sipped at the water.

Ben crouched down beside her, took the bottle from her and took her hands in his. Her stomach turned as she looked into his eyes. They were full of pity and concern, which made her uncomfortable and she glanced away. Rob being there worried her; it was a game changer. It made the whole surveillance feel different, more personal, more real. She'd suspected that he was up to no good, but had prayed that he wasn't involved in anything shady. He'd changed lately and she'd even thought that he might be having an affair, but drugs? What if he'd gotten into them, into the Ketamine? She closed her eyes.

'Kate, let's think rationally. He's a personal trainer, right?' Ben asked, again looking directly at her. 'That house.' He pointed out of the window. 'That house is big enough to have a gym in it and Isobel Reed is rich enough to employ him. After all, didn't she mention having a personal trainer at the hairdressers'?' He sat down on the van floor, his arm rested on her leg, and she purposely turned her gaze from his, once again holding the left side of her face away.

Taking a deep breath, she stared at the screen as Ben got up and started adjusting the dials, trying to enhance the grainy images that the remote camera sent back.

'Let's try and get some sound. This one cuts out background noise,' he said as a green line flashed across a screen. 'When the line becomes irregular it indicates that a noise can be heard and if it's distorted, turn this.' He pointed to another dial.

Kate nodded. Her hands still trembled. She sipped the water. 'What do we do now?'

'We just wait,' Ben replied. 'We have till three o'clock, that's when Patrick will come back for us. We'd have normally waited until after four, but I have a meeting that I can't be late for.'

'What, late lunch with your girlfriend?' Kate knew she shouldn't have asked and carefully watched Ben's face as he squinted at the dials.

'What girlfriend?' He looked genuinely puzzled and Kate rolled her eyes, knowing he wasn't going to answer her question easily. After all, why should he? It really wasn't any of her business who he snuggled up to on the settee, she just wished he hadn't been doing it when she'd walked in.

'The woman, you know at the office.' Kate stared at the clock waiting to see if Ben would respond. The clock ticked by slowly, but nothing happened. Rob's truck was still where it had been parked, yet he hadn't emerged from the house and she began to amuse herself, looking in the dials at the new hairstyle that curled around her face. She flicked it back over her shoulder.

'She wasn't my girlfriend, that was Rebecca, Julia's little sister. I've known her since she was a child. I used to babysit for her.' He laughed. 'We all used to be very close and with it being the anniversary this week, Rebecca wanted me to go to the cemetery with her. To take flowers.' He paused, sat back in his chair and Kate turned away from him in her embarrassment. She should have known that the woman was far too young for Ben, but as usual had jumped to conclusions without thinking.

'Sorry. It was none of my business.' She continued to look at the dials.

'Hair looks really good, by the way,' Ben commented, making Kate swell with pride even though she knew he'd probably said it to change the subject. She couldn't remember the last time she'd been to the hairdressers'; she'd stopped doing things like that after the accident. There hadn't seemed much point in trying to make herself beautiful, not after that.

Kate lifted a finger to her lips; she'd heard something on the receiver. The green line had begun moving up and down. It reminded her of one of those machines you'd get in a hospital that would show your heart beat pulsating on the screen. They both checked the surveillance cameras but nothing could be seen, except for perfectly pruned bushes.

A rustling came from behind the house, something banged and a mumbling could be heard. Then silence.

'Oh well, it was worth a try,' she said picking up the rucksack she'd brought from home. She dug in its depths for any crisps or biscuits that may be left. 'Twix or Snickers?' she offered Ben, who cheekily grabbed the Snickers, tore open the packaging and began to eat.

'Shhhhhh,' Kate whispered as she held her finger to her lips, leaning closer to the receiver. 'Stop rustling.'

The silence was almost deafening but she was sure that she'd heard something familiar. Suddenly the faint sound of footsteps padded over the radio.

A door opened and slammed, but no words were spoken and both Kate and Ben stared at the screen. There was a strange murmuring sound coming through that made them both move closer to the receiver, pressing the record button.

'Oh, baby. You're insatiable, you can't want it again?' Rob spoke, but still they couldn't be seen. Again, it went quiet.

'Please God, no,' Kate whispered. Her mind raced. She knew what she'd heard, but didn't want to believe what was more than apparent. Every emotion went through her body; devastation and disbelief hit her like a thunderbolt. It was true. Rob really was having an affair. And with Isobel Reed.

'My Rob, that's ... that's my Rob.' Kate's voice was wretched.

She moved to the far side of the van, crouched down in the corner and pushed her fingers in her ears in a stupid and vain attempt to block out any noise. She gulped in deep breaths of air and tried desperately not to vomit. She couldn't. Not in the van. Not in front of Ben. She tried to think rationally. There had to be an explanation. 'Rob must be Isobel's personal trainer, he's there working, that's all.'

Kate's eyes involuntarily closed as tears fell down her face.

Maybe he was just being nice; he was doing what personal trainers did, he was making his client feel good. That's what she paid him for, right?

She screwed her face up and thumped the floor. Who was she kidding? Her Rob was at the back of that house right now, making love to another woman and talking about how insatiable he thought her to be. She could imagine Rob's arms around the perfection that was Isobel Reed. He'd be holding Isobel in the same way as, on so many occasions, he'd held her. He'd be using his hands to tease, his tongue to make her feel hot and aroused. Kate heaved.

'Water?' Ben offered. She nodded her acceptance and took the bottle from his hand.

'Are they ... are they still ...' She gulped the water down. '... you know?' She looked back toward the dials which had now been turned off. She really didn't want to listen, didn't need to hear what was happening between them and was appreciative of the silence.

'I turned the volume down. I didn't think you'd want to ... you know. I can review it later, alone,' Ben said, looking down at the floor.

'How could he do this to me?' she questioned. 'I should have guessed. After all the things he's done recently, how could I have been so stupid, so blind?' She blinked back the tears. 'He's been sleeping on the sofa, on and off for months, then the other night, he ... he ...' She couldn't continue as she remembered the lovemaking earlier that week.

'Here, sit down.' Ben moved the camp chair closer to her and his hand reached out and touched her lightly on the shoulder. 'I'm sorry,' he said as she stood up and he pulled her into a hug. His arms felt safe, secure and she didn't want him to let go. But a knock on the side of the van indicated Patrick's arrival. The hug ended and they both sat back down on the chairs.

'All okay?' Patrick asked in his soft Irish accent. 'Sorry I'm late, had to get Eric to bring me in his car.'

The van started. The gears crunched and Kate sat in silence, staring at the floor as they drove back to the office.

Chapter Twenty-Four

'What do you mean, you're getting divorced?' Kate demanded as she stared at Elizabeth Duggan in disbelief. Her mother had suddenly announced that not only had she decided that she'd left their father, she was leaving him permanently. Kate thought of the conversation she'd had with Eve. Their mother adored their father, everything she did was for him. Her whole life revolved around his, and Kate found it hard to believe that under normal circumstances she'd ever be hearing these words.

'I can't live with him any more, Kate. I think he's a sociopath. He's horrid to live with.' She looked down at the floor as she spoke.

'But, you can't. You and Dad, you're a team, you used to be so good together. I remember how much in love you were. We all thought so. Besides, where the hell would you live?' Kate's mind reeled; the fact that her mother had chosen to run here of all places was enough of a warning sign to indicate that if she left her father, she might want to move back to Caldwick.

'I've wanted to tell you before. But your father insisted that I shouldn't, he said you had enough guilt on your shoulders about what you did to your sister, without thinking you'd split us up too. Besides, he's been working away a lot. It would never have been the right time to tell you.' She turned toward the cooker.

'Wait a minute,' Kate screamed. 'What did I do exactly? *Why the hell is any of this my fault?*' In her own mind Kate blamed herself for what happened, even though her rational self understood that it was just a horrific accident that was no one's fault, but to hear her mother actually accuse her was mind blowing.

Her mother rummaged through the drawer in search of utensils. 'Darling, if only you hadn't insisted that James drive you that night. None of this would have happened. James doesn't visit anymore; do you know that?'

Kate spun around on the spot. James doesn't visit? Was Eve right? Was her mother having some kind of breakdown? She stood for a moment and analysed her mother's words. She realised she had to tread carefully but couldn't help her next question. 'Why ... why would you even say that? I couldn't have predicted what would happen. I didn't know. I didn't crash the bloody car.'

'Darling, where do you keep the potato peeler? I can't find it.' Her mother slammed the drawer and opened another and Kate seriously wondered how on earth she didn't know where the peeler was, especially seeing as her mother had cleaned, tidied and reorganised all of her drawers during the past few days.

Kate sat down at the kitchen table and watched as her mother continued to search. She felt out of her depth and didn't know what to do. 'You really do blame me, don't you? You really think that I wanted all of this? Do you think I want you and Father to split up? Because I'll tell you now, it's the last bloody thing I want, because if you did you might end up coming to live here with me.'

Her mother turned and stared. 'Kate, we don't always get what we want. All I know is what we were left with and now we just have to make the best of things and make things right.'

'Right ... right?' Kate screamed. 'Good God, Mother, how the hell do you make any of this right?' She pointed to the scar on her face. 'James is ...' She didn't know what to say. Did she say that James was dead, should she insist on the truth? She once again pointed to her face. 'I have this and Eve is paralysed. How can any of us ever put that right?'

'Katie, don't be so dramatic. I'm leaving your father, lots of people get divorced nowadays and that's that,' she said as she chopped up carrots and carefully dropped them into the pot of boiling water. 'I can't live with him, he's been too bitter and twisted and I just wish I knew why,' her mother growled as she stood facing the range. 'Every time he talks to me, he says something nasty, something insulting and I don't like it.'

Kate laughed out loud and thought of the irony. She looked at her mother's back and wondered if she actually ever listened to what came out of her own mouth, and for just a moment it occurred to her how alike her mother and father really were. Besides, she'd never ever heard her father say anything nasty, not to anyone, and she wondered if her mother was imagining it.

'It's true that James was running late for his date,' Kate began to whisper. She was sick of shouting, her head pounded and she needed a drink. 'We were just doing what we'd always done. James always took us to town on our birthday; he was always going on a date and he always made out we were too much trouble, making him late. It's just something he did. He didn't really mean it.'

Kate closed her eyes and thought of the times her brother had teased his younger sisters, always moaned when they were in the same clubs as he was, but always invited them in a roundabout way. 'Don't you dare be in the Alligator club tonight, especially around ten o'clock,' he'd tease with a wink, which in his own way had really meant, 'be there and I'll buy you both a drink'.

'The car just spun off the road, it was no one's fault,' Kate said as she thought back to the accident.

'That's right, dear, no one's fault. That's why my son doesn't visit, you are scarred for life and my darling Eve now sits in a wheelchair,' Elizabeth said as she calmly continued

143

to chop vegetables for the evening meal. 'Of course, if you want to believe that pulling your sister from the car and crippling her was not your fault, then that's fine; it's you that has to live with yourself. Your father says that if you'd only caught the bus that day, none of it would have happened and he'd still have his precious law firm. Because of you he had no choice but to sell it.'

Kate was shocked. Eve was right, her mother really wasn't admitting to the fact that James was dead. And, even though she'd always suspected that both her mother and father had blamed her, it was the first time that she'd actually come out and said it. It was one thing blaming herself, but quite another to have it confirmed that her parents blamed her too.

Eve had said that mother had been crying the day before. But now there was no emotion, no sorrow, no sign of tears. The words she'd used had been said with so little feeling that her mother may as well have been reading out a weather report, telling her that Monday would have showers with a hint of sunshine, rather than the fact that she was divorcing her father. Kate didn't know what to do. Maybe she really was having a breakdown. She looked at her phone. Should she call a doctor, an ambulance, her father?

'Do you want boiled potatoes, dear, or roast?'

'*What?*' Kate slammed her hand on the table. 'Mother, stop chopping the bloody vegetables and sit down. We really need to talk.' Her chest heaved as pain and realisation tore through her body. She'd tried to put the accident behind her, even though every day she was reminded of the past and nothing made sense.

Had she really been responsible for crippling her sister?

All her thoughts raced around in her head, like a huge whirlwind spinning across her mind. In the course of one day she'd discovered that her fiancé was a lying, cheating rat, and she'd been told that both her parents blamed her for both the accident and for destroying their marriage.

'Mum, the accident. I think you should know ...' Kate closed her eyes. How did you reveal to someone that their son was actually dead and not just refusing to visit?

'I know, dear, you're sorry. But it was still your fault. Could you pass the gravy jug?'

'Are you bloody serious?'

Elizabeth Duggan walked past Kate, picked up the gravy jug, and then walked back to the range giving the gravy her whole attention, making Kate gasp. Her mother was unbelievable; she could have a nervous breakdown, and throw all of this guilt at her own daughter, but God help anyone who got in the way of making the bloody gravy. Kate walked over to the wine rack, studied the three bottles that sat there, like it mattered, pulled out a bottle of red and then poured a large glass, drinking it down in one gulp.

'Yes, please, darling, I'll have a glass. Now did you say boiled potatoes or roast? I think roast are so much nicer with beef, dear, don't you agree?' Elizabeth Duggan looked up from the gravy boat that she'd been polishing with a tea towel.

Kate felt her world begin to spin. She sat down quickly as her legs began to wobble. 'Mother! After all you've just said, do you seriously want to know what bloody potatoes I want? I doubt I could eat them,' Kate growled as anger took over her voice. 'Have you any idea how the accident ruined my life too?' She picked up a tea towel and began viciously rubbing the make-up from her face. 'That day ruined everything.' Kate held her chin toward her mother, pointed at the red puckered ridge that lined her jaw and watched as her mother quickly averted her gaze.

In the last twenty-four hours her life had turned from being predictably boring to being a complicated nightmare.

It was now an intricate web of deceit, of secrets and lies, that spread out in every direction and she had no idea how to control the outbreak.

Kate saw her mother's bottom lip quiver. 'I'm sorry.'

'Sorry? Does sorry even cut it? You need help, professional help. You need a doctor,' she said as she gulped down the wine. 'I need to phone Eve; she has a right to know what's happening, she needs to know about you and Daddy.'

Her mother nodded. 'She knows, dear, I told her this afternoon.'

'She knows? So what did she say? Is she all right, should we go to her?'

'Don't be silly, dear, Eve's fine. She certainly didn't react as childishly as you have.' Once again the comments came, as cutting as ever.

Kate held her head in her hands. If only her mother knew what an awful week she'd had, if only she could talk to her, tell her the truth, confide in her about Rob and let her know how her life had suddenly turned upside down. But if she knew it would only give her more ammunition, which undoubtedly she'd throw right back at her and Kate had no intention of giving her that privilege.

The whole conversation explained so much. At least now Kate understood why her mother had begun with the comments, the insults and the carefully placed accusations that had made her so unbearable for the past year.

Kate closed her eyes and wished that it had been her that had died and not James. In her eyes, he'd been the one to escape, the one who didn't have to be here, to live through the heartache and to cope with all of this. She opened her eyes and poured more wine into her glass.

'Darling, make that your last. No one likes a drunken woman, do they?'

Chapter Twenty-Five

Barely remembering the twists and turns of the country lanes, Kate drove into Bedale. The roads were uncharacteristically empty; the weather was drizzly, cold and windy for mid spring. Everything about the journey completely matched her mood. Tears rolled down her face as she pulled up on the cobbled road in front of the office. She simply sat and stared at the Victorian building before her.

A knock on the window made her jump and she looked toward the noise, but her eyes were misted and she could barely focus.

'Hey, what are you doing here? You okay? Is it Rob?' Ben's deep tone startled her. She shook her head. Opening the car door, Ben carefully pulled her towards him. 'What happened? Come on, you're all right. I've got you now.' His arms encircled her and she felt the strength within them.

He held her gently as she told him about the conversation she had had with her mother the night before, that she thought her mother was having a nervous breakdown and now she felt guilty for having left her alone in the house.

'Nervous breakdown or not, I can't believe she said all of that, and then expected you to sit through dinner,' Ben said. 'What kind of a person is she?'

Kate slowly shook her head. 'Apparently, she's a sick person. But I don't know how to handle her. I had no idea what to say, she isn't even admitting to James being dead.'

'Does she need medical help? Is she in any danger?'

Kate didn't know the answer, but Ben's voice slowly bore its way through the thick mist that had overtaken her mind. She stared into space. The tears had continued, stopped and then started again.

'Come on, I'll get you a drink,' he whispered. His arms were still supporting her protectively and her head leaned against him. She felt shielded.

'I don't need a drink,' she replied. Even though it was cold and they were both getting wet, she had no wish to move away. His aftershave overpowered her senses and she closed her eyes and breathed in the scent. She wondered what it would be like to be loved by someone like Ben. Her eyes burnt with the lack of sleep and she closed them. Her mind swam into a deep engulfing fog. Her whole body blended against his, as a deep sense of exhaustion enveloped her.

'Where's Gloria?' Kate heard the words as he shepherded her through the door and towards the settee. He helped her to sit, but her whole mind drifted into her own thoughts. Nothing felt real.

'Kate, it's Saturday. It's Gloria's day off, and yours.' She felt his hold loosen.

'Is it really?' She went to stand up, feeling embarrassed. Not only had she gone into work on the weekend, it suddenly occurred to her that after only a week she'd felt safer heading for the office than she had staying at home.

She pulled a tissue from a box on the table and blew her nose loudly.

'Oh my God, I'm so sorry. Not very ladylike, is it?' She tried to smile and lighten the mood. She eased away and pulled out a second tissue, but then sat back down as she became aware of how much she'd cried and the probability that her make-up had now been completely rubbed off.

'Look. I'm so sorry,' she whispered, feeling a sense of embarrassment. 'I need to …' She wanted to say that she needed to cover her scar, hide it from view, but couldn't find the words.

'Sorry for what?' A gentle, dazzling smile lit up Ben's face.

'Well, for bawling for a start. I shouldn't bring personal

problems to work, especially on what's supposed to be my day off. You hardly know me and you don't need this.' She tried to smile back at him.

'I think you had good reason. The past couple of days have been hard on you.' Ben sighed. 'Did Rob come home last night?'

Kate shook her head.

'None of that could have been easy for you. You are still in a relationship with him.' His words were calm and Kate once again blew her nose.

'Not for long. He won't hurt me again.'

Ben had sat back down beside her and once again Kate leaned against him and sobbed.

Ben sat back, pulled Kate into a hold and waited for her tears to subside. He breathed in and out as gently as he could, fearing that any sudden movement would cause her to move. He looked up as the door from the hallway opened and Patrick stepped into the room, took one look at Ben and Kate, then stopped in his tracks. Ben put a finger to his lips, waved a hand at him to retreat and Patrick took a step backwards, carefully closing the door behind him.

His hand gently stroked Kate's hair. It smelled beautiful and he noticed that she'd carried on curling it around the edges, just as the hairdresser had done. It suited her and added to her bubbly personality. A personality which had currently disappeared and been replaced by a blubbering mess, all because her family had happily pushed her into the line of fire and allowed her to take the blame for something she hadn't done.

He didn't know why he cared, she was right, he barely knew her, but somewhere deep within him, he felt the need to protect her; but he felt helpless and didn't know where to start or whether she'd want his protection. He remembered how helpless he'd felt when Julia had taken ill. He'd had to watch while the meningitis took over. Her whole body had been riddled with septicaemia, which had travelled through her like a fast flowing river. There had been nothing he could do to save her or the child that she'd carried inside. Yet still he wondered what his life would have been like. By now his baby would have been a toddler. He or she would have been walking, talking and calling his name. Calling him Daddy. He swallowed hard at the thought. He'd been happy, so very happy, yet one day, without warning it had all been taken from him. He'd spent the last four years wishing that she'd come back, and had waited for a ghost that couldn't and wouldn't return.

He closed his eyes and shook his head. Was this why he felt so strongly about what had happened to Kate? Was this why he felt the need to protect her? Because she too had had everything taken away, without warning? And the question was, could he protect her? Or would she be taken away from him too?

He looked down and realised that Kate was sleeping. Soft, gentle sounds of relaxation could be heard and he smiled, feeling happy that she'd felt comfortable enough to fall asleep, and that she'd trusted him to watch over her.

And now, for the first time he found himself fighting back feelings that he'd previously pushed away. He'd stayed away from other women, but Kate was different; she was feisty one minute, yet fragile and vulnerable the next. He wanted her to be more than a colleague, but the last thing she needed right now was someone else confusing her already bewildered mind.

He lowered his lips to her forehead, kissing her gently. He knew it was wrong. Now was not the time to make a move on her and he wouldn't. For now, all she needed was a friend and friendship was something he could happily give.

Kate stirred in his arms and suddenly sat up. She yawned, stretched, and her hand immediately went up to her scar. Ben noticed that she turned her face away, hiding it from his view. He tried to think; he needed to do or say something to relax her.

'Hey, sleepyhead. Listen, Patrick and I have to go on location today. And seeing as it's your day off, and you're here, I wondered if you fancied coming with us?' he asked as he leaned forward and stood up from the settee. 'We're going into Whitby to check out some of the fishing boats, see a few contacts and chat with one or two of the locals. Apparently, there's a boat there called *Red Lady*.'

Kate looked puzzled and concerned all at once. 'I really should go back to Mother and see if she's okay. And, if it's our day off, who'll follow Isobel?'

Ben winked. 'Don and Eric are watching Isobel today. They have a campervan. Anyone looking at them will think they're tourists, pulling up to make coffee and sleep. Besides, now that we know Rob could be around, we can't risk you being on site. And as for your mother, the space between you might be a good thing.'

'Don't Don and Eric get a day off?' Kate laughed at the irony. She'd been squashed into the back of a surveillance van that had no air, hot drinks or comfortable seating and on the one day that she wasn't watching Isobel, they'd not only have coffee making facilities and a proper toilet, but also daylight, windows and soft seating. But if she really thought about it, she didn't want to watch Isobel, not after the day before, and the thought of doing something other than going home gave her a huge sense of relief. The last thing she wanted to do was to have another battle with her mother, or run into Rob, and the thought of seeing him at Honeysuckle House again tore her in two. She smiled, as the thought of spending the whole day with Ben was more than appealing.

'They only work half day today; surveillance can't stop just because it's the weekend. We'll have different teams working around the clock. So, are you coming? Say yes. Patrick will be waiting.' Ben smiled. He picked up a folder from the desk, and tossed it in a briefcase. 'There's work to do.'

'My face,' she gasped. 'I've made a mess of my face.' Kate cringed as she caught her reflection in the glass cabinet. Her nose was bright red, her eyes were puffy and her make-up non-existent. The scar on her face stood out and once again her hand rose to cover it and she turned her face away from Ben's gaze.

'Okay. Take twenty minutes, get a coffee. Use the bathroom and all that. I'll meet you in reception at ... shall we say, ten o clock?' Without waiting for an answer he briskly walked out of the room and into William's office, where Kate could hear him chatting to his father.

Kate went through to the cloakroom, pulled her make-up from her bag and began the art of hiding her scar. Practice makes perfect and she was good at covering it up, but the puffy eyes were going to take quite a bit of work. She held the towel under the cold tap and applied the cool material to her eyes, waiting for the swelling to reduce. Fifteen minutes later she emerged with her dignity restored and she felt a little happier at the thought of going to Whitby for the day, and the fact that Ben was going too was a huge added bonus.

'Ben tells me you're going to Whitby?' William said with a huge grin on his face as Kate walked into reception. 'I love Whitby. Let's hope the sun shines for you.'

'Err, thanks.' Kate felt awkward. William was being nice and she wasn't sure how much Ben had told him, but by his new smiley mannerisms she got the impression that he was more than aware of everything.

'Oh, and make sure he pays for the fish and chips, on the company,' William said with a laugh as Ben entered the room, sporting a pair of jeans, boots and a jumper. A coat was casually slung over his arm as he strode toward the reception desk.

'Dad, do me a favour, check on Don and Eric in a couple of hours. If they need any help, get Daniel and Joseph over from Hawes, they're the closest.'

Kate watched as William walked to Gloria's desk, sat down and looked at the screen. 'Don't worry. I have the trackers and I can see who is closest. Now, off you go, enjoy the fish and chips and, Kate, make him take you to one of those posh restaurants, not the rubbish back street ones.' He winked at her and Kate smiled. Maybe working for William wasn't going to be as scary as she'd thought.

Chapter Twenty-Six

The wind in Whitby gusted over the cliff tops and right through the abbey car park where Kate stood, waiting for Patrick and Ben to finish talking. She pulled her coat tightly around her, checked her mobile phone and considered texting Rob. But she had no idea what to say to him.

'Okay. Plan is I'm going to ask some questions up there. There's a lady at the abbey that I've known some years. She works in the shop and she'll know if anything's been going on in the harbour,' Ben said as he too grabbed his coat and pulled it on.

Patrick looked over his shoulder. 'I'm going to go and speak to some of the shop owners down on the quayside. Shall we meet back here, at the car, at four o'clock?'

Ben checked his watch. 'Sure, all the boats should be back in by then. I'll check them out, ask a few questions. Maybe we could take a tour on one. See what they know.'

'Great. What shall I do?' Kate asked as she zipped up her coat and rubbed her hands together in anticipation. She looked hopefully between her two associates and waited for them to give her a task.

'You should probably stay with me.' Ben laughed.

Kate pouted. She knew it was her day off and she was still in training, but he could have trusted her with a small job to do, it wasn't like she hadn't done it before. And after her outburst that morning, she'd really wanted to prove herself. She waved to Patrick. He was back in the car and had already reversed out of the parking space, before disappearing into the distance and back towards the town.

'Come on,' Ben said as he pulled her along beside him. He

was smiling like an overgrown schoolboy. 'If you're nice and let me look at the ruins, I'll buy you those fish and chips.'

Kate laughed at his enthusiasm. 'I thought we were supposed to be working?'

'We are. But being undercover means exactly that. We need to look like tourists. It's called a pretext. We're here, pretending we're a couple. Doing things that couples do.' He paused. 'So looking around the ruins is allowed.'

He led the way to the abbey.

'This is the home of The Whitby Gladiator,' he said, ten minutes later, pointing to a statue that stood in the centre of the courtyard. 'As well as being the home of Dracula, of course,' he joked with an over exaggerated and evil laugh.

'Yeah, right.' She laughed, slapping his arm. 'You do know that it's just a story, don't you?'

'Is that what you think?' He grabbed her hand and pointed to the harbour. 'Many years ago, during a terrible storm, an old Russian schooner found its way into that very harbour. A man's corpse was strapped to the helm.' He spoke in a spooky voice, stared into her eyes and nodded. 'It's true, there was no one else on the ship.'

'So, how did it get to the harbour?' She looked nervously up at Ben, just as the wind whipped around them, giving Ben a full authentic stage on which to perform. He took great pleasure in going into full storytelling mode, his voice turned spooky, and Kate couldn't help but laugh.

'The dead man steered it here.' He pointed to the sands. 'As soon as the schooner hit the sand, a huge dog jumped from the ship and ran up that cliff.'

Kate looked at the cliffs that Ben pointed towards. There was a sheer drop to the harbour and there was no way that anything could have ascended it. 'It's impossible. No one could get up there, not even a dog.'

'Well, it's true.' He nodded. 'That night the killings began and some say that Dracula is still here,' Ben teased, grabbing hold of her shoulders and pretending to hide behind her, as he indicated the churchyard that lay in the distance. 'They say his grave is in there. We could go and look for it if you like?'

Kate shook her head and shivered at the thought. 'I don't think so,' she replied. She stood looking up at the architecture of the abbey. She'd never been here before and as Ben went into great detail to explain its history, she found the whole story amazing. It was more than obvious that he loved the place and she wondered if he'd ever visited here with his wife.

'Back in ten,' he said suddenly as he turned and walked into the exhibition, where he headed towards a woman. He hugged her and began chatting.

Kate turned away; she didn't want to watch Ben with yet another of his friends and she took great interest in looking through the cabinets of artefacts that filled the room.

'Come on, let's go outside,' he said as he gripped onto her elbow and led her toward the elevator. Once inside he spoke. 'There, no one can hear us in here. We're looking for a fisherman called Sharky. He's got a whole herd of children and has been working strange hours for the past few months, apparently. He's been seen fishing over the wreck of the *San Georgic* late at night.'

'What's wrong with that? He's a fisherman.'

Ben pursed his lips. 'Fishing isn't allowed there, so if he really was there, he had to be up to no good.'

'Maybe he was lobster potting, or catching a few extra fish. Just because he's out at night, doesn't really prove anything, does it?' Kate asked as the lift doors opened.

Ben smiled. Kate really was naive, in a good way. Even with all that she'd been through, she still looked at the world with rose tinted glasses. Still wanted the world to tick along without incident, and maybe she was right, it should.

It wasn't her fault, but she obviously had no idea how many hours these men worked, the strict hours that would be dictated by the tides, and if they were to add any more hours on into the night, they'd have to have good reason to do it. And good reasons normally meant lots of profit.

'One other thing: his fishing boat is called the *Red Lady*.'

Heading back into the fresh air, they walked back through the ruins and, even though the wind was bitterly cold, Kate loved what she saw. The whole abbey's remains were so much more than the big pile of old rocks that she'd imagined. There was an old arched stone window that stood overlooking the bay, great spaces where once the glass used to be and the view of sky where once there would have been a roof.

'Wow. I wish I'd been here before, it's amazing,' Kate said as she huddled into her coat, pulling it tightly around her as she walked towards the cliff edge and took in the impressive sight of the whole bay of Whitby, its harbour and the sea beyond.

The rain once again began to drizzle just as they left and they ran for cover as the tiny spatters turned into huge globules of water, falling heavily and then splashing up from the puddles as they ran.

'At least the rain has spared us looking round the gravestones,' Kate said with a laugh as they hastily, but carefully, ran down the ninety-nine steps and towards the street below, the water following them down the stairway in torrents.

'Mind, the steps are slippery,' Ben cautioned as he held out a hand to grab Kate's. He led her onto Henrietta Street, pulled her behind him and ducked into a doorway. Large puddles were forming on the cobbled streets and the smell of smoked fish drifted towards them from a tiny shop a little further along. A medley of cottages stood in long rows, all similar, yet individual. These types of cottages were often seen in tourist pictures, long terraced rows with white washed walls, painted windows and doors, all in bright, vivid colours.

Kate pulled a handkerchief from her bag, carefully dabbing the rivulets of water as they ran down her face. She pulled out her compact and checked her make-up, making sure that her scar was still covered.

Ben started walking again and Henrietta Street quickly led onto other narrow, cobbled streets with small galleries, cafes and curiosity shops.

'In here,' Ben said, quickly pulling her toward one of the shops and ducking through the low wooden doorway. The shop was quaint and sold old-fashioned sweets, all in tubs, symmetrically lining the walls with sweets of all colours and sizes. It reminded Kate of being a child again, searching the shelves for all of her favourites.

'Go on, pick some,' Ben said, his eyes shining like Christmas tree lights as he scanned the shelves. 'Look, there are flying saucers, Winter mixture, Bon Bons and humbugs,' he whispered as he picked up the jars and handed them to the rotund, grey haired lady who stood behind the counter. She smiled. Her cheeks were as red as beetroot and her glasses reminded Kate of the jewelled ones her great-grandmother used to wear.

'I like liquorice allsorts,' she said finally, after scouring her way through every shelf for her favourite. She passed the jar across the counter to the lady. 'They all taste just a little similar, but in reality, you never know quite what you'll get.'

'Wow, that's quite a surprise coming from someone with the worst OCD I've ever known.'

'I do not have OCD.' She turned and glared at him. 'Okay, maybe I do. A little. But I've only been this bad since the accident. It made me self-conscious and now I can't bear anything to be out of place.' She laughed, poking him in the side and watched as the sweets tumbled into a stainless steel bowl on the weighing scale, before falling from the bowl and into a white paper bag.

'I've noticed. Everything with you has a place. You line everything up. Even Don and Patrick have begun tidying their desks since you moved in,' he retorted as he passed a ten pound note over for the sweets, thanking the lady and telling her to keep the change. 'I think you've scared them into being tidy.' He poked Kate in the ribs, just as she had to him and pushed a humbug into his mouth, before once more ducking to avoid the low doorway, as they both stepped back out onto damp cobbles.

Kate was relieved that the rain had slowed down to a spatter and leaned just close enough into Ben that she could reach into his bag and steal one of his sweets.

'Hey, eat your own,' he grumbled.

Kate shook her head. 'Nah, forbidden fruit is much more fun, isn't it?' She pointed to the seagulls that were hiding under the eaves of the terraced cottages. 'You see, it's much more fun to steal one than to ask for permission.' She grinned, winked and moved to his left-hand side all at once, before practically skipping down the street beside him.

Walking over the bridge and down to the quayside, they paid attention to how many fishermen were moored. Some had already brought in their loads of fish, as others tried desperately to sell tickets for rides on the sea. They made promises of great coastline views, sightings of seals, dolphins and other spectacles that would probably never be seen through the rain and sea fog. Ben walked over and discreetly chatted to one of the older fishermen, as Kate pretended to look in a shop that sold everything from Whitby rock through to Dracula capes.

Did people really buy all of these trinkets?

'This way,' Ben said as he steered her along the quayside

and down some steps towards one of the boats. Before Kate knew it, she was being dragged onto a large fishing boat that was empty, other than the captain.

'Private tour, please,' Ben shouted as he jumped on board the *Red Lady*. 'And some rugs for our legs, if you don't mind.'

'Ben, no!' she shouted trying to protest. 'Couldn't you do this alone? I'm not sure my sea legs are up to it. Besides, I can see the cliffs from here.' She pointed to the cliffs and then to the sea, its rolling white water crashing against the rocks at the base of the cliff. 'I … I don't much like the water.'

'Where's your sense of adventure, Kate?' Ben whispered just loud enough for the captain to hear. 'Besides, it's our honeymoon. We have to do something crazy to tell the grandkids, when we have them.' He flashed her a smile. But, not just any smile, his whole face lit up. It radiated a warmth that Kate had never seen and for just a moment she wondered what it would be like for a man to smile at you like that every day.

Kate knew that Ben needed to get information about the boats, especially if this boat was the *Red Lady* that Isobel had mentioned. If the captain was riding the waves at night, they needed to find out why.

'But …' She looked at Ben, hoping he'd play along. 'I kind of need to go to the loo. I'm just wishing I'd gone before jumping aboard.'

'We have a toilet on board, miss, just through the galley.' The captain pointed to the doors that led inside and Kate excused herself, in search of the toilet – and some sleuthing on the way, if she could.

Back on deck, Kate noticed Ben handing money to the captain, who then went into the cabin, and returned with two huge fluffy blankets. He placed one on the wet seat for them both to sit on and then carefully tucked the other over both Kate and Ben's legs, who was still looking excited at the prospect of a boat trip. Kate loved the sparkle that had returned to his eyes, and settled herself next to him. Besides, beyond ending up a new wreck off the east coast, what harm could a boat trip really do?

She looked up at Ben. 'How much did you pay him?' Kate whispered as she pulled the blanket around her. It was clean, fluffy and Kate doubted it would normally be used, not unless the price had been right. The toilets had been spotless, as had the rest of the galley, making Kate think that the boat wouldn't have been used for fishing in a very long time. For a start, even the deck was clean and tidy. It was painted bright red, with black and white stripes, along with a bright yellow winch on the stern, all looking far too pristine.

'You have a very beautiful wife, sir,' the captain commented as he tipped his hat, then turned and began to steer the boat swiftly out of the harbour.

Kate blushed. Ben might have corrected him, but instead he winked at her. He'd already indicated that this was their honeymoon and even with the lack of a wedding ring, it appeared that the captain had believed him.

With the sound of the wind making it difficult to hear, Ben leaned in close to Kate and whispered, 'I doubt he gets more than a couple of private tours a day and out of what he earns, he'll have expenses. You know, the fuel, the harbour costs, etc.'

'Which means he must be making a living doing something else?' Kate looked over to where the captain stood. He was quite young and easily steered his boat over the waves and around the coastline.

'He probably does other jobs on the side,' Ben whispered as the boat took a dip on the waves making Kate shriek with nervous laughter.

'Just playing devil's advocate here, but what if there are no extra jobs?' she whispered back.

Ben pondered her question for a moment. 'Well, he'll

do what he can. Sometimes work is slow. Sometimes it's non-existent. Men like our captain here would have learnt how to take the good with the bad. It's like the rain, some people would be miserable and see it as a hindrance, others would take the opportunity to splash and dance through the puddles.' Ben had replied with a metaphor that Kate knew was directed at her. The past days had been difficult, but Ben was right. She should dance in the rain. She did need to put the bad things behind her. After all, as the saying goes, what doesn't kill you makes you stronger.

She thought of the accident, of what her mother had said the night before and of Eve. 'Oh no, I didn't call Eve.' She jumped up from her seat, but Ben pulled her back under the blanket and put his arm around her. The touch of his hand sent an electric shock down her spine, her legs trembled and her stomach did a somersault.

'Don't worry,' he said as his eyes searched hers. 'Eric said he was going over after work. He has an early finish today.'

'Seriously. Why would he do that?' Kate's voice was concerned. 'They've only met the once. Haven't they?'

'He said something about taking her to join his book club.' Ben smiled. 'Eric's harmless and probably very good for Eve. Trust him.'

'But she barely knows him!' Kate yelled as she searched frantically through her bag for her mobile phone.

'Kate, she's fine. Stop fussing.'

Kate hesitated before settling back down under the blanket. 'But they're so different. In fact, I'd say they're poles apart. I mean, do they even like the same kind of books?'

Did Eve like Sherlock Holmes novels? Why didn't she know this about her own twin?

Kate settled down in the arc of Ben's arm. They were pretending to be married and Kate had begun to quite enjoy the role play. Besides, it was the perfect excuse to curl up close. Ben made her feel secure, comfortable and wanted. He also made her feel safe as her stomach once again lurched but this time because the boat bounced up and down on the swell. The gulls swooped overhead in the hope that they might find food and the abbey loomed impressively on the cliff top. It rose up out of the rock, high above where they now sailed. Beside it stood the car park where they'd left Patrick earlier that morning, which reminded Kate that those steps would once again have to be climbed, before they'd be travelling back to Bedale.

Ben looked down as Kate slept. He'd hated seeing her so upset that morning. His heart had gone out to her and he'd have done anything within his power to take away her pain. Now she cuddled into him for the second time that day and slept. Had she felt safe in his arms, or had she simply been so exhausted that she'd practically collapsed with the movement of the boat on the waves? He hoped she'd felt safe, hoped she'd felt comfortable in his presence. He liked her, but she was broken and hurt, just like he had been. He looked down at her. Her hurt was far deeper and much more current than his. After all, he'd had four years in which to heal. He had internal scars, but none that showed, unlike her and he had no idea how she would ever come to terms with the scarring on her face, the crippling of her sister, or the death of her brother, especially when she knew that ultimately her whole family really had blamed her. Ben glanced down at the left-hand side of her face. The scar was clearly visible, yet it didn't alter the fact that she was still unbelievably beautiful. It had most probably faded a little over the past year and he lifted his hand to gently stroke her face, his finger carefully drawing a line across her jawbone and, for some reason, he felt an urge to magic it away, but to do that would change her and to him she looked perfect.

The boat came to a halt by the harbour. Ben looked up at the captain, indicating that he give them some time and Ben mentally kicked himself. He was supposed to be investigating the captain. But instead, he hugged Kate ever more tightly. It was far too soon to wake her, far too soon to let her go. She was exhausted and needed the sleep and he was content to sit and allow her to wake up in her own time.

Besides, for the first time in years, he held a woman in his arms. He'd missed the feeling and was more than aware that once she woke, he might never get to hold her this way again.

Kate stirred as she felt Ben's touch on her face. His finger drew a line along her scar, making her breath catch in her throat. Never before had she been comfortable with anyone seeing the scar up close and never before had she allowed anyone other than a doctor to touch it, but for some reason she didn't move. The boat rocked now rather than bounced. This indicated to her that they were back in the harbour and the boat had come to a stop. Keeping her eyes closed for just a few moments more, she felt Ben's face lower to hers, as he cuddled in. She was warm, comfortable and, for just a moment, she felt more content than she'd ever felt before. Then, she felt Ben's face lower to hers again. His lips gently brushed hers and she opened her sleepy eyes to look into his. They were jet black, deep, welcoming and shone like ebony. She held his gaze.

'You … you kissed me,' she whispered. The words were all she could manage to say as her fingers went up to touch her lips.

'I did.' He paused and Kate knew that he was thinking of his next words carefully. 'What was it you said? Better to steal one, than to ask for permission.' He nodded. 'Well, I was testing your theory and I think you are right; forbidden fruit really is more fun.'

She smiled. 'Touché.' Sitting up, she looked around to see where they were. 'I'm sorry I fell asleep again. I … I barely slept, you know, last night.'

'Don't worry. I understand. You've had a horrid few days, you must be shattered.' His hand reached up and touched her face and for a moment, Kate thought he'd repeat the kiss. But instead, he smiled, stood up, stretched and folded the blankets for the captain to retrieve, before winking at her and adding, 'Oh, and by the way, you snore like a train.'

Kate tried to playfully slap Ben as he jumped from the boat, and ran back up the steps to the quayside.

'Oh you're horrid, why on earth did I marry you?' she joked, knowing the captain was still watching from afar. 'And I'm starving, so if you don't buy me some fish and chips soon, I may consider divorce.'

Ben took the hint and steered Kate further along the quayside.

'Right. Wait here, just for a few minutes. I need to go back and pretend you lost an earring or something,' Ben announced as he turned back towards the *Red Lady*.

Kate caught his arm. 'Why?' she searched his eyes with hers, a look of amusement crossing her face.

'I need to get some answers. I was so content, sitting there hugging you, I totally forgot the investigation. I should have been looking for clues. If he is involved, there would have to be something. I won't be long.' Ben began to walk away and Kate burst into laughter and held up her mobile phone.

'Do you mean like photographs of maps, and compass points? Along with Isobel Reed's phone number, and a date and time of a meeting, along with quantities of drugs that are about to be dropped? I found it all scribbled on a pad, in the room beyond the toilet. It was locked at first, but it's amazing what a safety pin and a nail file can do.' She smiled, and looked pleased with herself as Ben studied the photos. 'What do you think I was doing? You know, when I went to find the toilet? Oh yes, that's right, I was being a private investigator.'

Kate had got her sparkle back, and chatted all through lunch to Ben about her love of North Yorkshire, and her visits to her grandmother's cottage as a child, along with Eve and James. They would have days when they would all drive for miles, just looking for the perfect picnic spot after going to the creamery.

'Grandmother would sit on the rug with a loaf of homemade bread, a pack of butter, our newly bought cheese and a big knife.' She laughed. 'She'd butter the bread fresh because she knew I liked it that way. We could eat the whole loaf between us.'

Ben smiled. He liked the way her face came to life when she spoke, how her hands became animated as she described how her childhood and teenage years had been before the accident. It was as though her whole life had been split in two. There was her life before and her life after the accident. But this he could understand.

He thought of the kiss he'd just stolen, of how Kate had reacted. She'd questioned it, but hadn't looked surprised or offended and he wondered for a moment if she'd thought it part of the act, of their pretending to be newlyweds. But then, as they'd stood together, he'd considered kissing her again, but in a real, more loving way. But he hadn't. It hadn't felt right. A first kiss should be special, full of hope, passion and trust and he decided that he had to think of a better way, a more romantic approach.

Chapter Twenty-Seven

'Hi, how are you?' Eve asked as she sat in the front seat of Eric's car. He had folded up her wheelchair and put it in the back, before getting in and starting the engine. She glanced at him and smiled. He was cute and kind of geeky and she'd fast come to the conclusion that it was a look that she liked.

'Are you as nervous as I am?' he asked, with a genuine look of concern.

Eve shuffled in her seat and nodded. She thought back to a conversation she'd had with Kate, the one where Kate had commented that Eric had reminded her of Clark Kent and now that she looked, she had to agree, he did. She couldn't get the image out of her mind, nor could she dismiss the idea that she'd like to take off his glasses and see if the man beneath lived up to her Superman expectations. She took in a deep breath and breathed out a little too heavy, making it sound like a sigh.

'I'm a bit of both. A bit excited, but a bit nervous too. I just hope I can get in and out of the house without too much of a problem. Do they know I'm disabled?' she asked as she indicated her chair before clicking the seat belt tightly into position.

'W-w-why would that matter? I'll help you,' Eric stuttered as Eve looked up and into his eyes. He really was nervous, nothing like the men she'd previously dated and, for that reason alone, she liked him.

'Great. Ever since the accident I've grown to love books. Don't think I've ever read as much in my life as I have in the past year. And the idea of a book club sounds fun.' She smiled and tried to sound positive. 'But ...' She looked at her watch. '... I do have to be home by four.'

'Oh, okay. Really?' Eric looked disappointed.

'I have a dog. Max. I need to get back to let him out. You can help me if you like?' She flashed him her warmest smile, a smile that she hoped would encourage him to stay for an hour or two after they got home.

Eric smiled back, a smile that lit up his face and made Eve forget all about Clark Kent.

Eric pulled the car up outside the home of Megan Ahearn. She was an Irish lady with a huge personality and her home was comfortable, but definitely lived in. There were old rugs on the floor, a big open log fire, magazines in piles under footstools and Royal Doulton china ladies on side tables. No one could call it untidy, but Eve found it overbearing. The thought of knocking Megan's ornaments over with her wheelchair terrified her and she kept her chair as close to the door as she could.

'Eat up, my dear Eve. Women should have curves,' Megan said, grinning as she handed Eve a second piece of cake. 'Your boyfriend, he needs something to grab hold of, if you know what I mean?' Her strong Irish accent sang out as she laughed, holding her hands up as though grabbing someone's backside.

The others in the room all agreed and Eve felt herself blushing as she looked over to where Eric sat with his head in a book. She was unsure whether to correct Megan, tell her that Eric wasn't her boyfriend, even though the thought of him being one did seem quite appealing. She decided to stay quiet and to say nothing.

'How are you doing?' Eric asked as he walked over to her and sat down on the chair to her side.

'I'm good, but so full of tea and cake I could burst,' she whispered, hoping that the lovely Megan didn't hear. 'I really hope she doesn't expect me to drink any more. I'm terrified of moving the chair, terrified of knocking things over and going to the loo at other people's houses can be a bit tricky.'

They chuckled together as the group took out their books and began to read out loud. Eve hadn't read the book but the whole afternoon was fun and for the first time in over a year she began to feel that making a circle of friends for herself wouldn't be that hard. In fact, it was something she really wanted to do.

On the drive back to Eve's, Eric tried to explain who everyone in the club was, adding his own opinions of them.

'Do you think they liked me?' Eve asked as she turned and looked at Eric, who'd now stopped the car, stopped talking and looked down, as though unsure what to say next.

'Eve, how could anyone not like you?' he finally said, turning toward her and carefully lifting his hand to her cheek. 'Actually, I'm sorry. That was inappropriate, I shouldn't do that.' He dropped his hand, making Eve stare at the uncertainty in his eyes. She'd enjoyed his touch. It had been the first time anyone had touched her with affection since the accident. It had been as though the minute she'd been seated in the chair, someone had put a banner around her neck that said, *Don't touch, incapable of sexual feeling.* But she was capable, and she did want the affection that Eric showed her.

'I don't break,' she said as she took hold of his hand. 'Honestly.' She lifted it back to her face, gently holding it to her lips. She gazed into Eric's eyes; he had a look of kindness, not of pity. It was genuine, caring and not a look that Eve had seen very often, and right now it was everything she needed to know as she raised her hands to his glasses, waited for just a second and then slowly lifted them from his face.

Chapter Twenty-Eight

'Come on then, tell all. How was your afternoon with Eric?' Kate asked as she and Eve spread out their picnic blanket. They'd pitched their spot on the central grassed area of Richmond Castle, while a very energetic Max, being out of harness, took the opportunity to run back and forth. He chased his ball, ran around in circles, and dodged the empty wheelchair while running and sniffing at the ground for scent.

Unlike the day before, the sky was clear and the sun shone brightly. The grass had dried, making it a pleasure to sit on. Both looked nervously toward the shop as they spoke, making sure their mother couldn't hear. She'd trundled in there the moment they'd arrived at the castle and twenty minutes later she still hadn't emerged.

'Eric's lovely. We had a great time,' Eve replied in a whisper as Kate began to take out the fresh bread, slicing it and buttering it, just as her grandmother had done so many years before. Placing the bread on plates, she unwrapped the ham, coleslaw, scotch eggs and quiche. The sight of which made Max stop running around. He instantly took a liking to the idea of food and sat before them both, patiently waiting to be given a treat.

Eve lay back on the blanket. 'We're reading *The Secret Keeper* by Kate Morton. It's really good.' Kate noticed that Eve sounded excited, maybe for the first time in a year. 'It's two stories, set in different times. A young girl witnesses a crime while she's hiding in a tree house and fifty years later it all comes back to haunt her.'

'Eve, I don't want to know what you're reading, silly. I want to know how all this happened. You only met Eric the other night and now you're going out on dates with him?' she asked, amused that her sister would do something so completely unpredictable.

'Kate, I have been on a date before. Quite a few, actually. Eric asked and I said yes. It wasn't a secret.' Eve smiled shyly and for a moment she once again resembled the young and carefree teenager.

'Will you be seeing him again?' Kate asked hesitantly, hoping that Eric had enjoyed the day as much as Eve had.

'Of course. He's taking me out to dinner tomorrow,' she responded enthusiastically and flicked her hair in a way that Kate had not seen her do in years. 'A carvery at the creamery in Hawes.'

Kate smiled. It was good that Eve had a new friend. Her sparkle had returned and by the look of how she blushed, he'd already become a little more than just a friend.

Eve lifted herself back up into a sitting position. 'So, are you going to tell me about Ben?'

Kate sighed. She thought of the lovely day that she'd spent with Ben, the trip to the abbey, the lovely cuddly boat ride, the stolen kiss, the fish and chips and the way he'd playfully chased her up the ninety-nine steps, even though the run had just about finished them both off.

The whole day had made her think about Rob, about his involvement with Isobel and about moving on. After what she'd heard outside Isobel's house, she never wanted him touching her again. She wanted him to leave and, as far as she was concerned, the sooner the better. He'd barely been home for weeks. But Kate didn't care; not any more.

'I'm back,' her mother's voice bellowed as she wove her way between other groups of people who lay on the grass of the castle grounds. She had a bottle held tightly in her hands. 'Mead, darling, your father and I love it.' Kate stared in disbelief and confusion, as she watched her mother carefully pack the bottle into her bag. 'I thought I'd buy him a bottle, it'll make him so happy.'

Mother was acting as though nothing had been said, as though she was about to pop home as soon as they were done with the picnic and take the husband that she was supposedly divorcing a bottle of mead. Kate crossed her fingers, knowing that her father would know what to do. She really hoped that he would persuade her to see a doctor, get some medical help or at least talk to someone. She also hoped that, with any luck, he would come and take her back home soon.

But Kate still felt bitter. She still couldn't believe how nasty her mother had been, and how she'd admitted that she blamed her for the accident. By the end of that day, Kate had not only hated her mother, but she'd hated herself too.

'So, does this mean you're going home?' Eve asked hopefully. Saying exactly what both twins were thinking.

'No, dear. Your father's working away. Why did you think I'd come? He wants me to stay here, it was him that told me to come. He thought I'd be better with you two, rather than being home alone and it's just for a few more days,' she said as she sat down on the grass. 'He has a reason for everything, you know that and I've found it easier over the years not to argue.'

Both Kate and Eve glanced toward each other. They had a way of communicating without having to say a word and both had picked up on the news that their father was away, which was why he hadn't been answering the house phone and his mobile seemed to be permanently switched off. No longer was she threatening divorce, nor was she calling him a sociopath, and just one look between them created a silent acknowledgment to keep quiet on the subject.

Kate's mobile buzzed and she checked the message that popped up.

Hope you are having a good day. Ben x

A smile turned the corner of her mouth. It was only the second text that Ben had ever sent and, what's more, for the second time, there was a kiss at the end of it. Kate felt herself glow inside. She liked him, but still found it hard to believe that a man like Ben would be so nice to her and wondered if she'd somehow mistaken his affection. Brushing the thought to one side, she picked up the phone and replied quickly.

Today is a good day, but yesterday was better x

She closed her eyes as she pressed Send. Was it best to take a chance and say exactly what was on her mind or should she have been a little more casual and play it cool?

She lay down on the grass, allowing the sun to warm her face.

'Mmmmm sounds like you had a good day yesterday too,' Eve teased as she picked up Kate's phone and read the text message. Kate grabbed the phone from her hand and they both simultaneously pulled a face.

'Shush,' she whispered, ensuring that Mother hadn't paid attention to the exchange.

Kate's phone began to ring. The theme tune rang out and Eve began quietly humming the wedding march, as Kate glared at her to be quiet.

Rob's name flashed up on the screen and a sudden nervous reaction made Kate feel as though someone had punched her in the stomach.

'What do you want, Rob?' she snapped. The only way to not break down was to stay in control. The memory of him being with Isobel was still clear in her mind and she was unable to contain her anger. Besides, he'd stayed away from home for two nights now and, at a guess, he'd been at Honeysuckle House, in Isobel's bed. But then again, had he? If he hadn't stayed at Isobel's, where had he stayed? After all, hadn't it been Luca's brogues that Eric had seen in her hallway, not Rob's expensive Nike trainers?

'Hey, baby, what's wrong? I just called to check you were okay and you go snapping my head off.'

'What are you up to, Rob?' She stood up and walked across the grass, ensuring she was out of earshot of her mother who was currently leafing through a magazine. 'You haven't been home for days, *again*.' She had to be careful what she said. Isobel was still under investigation and Kate couldn't confront him, not about her. It could blow the whole case and, if it did, the reward might be lost to Parker & Son.

'Come on, baby, so I haven't been home for a day or two. It happens. You know what I'm like.'

'Yes, I do know what you are like, Rob, and I don't like it any more. What are your secrets, Rob? What are you hiding?'

'Me, why would you think that, baby?'

'As the saying goes, Rob, tell me no secrets, and I'll tell you no lies. Problem is, I can't keep up with all your bloody lies, and I no longer want to.' The words were spat down the phone like venom. She'd had enough and this time he wasn't getting away with feeding her the normal bullshit that fell out of his mouth.

Rob went quiet and Kate could hear his deep breaths. She knew she'd caught him off guard and, knowing Rob, he was contemplating the situation and deciding what retort he'd come back with. 'What's got into you, Kate?'

'I want you out, Rob.' She couldn't help herself. The words had just fallen out of her mouth like an erupting volcano. 'I want you out of my cottage and I want you out of my life, permanently. Do you understand that?'

There, she'd said it. Relief flooded through her and suddenly she realised that it was what she wanted more than

174

anything else in the world. There was no way she could ever trust him again. Now that she knew about him and Isobel, and about her numerous sexual partners, the last thing she wanted was him sharing her bed.

'Err, what? Where the hell …?' Rob shouted. 'Why the hell would you say that?' He felt the panic rise within him. Where had the 'grateful to be loved' Kate gone? She couldn't throw him out. It was imperative that he lived in Yorkshire, and more than imperative that he lived with Kate. To the outside world he was a personal trainer. He was a man engaged to be married to the daughter of a barrister. To the outside world they appeared happy, content, and that couldn't change, not now. It gave him a certain standing within the community. Men trusted him with their wives. If he were single, the trust would be lost and the drugs wouldn't get sold.

'Baby, we can sort this out. You know how much I love you,' his voice quivered and he tried desperately not to lose his temper. 'We're good together, Kate, you know that. What about the other night, you know, the night in the bathroom? It was good, wasn't it?'

He had to make his sweet talk work. After all, why wouldn't it? It had always worked before. He'd always been able to talk her round and make sure she kept loving him. Besides, she was lucky to have him. What woman wouldn't want a man like him? Especially since the accident, she should be thankful that anyone wanted her at all. He remembered the day he saw her at the hospital. Her car wouldn't start and she'd looked sad and broken, sitting there in the driver's seat with a car that was going nowhere.

Unbeknownst to her, the whole situation had been engineered between Giancarlo and himself. They'd found her, watched her and targeted her home as a safe house. A woman who'd inherited a cottage would be reasonably well off and, as the local PCSO, she was well known to the community, which was a bonus in itself. But then the accident had happened. Things had gone wrong and it had been unfortunate that her brother had been a casualty, but the accident had been part of the plan. The car had been supposed to run off the road, no one should have been injured, no one should have died and he should have been able to rush in and save her. She was supposed to fall in love with him for being the hero, and then they were supposed to live happily ever after. At least, for as long as Giancarlo allowed them to.

Their brother, James, was dead and murder hadn't been part of the plan. He'd pulled both her and Eve from the wreckage and without a second thought he'd gone back for James. But it was too late, he was already dead and there would be no super hero moment, meaning that Rob had had no choice but to leave the scene and abandon the plan.

But when Giancarlo says that something has to be done, no one argues and it wasn't long before he'd been ordered to find a new way to get close to Kate. And tampering with her car and making it look like a breakdown had been a perfect plan. He'd turned on the charm, had asked her out on dates and had allowed her to believe that he'd been falling in love with her. Because by pretending to fall in love with her he'd been given the perfect way of infiltrating the village and its people.

'As I said, I want you out, Rob, and I want you out before I get home,' Kate shouted, her voice angry but controlled.

She quickly looked over her shoulder. The last thing she needed right now was the 'I told you so' talk from her mother. The less she knew, the better. 'Get your things and get out. You should easily find a bed for the night, after all you don't normally have a problem, do you?'

She knew that she should be upset. There had been so many times when he'd been tender, warm, gentle and affectionate toward her. Yet still, she could think of no reason why she'd want to stay with him. He didn't love her. He couldn't love her. If he did he'd come home at night, rather than spending nights away with women like Isobel Reed. God only knew how many other women there were or had been. She tried to think of how many women would have been on his books. How many training sessions he took each week and his constant showering and changing of clothes between each one. How many of his clients had he slept with?

'Rob, did you hear me?'

'Oh, I heard you,' he shouted with a high-pitched shriek that could have shattered glass and Kate pulled the phone away from her ear. 'You can't do that, you bitch. I stood by you, Kate. It was me that had to look at that disgusting scar, me that had to make love to you looking like that, yet still, I stayed.' He paused, giving Kate the chance to draw breath.

'*Had to? Had to?*' She couldn't believe her ears. '*Get out ... I want you out, and I want you out now!*' she screamed. At this point she didn't care who heard, she just wanted him to realise that she meant what she said.

'Ohhhhhhh, I get it. Who ... who is it? What's his name?'

'Don't try and turn the tables on me, Rob.'

'Who are you shagging, Kate? There must be someone, I mean come on, why else would you throw me out?'

'Rob, you're being both cruel and ridiculous. I don't have to justify myself to you. Now get out of my grandmother's cottage before I get back. I don't want you there anymore and I'd rather be alone than be with you. Is that clear enough for you?'

Rob went quiet and Kate pulled the phone from her ear and checked the screen. For just a moment, she thought they'd been cut off.

'Have you been dieting, Kate?' Rob said completely out of the blue. 'The jeans you have on, are they looking a little loose?'

The words made her panic. Where was he? What did he mean? The jeans did look loose, but he hadn't seen her for days. And how would he know she was wearing them today? Her breathing escalated and she spun around, her eyes searching, looking for Rob.

Where was he?

'Are you watching me?' Her eyes were fixed on the castle's turrets; it was the only place he could hide. 'Would you stoop that low, you bastard?'

She spun around once more, and then relaxed as she saw the area around her was clear apart from Eve, her mother and Max. All the other people appeared to have left and there was no movement around the turrets.

'Where are you, Rob?' she murmured. Her soft voice and attempt to keep calm made Rob give off an evil laugh that went on forever.

'I'm everywhere, Kate, and don't you ever forget it.'

She stared up at the sky, trying to clear her mind. What if she'd been seen in Whitby, what if he'd seen her with Ben? But, then again, why would that matter? Rob didn't love her, so why should he care?

He was making her angry. 'Everywhere, are you? Rob, you might think you are, but in reality you are nowhere, you are no one. You're not important to anyone, especially to me. I really do want you out. I want you gone and what's more, I never want to see your evil face ever again.'

'Who's telling you to do this, Kate? Is it that new boss of yours, or your good for nothing mother? If it is, they'd better watch their backs.' He paused. 'Or, actually, I get it, could it be that pathetic crippled sister of yours? It's her, isn't it? She's never liked me. If it is, mark my words, I will make her pay.'

Kate reeled at the multiple insults. She didn't much like her mother, but she wasn't going to listen to Rob or anyone else saying anything bad about her. He had no right to threaten her and as for threatening Eve … and Ben.

'Do you really think that I don't know my own mind, Rob? Do you think I can't live without you? Well, I've got news for you, I can. Now get your filthy cheating backside out of my fucking house.'

'Cheating? Is that what you think?' He paused. 'What the hell makes you think that?'

Kate inhaled. She had to be careful and not reveal what she knew about Isobel Reed.

'I'm not naïve, Rob, whatever you might think. Why else would you not be coming home at nights? I've had enough and I want you gone.'

'You might think you've won, Kate, but I can guarantee you one thing. There's nobody else that would ever want you. You think that tidying the house within an inch of its life will ever make up for that mess on your face? Do you?' The words had been carefully chosen, vindictive and meant to hurt, but Kate was past hurting. She knew her scar was ugly, red and puckered. She didn't need him to tell her that. She saw it every time she caught her reflection in the mirror.

She was absolutely determined that Rob would never humiliate her again. She was sure that Ben cared, but if he didn't, it didn't matter. Yesterday he'd given her hope and that was all she'd needed to move forward.

'That's where you're wrong, Rob.' She looked up to the sky as a drop of rain landed on the tip of her nose. She smiled at the irony. It reminded her of her chat with Ben and the advice he'd given. She laughed. 'Do you know what, Rob? I don't need you. But it's raining and what I do need to do is to go. That's right. I need to go and I need to dance in the rain.

179

Chapter Twenty-Nine

Kate pulled up outside the house to see Rob's truck clearly parked on the drive. She sat for a while, watching and hoping that he'd leave, but knowing deep down that he wouldn't go, not without a fight.

Thankfully, her mother had agreed to stay with Eve for a few days, much to Eve's disapproval. She'd been invited to go back with them, watching DVDs had been mentioned, but Kate had been tired and after her confrontation with Rob had opted to go home in favour of an early night instead.

Taking a deep breath, she stamped up to the back door and walked in. She fully expected Rob to be packing, or that he might have already packed and would be ready to go. But as she entered the kitchen, she stopped in her tracks.

'Hey, baby. I've cooked us some food.' He spun on the spot, picked up the tea towel and threw it over his shoulder. 'We have a chicken stir fry, with garlic bread and roast courgettes, with garlic, tomato and Parmesan.' He smiled, took a sip from a glass of wine and passed her the bottle. 'Here. It's cold. Just out of the fridge.'

'I'm not hungry.' It was all she could think to say. She stood and stared at him. He was cooking, wiping down and sipping wine, like nothing had been said. What made the image even worse was that he never cooked, he never cleaned and he never normally drank.

'Come on, sit down. I have it all ready.' He took two pasta bowls from the cupboard, placed them on the table and opened the oven, where roasted courgettes sizzled in a dish.

'I said I'm not hungry. Besides, what are you still doing here? I told you to get out.'

Rob immediately spun. His eyes pierced hers. 'Come on, baby, I'm trying to be nice. Now, please, sit down and bloody well eat.' He put the hot dish containing the courgettes down on the oak table and Kate knew that a scorch mark would be left behind. She stared, and sat down, not daring to speak. She could feel her whole body tremble and looked towards her bag, wondering if she could get to her phone, and who she would call if she could. It was hardly a police matter. She'd asked him to leave, he hadn't. Instead he'd cooked supper and she just knew that the police would say she was wasting their time.

Kate's stomach contracted as she picked at the food. She didn't want to eat and eyed the food suspiciously. She'd never known him to cook and it occurred to her that he could have found a way to poison the meal. But she quickly dismissed the idea, as he was far too busy tucking into his own and he wouldn't have had time to poison one portion without the other.

'Rob, I ... I'm really not hungry. I ... I think I'll take a bath.' She stood up, grabbed her bag and headed for the stairs, fully expecting him to follow and felt a huge sense of relief when he didn't.

Closing and locking the bathroom door behind her, she reached for her bag, grabbed at her phone and sent a text to Ben.

I asked Rob to leave. But he's still here. He's acting all strange. I'm locked in the bathroom. I'm scared. x

Kate ran the water. She knew she had to at least sound like she was doing what she'd said and her mind suddenly went to the last time she'd made love to Rob, in this bath, in this bathroom. She heaved.

Sitting on the floor, she watched her phone, willing Ben to return the text, praying that he'd see it. But even if he did, what could he do? She should have stayed in the car, driven off and waited until the coast was clear. But the last thing she'd expected to do was to walk into her kitchen and find Rob cooking and acting as though nothing had been said.

She heard Rob's footsteps on the stairs and panicked. She jumped up and picked up her work phone, and pressed in the panic code, just as Ben had taught her.

The door handle moved and Kate froze, staring at the door.

'You in the bath, Kate?' Rob questioned as the handle repeatedly went up and down.

'Let me be, Rob. I just want to take a bath in peace. I think it's time you packed and left.' She swished the water around to make a noise, in the hope he'd leave her alone.

'Oh, it is, is it?' A loud noise made Kate scream. The door burst open and Rob stood, with his frame filling the doorway. 'You won't let it go, will you? You just won't let it go.'

'Rob, I want you to leave. Please.' She looked over his shoulder; she needed to get past him, but he blocked her escape, making her take a step back. 'I really don't want to fight, Rob. Please, just go.' She backed herself into the corner. 'I've phoned the police. They're on their way and you need to leave before they get here.' She called his bluff, but saw the way his eyes dilated, deep black and cavernous.

'Why, baby? Why would you want to do that?' He moved towards her. 'Kate, I love you. And you know that you love me. Am I right? Come on, baby, let's try again. I'm begging you.'

'Love me? You've never loved me, Rob. Now, get out of my way and go to hell,' she said, fear coursing through her body.

Rob just stared at her, his eyes devoid of all emotion. 'I thought you said that you wanted to dance? Well, come on then, dance with me.' He grabbed at her hands and began moving them up and down. He put his hand on her waist, and began moving erotically against her.

'Get off me, Rob. Please. Leave me alone.'

He did as she asked, dropped her hands and stood back. His hands rested on his hips and she saw him take in a deep and prolonged breath. He slowly shook his head, side to side. 'That's what it is.' He smiled, shrugged his shoulders and stepped towards her. 'I'm doing it wrong, aren't I?' He laughed, a long, evil laugh that made Kate begin to shake relentlessly within. 'I'm not dancing right, am I, Kate?' He grabbed at her shirt, tearing it in the process. Kate screamed. 'You wanted to dance in the rain, didn't you?' He turned to look at the bath water. 'And when you dance in the rain, baby, you get wet, don't you?'

Panic rose within her, but Rob was far stronger than she was and he dragged her effortlessly towards him. The next moment, he had put her in the bath and pushed her head under the water. She held her breath, her lungs began to burn, she was sure they would burst and she could feel Rob's hands holding her down. Panic surrounded her every move, her hands grabbed at his hair, his face, and then the image of James came into her mind; her brother's glazed, cold eyes stared back.

And then she heard a noise. A bang, a shout, a loud noise that came from everywhere all at once and then her head emerged from beneath the water. Rob's hands were gone, and she gulped at the air, trying to pull as much as she could into her lungs, but began to cough, choke, yet still attempted to pull in the air that didn't want to go in.

'It's okay, it's okay. He's gone.' Ben was there. His arms were around her and she felt relief, followed by hysteria, as she felt herself being lifted from the water.

Chapter Thirty

Ben's voice woke Kate. She felt drowsy, confused and, for a moment, wondered where she was, and then she remembered.

'How are you feeling?' he asked, his hand brushing the hair away from her face, which for once wasn't covered in her usual make-up. She didn't care what she looked like. All she felt was a deep, overwhelming sadness. A disbelief that Rob would try to kill her and thankful that Ben had turned up when he had.

'I'm all right. I could have done without the five hours we spent at the hospital last night, and the interview by the police, but other than that, they said that I'll live.'

'You need to eat,' he said. 'And on the menu today is a bacon sandwich. Would you like it up here, or downstairs?' He smiled and walked back to the door. 'Do you want coffee?' he asked.

'No, I'll come down and, yes, please, thank you,' she managed to say. 'Coffee would be great.' Her throat was sore, her arms and legs ached and she stretched her arms above her head, wincing with the pain.

She walked around the bed, looking down at the borrowed pyjamas that hung loosely from her body. She remembered rolling the arms and legs up to allow her hands and feet to move easily, but now they'd unravelled and hung so long that at least a foot of material hung at the end of each arm. She waved them up and down and tried to laugh, but tears sprang into her eyes. She looked around for her bag, a small bag that had been hurriedly filled with a selection of her clothes, underwear, but strangely not pyjamas. She shook her head and looked at its contents, hardly the items she'd normally choose. But at a time of panic, it was amazing what had seemed like a priority and what had not.

Trying to make the best of what she had with her, she dressed quickly. Her stomach rumbled and she went in search of the sandwich that Ben had tempted her with. His voice could be heard humming a tune and she padded her way down the stairs, along the hallway and toward the noise.

'I just love your house,' she managed to say as she entered the room. 'Thank you for, you know, bringing me here.'

Ben looked her up and down. 'Coffee's coming up and, technically, it's a very small house. It has just two bedrooms, but I use one as an office. I sold the big house after ... after Julia died. It felt too big, and far too empty.'

Kate nodded. 'I'd have probably done the same.' She tried to imagine how he'd felt about walking through the same rooms, and fully understood, especially after losing James and how she'd felt about taking his job.

Ben's house was modern, masculine and it suited him. He looked at home behind the counter and she smiled as he twisted the knobs on his coffee machine, which looked far too technical and she wondered if boiling a kettle would be easier.

She thought about Rob, of what he'd done, and of how she wanted him out of her life. But now it seemed that he'd disappeared and she prayed that he'd never dare come back. It was a strange feeling, the end of an era and she didn't know whether to be happy or sad that a part of her life was over. Her whole body felt bruised, on both the inside and the outside. She had a feeling of numbness, surrounded by an ache that wouldn't go away.

'Is fresh coffee okay? I don't have instant,' Ben suddenly said as he flashed a smile. He stood by the stove. His tracksuit bottoms hung from his waist and a tight, white T-shirt covered his chest. His arm muscles escaped the material and showed a polished shape that Kate hadn't noticed before. It was the first time she'd ever seen him dressed so casually and she had to admit, it suited him.

'That'd be lovely. Thanks.' She inhaled deeply. 'What smells so good?'

He turned and stirred a pan. 'Home-made chicken noodle soup,' he announced proudly. 'Mum always used to make it for me as a kid. It always seemed to make me better, when I didn't feel very well.' He paused before walking across the kitchen, and placing a cup of coffee before her. 'After the few days that you've just had, I kind of thought you looked as though you might need some.'

Kate sipped at the coffee, and slowly chewed at the bacon sandwich that Ben had prepared, swallowing with care. Her stomach growled and she hadn't realised how hungry she was until she'd begun to eat, but her throat still hurt. 'I'm sure food tastes better when someone else makes it for me.' She began to laugh and then stopped suddenly, thinking of Rob cooking for her, as though that would make everything all right.

Ben looked thoughtful. 'I was worried about you last night. When I saw your text, I didn't stop to reply. I just jumped in the car and drove. And then the panic alarm went off. I was terrified. I knew you wouldn't have keyed the code for nothing and, well, I just burst in and ran up the stairs.' He raised an eyebrow and exhaled. 'What if I'd got there just a few moments later?' He shook his head and then turned back toward the pan. It stood on a large cream Aga, which was set back in what looked like a brick chimney breast, but Kate knew that a chimney in a modern house was improbable. The kitchen was modern and pristine. Beams covered the ceiling and black granite worktops sparkled with a shine that stood out against the contemporary walnut cabinets. A mixture of old and new blended perfectly against the pure white walls.

'Looks like your mum taught you well,' she said as she picked at the bacon. 'Smells like you're a great cook.'

'Sure I am.' He smiled. 'I always showed an interest as a kid and she was more than happy for me to help. Gave us some time together, if you know what I mean, and as a willing individual, I always got to eat the proceeds.' He smiled again as he stole a small piece of bacon from her plate, then happily munched it, before turning around and stirring the soup once again. 'Another twenty minutes and I'll add the sweet corn and the noodles.'

'What's she like, your mum?' Kate asked, genuinely interested. She knew his father and knew how much like him Ben was, but couldn't ever remember Ben mentioning his mother before.

Ben chuckled as he picked up the tea towel. 'Are you serious?'

'What did I say?' she offered, holding her hands out as though waiting for an answer but once again Ben flashed her a smile and shook his head, before walking towards the door, chuckling as he went.

'Kate Duggan, you are so naive. I'm just going to throw some proper clothes on.' He left the room and headed up the stairs and towards his bedroom, the room she'd slept in the night before, and for the first time she wondered where he might have slept.

She wandered from room to room. The kitchen made way to a dining area. A long oak table stretched before a four-panelled concertina glass window that took up a whole wall and gave way to views over the countryside. The house might be small, but everywhere she looked it screamed money, class and perfection. Nothing had been done by half and Ben's personality showed in every minute detail.

A noise behind her made her jump. She spun around to see Ben leaning against the doorway; his wide disarming smile lit up his face and took her by surprise. He wore a blue cotton shirt, with jeans that hugged him just a little too comfortably, making her eyes dwell for just a little too long on their contours.

'You're laughing at me. Why do you say I'm naive?' she asked going back to his earlier comment.

'Because I think you are,' he replied, and then walked back to the kitchen and refilled his coffee. 'Some days, I really can't believe how clever you are and other days, how really naive you are.'

Kate followed him, sulking. She crossed her arms and sat down on the stool. 'Fine. Insult me, but I have no idea what I've said wrong.'

'Kate, Gloria is my mum. I can't believe you hadn't worked that out.' He chuckled again as Kate suddenly registered what he'd said.

'Gloria?' she asked in disbelief. 'What, really, how come?'

'Well, my mother and father, they met, fell in love and then I came along.' He ducked as a napkin narrowly missed his head, landing just short of the chicken soup.

'When you came to work for Parker and Son, Kate, did you just think it was me and Dad?' Ben walked over to where she stood.

'Of course, the name above the door indicates that, doesn't it?'

Again, Ben smiled. 'No it doesn't. It says Parker and Son. Gloria was the original private detective, and then I was born. Hence, Gloria Parker and Son. My dad, he was an accountant and still to this day tends to run the workload and the accounts at the office, albeit Mum did teach him the tricks of the trade and he became a really good detective. She taught me a lot of what I know too.' His hand reached out, toward her face, but stopped just short of touching her.

Kate was a little shocked but amused. It was true, she had presumed that the name was directed at William and Ben. William had been there on her first day, he'd spoken to her with authority and Gloria had appeared to be far too lovely to be the boss's wife. There had been no airs and graces, no attitude and definitely no acting like she owned the place.

She looked towards Ben's hand, knowing that once again he'd almost touched her face. She took in a deep breath and stared up and into his eyes.

'Kate ...'

'It ... it kind of makes a lot of sense, about Gloria, now that you've said,' she murmured, changing the subject and jumping down from the stool. She was nervous of what he would say next and looked toward the door. She shuffled from foot to foot.

Ben stepped forward. 'Kate ...?' he said again as he pulled her into his arms. His hand lifted to stroke the side of her face. Her breath quickened as her senses took over her mind. Ben's hand cupped her chin. Her feelings intensified and the tension rose in her stomach. She felt sixteen again. Eager to be held, yet petrified of what would come next. She felt the heat from his lips as they travelled just millimetres above hers. She breathed in deeply; the musky aroma of his aftershave surrounded her senses.

'Ben, please, don't ... don't pity me,' she said, lifting her face toward his. Her eyes now looked directly into his.

Ben's eyes gleamed at her like volcanic rock and she felt him inhale. Then slowly, as though he understood her dilemma, he traced the scar with his finger. 'I don't pity you. You are so beautiful,' he whispered as he pressed his lips gently to hers. The mere graze of his lips sent shock waves through her entire body. Sensing Kate's mood, Ben began to move slowly but rhythmically, his lips travelling passionately over hers, leaving her mouth burning with desire.

But then, the heat was gone. Ben had stepped back and Kate could see him taking deep, deliberate breaths.

'What … What's wrong?' she asked tentatively, unsure she wanted to hear the answer.

Ben smiled. 'Nothing. Nothing's wrong. I just …' He closed his eyes, just for a moment. 'It's not the right time and I promised myself that I'd wait until it was. You, you don't need this, not after last night.' He paused, walked over to the soup and stirred it again. 'Do you know what? My timing sucks.' He laughed. 'I really wanted to court you, take you out, send you flowers. And I was waiting for the right time. Waiting until you were free, but then after last night, after I almost lost you.' He shook his head. 'It keeps going round in my mind. What if I'd got there just one minute later?'

'Have you heard anything from the police? Have they caught him?'

Ben looked concerned. 'No. I dragged him off you, and he ran. Sorry. I was more concerned about getting to you than I was about catching him.'

'So, he's still out there.'

Ben climbed into the shower while Kate slept. He turned the power up as high as he could. The water was cold and pummelling, making him take deep breaths, as he allowed the water to fall on his face like the torrents of a waterfall, crashing upon him where he stood.

He wanted Kate so much and the thought that they'd just kissed, with so much promise of passion, had aroused him in a way that he hadn't known for years. He leaned back against the tiles.

'Fool,' he whispered, clenching his fists. 'You did it all wrong.' He'd thought of kissing her the first moment he'd seen her, sitting in the reception at the office. He knew she'd been unnerved by his actions and he also knew how much courage it would have taken to sit there so calmly, especially when he'd purposely led her to believe that he was the boss. After all, she had just wound her window down and called him a moron. Which can't have been the best start, but the fact she'd sat there, without flinching, showed him that she was tough. It showed she had character and he'd immediately admired her integrity.

And here he was, in the shower, trying to calm his arousal, after one single kiss. He asked himself why he'd done it, but he knew why. She was witty, funny, feisty and caring, along with being vulnerable and naive. She had so many qualities and insecurities, they would be impossible to count. But all of that put together was what made her so very special. He wanted to fall into those big doe eyes as they'd looked up at him. He wanted to create a world from which she'd never want to leave.

He jumped out of the shower, grabbed a towel and quickly dried himself. It was time to move on, to move forward with his life and he hoped that he knew exactly how to do it.

Chapter Thirty-One

Eve took in a deep breath and used every muscle she had to pull herself up to stand at the kitchen unit. The one thing about being paralysed below the waist was that the upper body got used to taking the burden and she could easily use her hands on the units to take her weight. Her legs were weak and trembled uncontrollably as she concentrated on standing. She loved the days when she knew that there would be no interruptions, the days when she could work on her physiotherapy and the days when she knew that the effort would help strengthen her legs.

Mother had returned to York with their father, who'd arrived out of the blue that morning to collect her. As she left she said something about Kate not wanting her and that she was sure that Eve hadn't wanted her either. Then she had gone, just like that, no mention of Father being a bully or a sociopath, and certainly no mention of a divorce.

Eve had tried to look sad, but inside she'd been jumping for joy. The thought of Mother living with her had been a nightmare and she'd dreaded the idea that her physiotherapy would have been brought to a halt, knowing how much work it would take afterwards to get back to where she'd previously been.

Looking down at her feet, Eve prayed for them to move. She concentrated as hard as she could and felt overjoyed when she saw the smallest of movements. She'd painstakingly taught herself to stand over the past year, and knew now that all she had to do was build up her strength and spend days working her muscles.

Eve sat back down in her chair, closed her eyes and thought of the call she'd had from Ben the night before. He'd been at the hospital with Kate and had explained what had happened.

Kate had asked that she did not tell anyone – especially their parents. Fury overtook Eve; she needed to be strong, needed to be capable and, if necessary, she needed to help her sister, not be a burden to her. She looked up to the ceiling and prayed.

'God, if you give me back my ability to walk, I will be the best sister that Kate has ever wished for. I'll help her, look after her and make sure that no one ever hurts her again.' She looked down at Max and ruffled his fur. 'Won't we, Max?' She patted her knee.

'Come on then,' she encouraged as Max put his front paws up onto her lap. 'Oh, and God, if you're still listening, I'll take better care of Max too. I'll groom him myself and walk him myself rather than wait for Zoe to get here.'

Max nuzzled her lap and then jumped up on the settee, lying down ready to snooze.

'Oh, no you don't. Get down. Not today,' she said to the dog that looked up at her with big, dark, sad eyes. 'Eric's coming later. Oh yes. You like Eric, don't you, Max?'

Eric would be picking her up in a few hours and she wheeled herself through to the bedroom and opened her wardrobe, searching for something to wear, something to give her the edge. She wanted to look good, sexy even and chose a pair of jeans and a skinny T-shirt that casually hung from one shoulder.

'Would this be the outfit to turn his head?' Eve held the top up to Max, who'd followed her into the bedroom and now lay on the bed, where he continued to snooze. She knew that Eric liked her. He'd kissed her but that was as far as it had gone and for once she needed him to look at her in a different way, not just as a friend.

Eve smiled. 'Are you sure you don't want a visit tomorrow?' Zoe had questioned earlier as she'd helped Eve to straighten her hair. But she'd shaken her head and thought of the evening she'd planned to spend with Eric.

Chapter Thirty-Two

'Eve, calm down,' Kate whispered as she sat up in bed, and tried to look at the clock through eyes that were glazed and didn't want to open. 'What's happened?'

'Eric kissed me,' Eve sobbed.

Kate switched on the bedside lamp and flopped back against the pillows. 'Okay, and that's a bad thing because …?' Kate sighed as she unhappily pulled back the duvet and slid her feet out of bed. She was still at Ben's house, and she still found it strange to feel the floor boards and rugs underfoot, rather than the carpets in her cottage.

'Because it was a real kiss, Kate. A real passionate one, not just a peck and I really like him, but what if I'm not good enough for him, Kate? What if I'm not enough?' Eve continued to sob down the phone. 'One of the women at the book club, I saw how she looked at him.' She paused and Kate heard her blow her nose loudly into a handkerchief. 'And what's more, she's slim, tall and has the most perfect figure. What if she makes a move on him, Kate? What if he likes her more than me? He might take the better and easier option, don't you think? He's not going to want to push me around in a bloody chair forever, is he?'

Kate deliberated for a moment. Eve was more fragile than she'd thought and she needed to think carefully before giving out advice.

'Eve, do you ever look in the mirror?' Kate hesitated and just hoped for once that she could say something that would make her sister feel better.

Eve answered with a loud grunt. Kate waited a few moments before continuing. 'Well, do you?' She sounded more like their mother on one of her lectures, but she knew that being stern would be the only way to get through to Eve.

'Yes.' Eve's answer was whimpered and pathetic. Kate's heart cried out as she could feel her twin's anguish. It was as though they were connected, heart to heart by a string that tugged between them. Every time Eve's heart lurched, so did Kate's.

Kate closed her eyes and wished for teleportation. She'd have given anything to be curled up with Eve, on a bed like spoons, cuddled up together, as they'd done so often over the years. At least then she'd have been able to reassure her, help her and convince her that she was beautiful and that Eric would be a fool not to see that.

'What do you see when you look in the mirror, Eve?' The question was direct and meant to provoke.

The phone line was silent for a few seconds. She knew that Eve was thinking about her answer and could almost guess what it would be. After all, Kate knew that when she looked in the mirror herself, all she saw was the scar. A huge, puckered red scar, something that everyone noticed, but most were too embarrassed to mention.

'I see a great big lump of metal on wheels, Kate,' she finally replied. 'I just see the bloody chair.'

'Well, that's the problem, Eve,' Kate snapped. 'I never see the chair. When I look at you, I see a woman, a beautiful woman in the prime of her life, with so much to give. And do you know what, Eve? I'd say that Eric is a good man and he sees exactly the same.'

Eve sniffed loudly. 'But—'

'There are no buts. Tell me what happened?' Kate asked. The words were a question that got no reply. 'Eve, when did he kiss you?' she continued as she once again checked the clock. It was six o'clock in the morning. So unless Eric had stayed the night the kiss must have happened the night before. She thought of the kiss that she'd shared with Ben, the kiss that had brought her so much hope for the future.

'Last night,' Eve acknowledged. 'He kissed me when he brought me home from having dinner.' She sobbed. 'Actually, I think that I may have kissed him.'

Kate began to daydream as she perched the phone under her chin. She wondered what it would be like to kiss Ben every day, to see that sparkle light up his face and to gaze into those cavernous eyes.

'But you said that you and Eric have kissed before?'

'Yes, we have. But not like this. I've been thinking about it all night, Kate. I've barely slept.'

'Okay. Let's think rationally. Have you heard from Eric since the kiss?' Kate said as she walked down the stairs, into the kitchen and turned Ben's coffee machine on, before digging in the cupboard looking for coffee.

'We've been texting back and forth all night,' Eve replied.

Kate closed her eyes. The coffee machine was more trouble than it was worth and she opened the fridge and looked for the orange juice.

'Eve,' she said with a sigh. 'So, you should be happy. What's the problem?'

'I'm frightened, Kate. We kissed, everything got a bit heated and then he got all nervous and left. I hoped he'd want to stay. I was disappointed and relieved, all at once. But then I started thinking about sex and, you know, what if he wants me to have sex with him? What if I can't do it anymore?' She stopped as she began to take in huge gulps of air. 'I'm not sure how much I'll feel.'

'For goodness' sake, Eve. One kiss does not equate to sex.' Kate tried to keep calm. The phone slipped from under her chin and almost landed on the floor. Grabbing it quickly, she held it tightly in one hand, as her other picked up the juice.

'Eve, you had sex before the accident.' She laughed. 'I

know that for sure because I've lost count of how many times I walked in on you, or caught you doing it in the back of the car on our parents' driveway.'

She heard Eve begin to laugh. 'Oh my goodness, I did do that, didn't I?'

'Well,' Kate continued, 'it can't be so different, can it? I mean, it's not all about the actual sex act is it? There are so many ways of pleasing each other ...' She was suddenly aware that Ben was in the house and probably listening to their conversation. She looked over her shoulder towards the lounge, where, being the perfect gentleman, he slept on the settee.

Kate was tired. The past two days had completely drained her and all she wanted to do was go back to bed, to Ben's bed, which still smelt of his aftershave.

'Eve, I'd come over, but I'm not sure I could face Mother, not at this time of the morning.'

'She isn't here.'

Kate had begun walking back to the bedroom, but stopped in her tracks. 'What the hell do you mean, she isn't there?' Kate panicked at the thought that their mother could have gone back to the cottage.

'I'm not her bloody keeper, Kate. Father had been working away, but now he's back and he came over yesterday. He promised to take her to see a doctor. And she said something about not staying where she wasn't wanted, didn't she, Max?'

Kate felt a sudden sense of relief. 'Father, he came?' The news that their mother had gone back home explained so much. Closing her eyes, Kate thought of the bed that was just a few paces away; she thought of how amazing it would be to crawl back in, and even wondered what it would be like to drag Ben into the bed with her, but she knew deep down that she needed to go to Eve. She needed to curl up with her, hug her and tell her that it would all be all right, even if in the back of her own mind, she couldn't promise.

Kate glanced into the lounge and checked that Ben was still sleeping. Satisfied that he was, she went up to the bedroom and changed. 'Eve, I'll tell you what, give me half an hour and put the kettle on. I'm dying for a decent coffee.'

Chapter Thirty-Three

'What do you mean, the bloody shipment's gone?' Isobel screamed down her mobile. She walked from lounge to kitchen, out through the back door and entered the pool house, where Roberto ran on a treadmill.

'Half of the shipment was impounded. Martin was stupid, he's been arrested,' Giancarlo whispered. 'But there's nothing I can do. Not from here.'

Isobel panicked. 'Where are you?' She held the phone tight to her ear. She heard him cough and for a moment she thought that he'd gone, but then realised that someone must have walked too close to where he sat. It was a signal they'd used numerous times before, to cough and to begin again once they could speak.

'I have to leave the country for a week or two. The police are onto me and it's me they will follow, so the further away from the rest of the shipment I am, the better.'

'But, Giancarlo, you can't leave. What will we do? Will Martin talk?'

'No, it'd be the last thing he'd ever do,' Giancarlo whispered. 'I've given Roberto all the details of the next drop. Customs are watching the airports and docks for us. It's too dangerous to bring it in that way and hopefully they'll follow me, thinking I'm doing the pick-up. We have to bring the drop in by the alternative route. It's all planned with the *Red Lady*. We've spoken of this. It's more dangerous, but both Luca and Roberto know what they are doing.'

Isobel knew that the Bellandinis had always stuck together. They were like a pack of wolves, all working towards a cause and all of them did what Giancarlo said, whether they liked it or not. She actually felt sorry for Martin. Giancarlo would get his revenge and when he did, she wouldn't like to be in his shoes.

'So, what happens next, Giancarlo?' Isobel questioned. 'I have dealers screaming at me.'

'Calm down, calm down, all will be well.'

Isobel walked around the pool, crouched down and ran her fingers through the water. 'So, it's still coming in by sea? Still midnight? When?' she quizzed without looking up at Roberto who continued his run on the treadmill. He was in a zone of his own, had been for days, but Isobel still hadn't worked out why.

Again there was a pause before Giancarlo said, 'Roberto will tell you everything. You have to be prepared, my darling girl. I could be gone for a while.' His voice sounded calm, yet defeated.

Isobel closed her eyes and sobbed. 'And Elena, is she to go with you?'

Giancarlo didn't answer, which told Isobel all that she really needed to know. She'd loved Giancarlo for years, even though she knew that he'd never love her in return. He loved his wife, and had made it very clear that he didn't need another.

Why had she allowed it to continue? Why had she been so weak that for the small amount of attention that he chose to give her, she'd not only become deeply involved with him, but she'd ended up in deep with the drugs? And now the dealers were screaming, they wouldn't wait forever and she feared for what they'd do to her, if the shipment didn't arrive.

Of course, she'd played around with Luca, and with Roberto. They were all part of the same family, all conquests, like trophies she'd needed to win, but all had been to make Giancarlo jealous, although none had and now he was gone. Isobel sobbed.

'Hey, *bello piccolo fiore*, do not cry for me.' He chuckled as he spoke. 'I'll be back before you know it, there is a plan. If the shipment goes wrong, you need to do what Roberto says. You need to go with him to the safe house and wait for me.'

His Italian words of 'little flower' rang out in her ears as Isobel remembered the hushed plans often spoken between Giancarlo and Roberto. They'd looked at maps, discussed co-ordinates and had taken trips away without explanation. It was obvious that elaborate plans had been made but none of the details had ever been made clear to her and right now she was pleased that they hadn't.

The less that she knew the better.

'Giancarlo, I'm scared. Please promise me you'll come back. I don't know how we'll survive, not without you.'

'My girl, just do as you are told. Roberto will look after you.'

Isobel stared at where Roberto now sat on the edge of the pool, his eyes just staring into space. It was as though she didn't exist and she immediately knew that if she were to rely on him to keep her safe, she'd be waiting a long time. She swallowed hard, and realised that if she wanted to be looked after, she'd have to do it for herself.

Chapter Thirty-Four

Kate walked in through the front door and immediately noticed that there was a different atmosphere in the office. She looked at her watch. It was still only nine o'clock and even though Ben had said she should stay at home; the early morning wakeup call she'd had from Eve had been the push she needed to leave the house. She'd spent the last two hours trying to boost Eve's self-confidence where her love life was concerned and now felt it was time to go to work.

'Hey, how are you?' Kate asked Gloria with a beaming smile.

'I'm great. More to the point, how are you?' Gloria gave her a brief look, then walked over to a newly-installed coffee machine that now stood behind reception. 'I don't know why Ben bought this thing. He has one at home, you know, and says it will make my life easier.' She tutted and pointed at the machine. 'You want it normal, cappuccino or would you prefer one of those latte ones?' she asked, raising her eyebrows and waiting for Kate to make a decision. 'Now, sit down. You should rest.' Gloria pointed to the settee with authority and Kate knew that Ben had already filled her in about the attack.

'Normal coffee is fine, thank you. Where's Ben?' she asked, changing the subject.

Gloria pointed towards the wall, indicating that he was in the next door office. 'He's in there with William,' she replied as Kate moved towards the door. 'It's about the case, I don't think they'd mind if you joined them.'

'Ben, do you want to fill me in? Because right now I don't understand.' She sat down in the tub chair that stood before

William's desk. The door opened and Gloria entered with a tray.

'Finally, I got that damned machine to work.' She placed the tray down on the desk. It held carrot cake, chocolate cake and three steaming mugs of coffee. 'I'll be going back to my kettle before the end of the day, mark my words.' She laughed and then looked affectionately at Ben.

'Thanks,' they all said in unison as they picked up the mugs and immediately began to drink.

Kate felt her heartbeat calm as she sat back in the chair. It seemed so long since she'd first come to work here. Yet, in real time, it had only been just over a week. Since then her life had changed considerably. She still couldn't believe that Rob, of all people, was involved with drugs. He'd always been so very strict about everything that he'd put into his body, even his daily amount of calories was dictated by every minute of exercise he'd done during the day. But then again, she wouldn't have thought him capable of trying to kill her either, but he had.

'It's time to turn the case over. We're done.' Ben stared at his father. 'We won't put you at any more risk. It isn't worth it.'

'But we're so close.'

William stood up. 'Don't worry. We have all the information we need. All we have to do now is pass it over and wait till the authorities take them down.' He looked at her, lips pursed. 'Ben's right. We won't put you in danger. Besides, do you remember the day in Whitby?' He placed his mug back on the tray. 'Well it seems that your day was quite productive. You were spot on about the *Red Lady*. And what's more, those photographs you took have given us times, dates and co-ordinates. We know that the drugs are coming in by sea and it'll be the *Red Lady* that picks up the load.' He patted the evidence folder. 'A fishing boat coming in from France will drop the drugs over the *San Georgic*, the wreck we spoke about before. This way they won't have gone through customs. They'll use a basket, similar to a lobster pot with a weight attached. It stops the basket from drifting off. From what we've heard the drugs will be picked up by two divers, one of them will probably be Roberto Bellandini. He will use scuba gear to retrieve the baskets and take them aboard the *Red Lady* tomorrow night.'

'Who?' Kate was puzzled.

'Roberto Bellandini, my dear Kate. The man you know as Robert Bell, his real identity is that of a Roberto Bellandini, a twenty-eight-year-old drug dealer, related to one of the most notorious Italian families that we've ever heard of.'

Kate threw her hands in the air. Was there anything else she didn't know about the man she'd been about to marry? 'As far as I'm aware, he has no idea how to scuba dive. He's quite fond of the shower, but not the sea. Trust me, I've had to clean the bathroom after him for over a year.' She laughed at the thought.

'Yes, Kate, he can. He's a scuba diving instructor, capable of teaching people from their first breaths, right through to teaching them how to become instructors themselves. He's quite an expert; been diving for years,' William replied, filling her in on another part of Rob's life that she'd known nothing about.

'I feel so stupid. I had no idea who the hell I was engaged to.' The thought of Rob made her shake; every part of her trembled and she wondered how long it would be before the feeling would go.

Ben stood up and walked over to where she sat. 'You are not stupid. Far from it.' Ben held out his hands to take hers. 'You're shaking. Why don't you go home? We can manage things here.'

She shrugged him off as anger took her over. 'Do you

know what, Ben? I don't want to go home. I mean, where is my home right now? I can't keep staying at your house, yet I don't feel that I can go back to the cottage either. No, I'm staying here. What I really want is to see Rob put behind bars, along with Isobel, Luca and whoever else is running this bloody circus.'

Isobel paced up and down the living room. Fear and anguish raced through her as Roberto sat on the settee, head hung, hands clasped.

'So, they arrested him?' Isobel asked as she desperately looked around her to find something to do with her hands. She picked up a packet of cigarettes, pulling one out. She lit it.

'Put that out. Smoking isn't going to change what's happened,' he said as he looked up at her in disgust. 'You know how much I hate you smoking. It smells disgusting.' He stood up and opened a window, standing beside it until Isobel relented, crushing the remnants of the cigarette into an ashtray.

'Roberto, you're such a bloody hypocrite. In fact, you're a drug dealing hypocrite.' She pushed out her bottom lip and sulked. 'How did they finally get Giancarlo? God knows they've tried for years,' she cried. 'Will he go to prison? He won't survive surrounded by villains.'

Roberto laughed and shook his head. 'That's where you're wrong, Isobel. He would survive and those villains, my dear, are people like us. Drug dealing criminals.' He paused before moving away from the window. 'But stop worrying, they can't pin anything on him. He'll be clean, he'd have made sure of that. After thirty-six hours they have to release him.' He walked to the door. 'I'm going for a swim.'

'*Swim?*' she screamed. 'Giancarlo, your uncle, is rotting in a foreign police station and all you can think of is going for a swim.'

Roberto moved quickly, his hand grabbing her by the throat. 'Don't ever challenge me about my family ever again. I've told you, he's clean,' he hissed, before dropping her like a stone. 'Plans are already in place. He'll be out before the end of the week. Now, I'm going to the pool. I need to check the scuba gear out.'

Isobel massaged her neck. 'Touch me like that again and I'll cut your air supply, you bastard.'

Roberto looked directly at her, his eyes widened. '*Don't* give me ideas, you might just regret it.'

Chapter Thirty-Five

Kate looked up at the new moon.

'You'd think they'd wait for a full moon, wouldn't you?' she said to Eric, who drove as slowly as he could. He'd switched the headlights off and navigated the lane with a torch, until he was sure that he'd reached the cliff top car park.

'What?' He turned to look at her.

'The moon. It doesn't give off much light, does it? You'd think they'd wait for a full moon.' She tipped her head on one side and studied the moon with interest.

Eric laughed. 'Noooooo, it's the last thing they'd do.' He pointed up into the sky. 'You see it's the moon that dictates the current. When it's a full moon, the currents in the sea are stronger and more treacherous.' For once he looked as though he were preening himself and Kate smiled, pleased that her lack of knowledge had given him the opportunity to do so.

She and Eric sat in the car. They were pretending to be a courting couple and kept low, covered with blankets, hoping that no one was watching. They kept a close eye on the clock. They'd been told to stay hidden until at least eleven o'clock. Then and only then were they to crawl to the edge of the cliff and lay in the undergrowth to watch the sea. Kate thought of her jeans and how dirty they would be by the time she'd crawled through the mud. It would be another pair that she'd most probably throw in the dustbin. Or would she? Being dirty hadn't killed her before, nor had it hurt her, and she'd come to the conclusion that keeping her obsession under control was something she needed to do.

'Let's go,' Eric said at last as the clock ticked over to eleven o'clock and he carefully opened the car door retrieving a bag from the back seat. 'Here, I brought you a rug.' He passed it to her. 'I knew how worried you'd feel about lying in the dirt.'

They moved in total darkness through the undergrowth. Only the lights from the moon and stars lit up the ripples and shimmer of the waves that glistened back at them like a mirror lying on its side.

'Can you see anything?' she whispered to Eric as he shuffled like a snake toward her through the grass. The abbey stood eerily to their left and below them a cliff face that dropped eighty feet to the sea.

'Follow me. I can just about see the edge,' Eric murmured as a noise from the cliff top made them both stop in their tracks. Kate felt her heart pound. They waited and listened for the noise to repeat itself, while staring at one another, unable to move. They watched and waited silently. The noise had gone, yet still they waited, until they were sure they were alone.

'Where are the police?' Kate asked as she tried to peer through the darkness.

'They're down on the quayside, hiding in that boat.' He pointed to a huge fishing boat that sat in darkness.

'Is Ben with them?'

'He is. Look, you can just see one or two of them on the deck. Also, look over there.' He pointed to the abbey. 'They have look outs just beyond the ruins.'

Kate watched in awe as the men moved silently along the cliff. 'My word, you really would have no idea that they were there, would you?' She turned back towards the sea. 'Is that the *Red Lady*?' She pointed to an object, its position only just seen by a distant glint in the moonlight as it floated out of the harbour walls.

'That's kind of the point, Kate. They're not supposed to be seen. I'd been told where they'd be, or I wouldn't have noticed them either. As soon as the *Red Lady* pulls back into the dock, they'll arrest all on board, including Rob, and then you'll finally be free of him.'

Kate sighed. Eric sounded sincere and it brought a lump to her throat. 'Really wish we could have been down there, in the thick of it.'

'It was impossible. Ben's taking quite a risk allowing us to watch from here. If the authorities knew, they wouldn't be best pleased with him,' Eric whispered as he indicated toward the harbour.

'Do you think they'll catch them?'

'Certainly they will, it's a sure thing. Apart from our evidence, the authorities got a tip off, but they only have one chance and they have to catch them in possession of the drugs. Timing is imperative. So you can guarantee they will all be in exactly the right place to jump as soon as the boat gets back.'

Kate's mind went to Rob. She'd really thought she'd known him. She thought he'd loved her, but all the time he was dealing drugs, possibly from her house. Her stomach turned when she thought of all the drugs raids she'd been on in the force. The times the occupants had pleaded with her, saying how they knew nothing of their partner's deceit and how she'd disbelieved them. She hadn't thought it possible that someone could have a house full of drugs without the other knowing. She sighed and wondered how many of Rob's friends had been collecting them from her house, when they'd just dropped in for coffee. She'd been nice to these people, made them drinks and more often than not had left them sitting at the kitchen table chatting with Rob.

'I know where I'd rather be right now,' Kate whispered, 'and to be honest, Eric, it's not lying in the grass with you. No offence intended, of course.'

* * *

The *Red Lady* drifted over the surface of the sea. Its engine had been cut and it was slowly being pulled along by the current as Isobel sat by the wheel, using it to slowly manoeuvre the boat in the direction she wanted.

The captain had been bound, and pushed into the small space beneath the seating. His eyes were like saucers, as he stared directly at where Isobel sat.

'You can't do this, I've done nothing wrong,' he pleaded. 'I have children, five of them, they need me.'

His voice had turned from a soft whimper to a screech and Isobel glared into the darkness where she could clearly see him staring back at her. 'Shut up or I'll throw you in. Do you think we don't know what you did?' she growled, as her foot kicked out at him. 'Roberto, are you sure it's still safe to go ahead? Do you really think he spoke to the police?' She pointed to the captain.

'It had to be him. Who else knew? Giancarlo says we go ahead and, as for him, he'll pay for what he did. Giancarlo will make sure of that,' Roberto said.

Isobel was not convinced and turned to see Luca stare down at the captain. Their eyes connected and Isobel watched as the captain's eyes pleaded with him. It was a look of knowing, followed by one of need.

'What the hell's going on?' she demanded, glaring at them both.

Luca shrugged. 'What do you mean, what's going on? Nothing's going on.' He walked up the deck and began checking the dive cylinders for air, but Isobel knew him better, knew he was up to something and didn't like it.

'I saw that look. You're in it together, aren't you?'

'Isobel, you're imagining things, now can we get that engine started, or are we waiting for dawn to break?'

Isobel bristled. 'We'll have to wait till we get away from the shore before we start the engine, you know that.' She studied the water, watching for her opening on the tide. 'Shame it's not raining, it would have given us a lot more cover,' she said as she turned to Roberto and allowed him to zip up her dry suit. 'Roberto,' she whispered. 'I think Luca could be the snitch, I think they're in it together.' She pointed to where Luca stood, weight belt in hand. She clicked the engine into life, masking her words with the noise. 'I don't like how he looked at the captain, it's as though they're up to something, I just don't know what.'

'You're imagining things, Isobel. Luca is family. He wouldn't grass on us. Giancarlo would kill him.'

Isobel shrugged. 'Only one way to find out. You have to speak to him,' she said with a knowing look and watched as Roberto strode towards where Luca stood.

'Come on, Luca, what the hell's going on? Did you snitch, because I swear that if you did, I'll kill you.' Roberto squared up to his cousin.

But Luca backed off and paced nervously. 'Don't be stupid. Why would I do that?' Once again he looked at the captain and again their eyes connected.

But Roberto laughed and patted him on the shoulder. 'You'd always look after the family first, right?'

'Right,' Luca responded and breathed out heavily as though relieved. He glared at Isobel and then turned his attention to the dive gear.

But Roberto stood his ground and stared at him, while nodding and smiling. 'Okay. No hard feelings, then?'

Luca held out his hand to shake Roberto's. 'No, no hard feelings, not from me, cous.'

Roberto shook his hand, holding on tighter and for just a few moments more than needed. 'Good, now throw the snitch overboard.'

Luca spun around on the spot. 'But ... I ... I ... I don't want to kill anyone. What if he is innocent, what if he didn't snitch?'

The panic was clear in Luca's voice and Roberto knew it. He strode back over to where Luca stood and in one fast swing, his fist connected with Luca's face and Roberto watched as he fell to the deck. 'It's either him or you that snitched, who else would it have been?' He rubbed his hand. 'So here's the deal, throw him over or I throw you over, which is it to be?'

'Roberto, come on. We grew up together, like brothers. I wouldn't rat on you, you know that.' He looked up. 'Okay. You win. He goes overboard. But you'll need to help me.'

Isobel shook with anxiety as she watched Luca and Roberto drag the screaming man along the deck and with one splash, he was flung over the side, still bound, like a piece of discarded rubbish that no one wanted. Her throat constricted and she began to gag repeatedly, knowing that their drug dealing days had just turned into murder. 'I wasn't a part of that … not me, I didn't agree to murder.'

Roberto walked over to her and pulled her into his arms. 'No you didn't and I'm sorry, but it had to be done.' His voice was calm and Isobel shook with fear; it was more than obvious that killing was natural to him. He showed no remorse, unlike Luca who was now throwing up over the edge of the boat. 'I need you to focus, Isobel. I need you to steer the boat.'

She nodded, knowing that right now her main prerogative was to stay alive and navigate the boat safely through the waves. Turning devices on, she set the compass to hone in on the wreck. The days of guessing and working to landmarks were a thing of the past.

'Nearly there. Are you ready?' she queried and looked between Roberto and Luca as they tightened their weight belts. 'Roberto, do me a favour, drop the anchor,' she shouted as she cut the engine and turned the boat against the waves.

'Isobel, I'm not dropping it, it's far too deep here, the swells too high. The anchor wouldn't hold,' Roberto replied, then turned and pointed to the water. 'Me and Luca will take care of the drugs. Just keep the boat in this position while we're gone. You know the dive plan. Twenty minutes and we'll be back up.'

'What if ...' She was going to say, *What if Luca is the traitor?* but stopped herself.

'Pre dive check?' Luca queried and turned to Roberto for help.

'Sure,' he replied as he moved in front of his dive buddy and began to check the kit.

'B.W.R.A.F,' Luca said as the check began. 'Burgers with Relish and Fries,' he continued with a laugh, as though trying to ease the tension that showed all over Roberto's face. 'It's a way of remembering the initials.'

Roberto glared. 'I know what it stands for, now turn around, let me get on with it.' He began checking his buoyancy aid, weights, releases and air. All were secure and all his instruments were clipped into the central zone.

'You look good to go,' Roberto said as he moved away. 'Have you got the lift bags, SMBs and markers?'

'Sure do. I've even got three different torches, just in case we need them,' Luca replied, patting his pockets in a final check to ensure they were there. 'You want checking?' he asked as Roberto moved away, turning his back as he looked over to where Isobel was tapping the dials.

'I'm okay, thanks. I like to do my own checks. Don't you worry about me,' he said smugly. He glared at Luca, spat in his mask, rubbed the spit into the lens and then leaned over to rinse it in the bucket of water that stood on the deck. Pulling hoods and gloves into place, the mask was positioned, its skirt safely tucked under the edge of the hood.

'Ready?' Isobel asked and both Luca and Roberto held up their hands signalling they were okay and ready to go.

'Regulators in, air out of the jackets. You need to go in negative and descend quickly.' Roberto looked at Luca and waited for his signal.

Isobel turned to Roberto. 'Okay. You'll be over the wreck in five, four, three, two, and go,' she whispered, and watched as they both dropped backwards off the boat and into the sea. Both were in unison, both equalising as they went.

It had been twenty minutes since Isobel had watched the large orange balloons float to the surface, and she knew that a lobster pot of drugs would be tied below each. They were just too far off the boat for her to reach and with divers below, she knew better than to start the engine. Roberto and Luca should have been back by now. Their planned dive time had been twenty minutes and that time had now doubled since their descent. She looked back to the shore, paced up and down the deck and wondered what to do.

The plan had been to retrieve the drugs, but no one had spoken of what to do if Roberto or Luca didn't return. She couldn't leave, but didn't know how long she could stay. Either way, Giancarlo wouldn't be pleased. She'd seen what he did to people who disobeyed and she had no intention of joining the exclusive group of people who were now missing, never to return.

She looked at where the drugs floated on the surface, constantly checking for air bubbles, hoping and praying that the men would surface and soon. The lift bags began drifting towards her and she reached over the side in an attempt to grab them. The tide pulled it back and forth, but each time they just managed to elude her grasp. Cursing she grabbed hold of a rope and began throwing it toward the bag in the hope that she'd alter its path and steer it closer to the boat.

Reaching out she attempted a grab, missed and grabbed again. Then, from nowhere, an arm came from beneath the waves and dragged her over the side and into the water.

Luca surfaced. He was some way from the boat and after pulling his mask from his face, he stared at the surface of the sea, watched for air bubbles, and prayed that Roberto hadn't noticed the direction he'd escaped in. Surely by now he'd have realised, surely he'd be looking for him and his only hope was that Roberto might think he'd been lost at sea, trapped within the wreck and drowned. The last thing he wanted was to face either him or Giancarlo, ever again. Both were ruthless and, family or not, he'd be living on borrowed time, watching his back and waiting for the inevitable. No, it was better to escape now, to make a permanent getaway. He wasn't going to wait for Roberto to turn on him again and he wasn't a hardened drug dealer or murderer, and if that was what his family expected, then he couldn't do it. He had to leave the family, and he had to leave tonight.

The *Red Lady* bobbed up and down in the distance. The waves lapped up against her side and he squinted in an attempt to make out where Isobel stood. And even though the bright orange lift bags still floated around on the surface, neither Isobel nor Roberto were anywhere to be seen.

A wave splashed over his face and, taking in a deep breath from his regulator, he replaced the mask, deflated his jacket and dropped below the surface.

He began heading for the shore. Only from there could he escape to safety.

Kate watched through the binoculars.

'I'm freezing cold and bored. I can barely see a thing, Ben and the authorities are still hidden, and we're lying here on a cliff top, when we could be in bed,' she whispered and then laughed. 'Not together, I might add.'

Eric lay on his back looking up at the stars. He'd long since got tired of watching the waves. 'I haven't seen anything of interest since we got here. I was just thinking about the fact that right now, I should be curled up in bed with Eve in my arms,' he said dreamily as once again he picked up his mobile and checked for messages.

'Err, hello, what did you say?' Kate squealed a little louder than was necessary.

'Oh, err, no, no, sorry, I shouldn't have said that,' Eric rambled. 'It's more of a wish list. Sorry, I shouldn't have said that either.' He turned over and once again began to take great interest in what was happening on the water.

Chapter Thirty-Six

It was some hours later that Eric and Kate had given up the watch and arrived back at the office. Patrick was in reception, trying to operate the coffee machine, but stood back contemplating the buttons.

'What the hell are you doing here? Don't you have a home to go to?' Kate asked as she pushed past him. She'd watched Gloria that morning and, like an expert, pressed all the right buttons and watched as the coffee poured into the mug. 'There, is that what you wanted?' she said smugly.

'Ben rang. He said we all had to wait here till he gets back,' Patrick said quietly as he sipped at the coffee, and Kate noticed that he was looking everywhere in the room except at her.

Something was wrong. There was something she wasn't being told, but for now she chose to ignore it. 'I'm so tired,' she said, pulling a big fluffy cardigan from the back of Gloria's chair. Wrapping it around her, she lay down on the leather settee. 'Wake me up when he gets here,' she whispered as she moved a cushion, rested her head on it and allowed her mind to drift into a deep and peaceful sleep.

It was two hours later when Ben's voice woke her.

'Kate, Kate, wake up, we need to talk.' He spoke calmly and stroked her cheek, waiting for her to wake. He then closed his eyes briefly, before continuing. 'Rob, Luca and Isobel, they either got away, either that ... or ... or they are all missing at sea.'

'Could they be dead?' Kate whispered the words, barely able to say them out loud. 'Is Rob dead?' She'd hated Rob after what he'd done, but now, thinking that he might have died confused her. She had no idea how she should feel and curled her legs up before her on the settee, hugging them as closely as she could.

'The truth is, I don't know, but I doubt it,' Ben said, his hand resting gently on her knee. 'The drugs were missing and the authorities suspect that Rob took them with him.'

'Do you think Rob killed the others?' Kate already knew the answer before Ben spoke.

Everyone sat in reception and stared at the walls, while Ben explained what had happened over the course of the night.

'A decision was made to go out to the *Red Lady*. It'd been stationary for hours and intelligence decided to go out to it. When we got there, they'd all gone, even the captain of the *Red Lady*, Sharky. The underwater search teams have gone in. But it will all take time.'

'Do you think they got spooked, you know, maybe they knew we were watching?' Kate asked what everyone else was thinking, and they all looked toward Ben for an answer.

Ben shook his head. 'I don't know, but whatever happened, they certainly had a plan. They could still be out there, and for that reason alone, tonight I think you should come home with me,' he said directing his words at Kate. He then turned to Eric. 'And you, young man. You need to go and stay with Eve. Don't leave her side, not until they're found, just in case.'

Eric agreed and immediately picked up his coat. 'Ring me if you hear anything.' He held his mobile up and waved it around in the air, before walking out the door.

'What do I do, boss?' Patrick asked as he looked toward Ben for instruction.

'Patrick. I need you to go over to Isobel's. Take the small van. I need to know if any of them go back there.'

'But if Rob isn't dead, do you think he'd hang around?'

Kate suddenly said, worry spreading all over her face. 'He'd be crazy to hang around, wouldn't he?'

Ben pulled her into a hug. 'I don't know, but I'm not taking any chances. I need to keep you close for my own sanity. I can't risk him coming after you. I couldn't bear to lose anyone else that I love.'

Ben kissed her on the forehead and Kate allowed him to hold her. It occurred to her that he'd used the word love. Did he mean her? Or was he talking in general, about everyone at the office?

Kate followed Ben through his house and towards the stairs. Early morning sunlight was already making an attempt of creeping through the windows and had begun to light up the stairwell.

'Kate, do … do you trust me?' Ben softly asked her.

'Of course,' Kate replied, and all at once she realised it was the truth. She did trust Ben more than she'd ever trusted anyone in her whole life. After all, if it hadn't been for him saving her, she'd already be dead.

She turned into his arms as a light kiss was placed on her forehead. Taking her hand, he led her to his bedroom. The curtains were closed and the security lamp was already lit, and the room offered a soft welcoming glow.

Ben padded over to the bed and pulled back the duvet. 'I really don't want to leave you alone tonight. Not after what he did to you before.' He paused and looked at the clock. 'Let me stay with you, I'd say tonight, but it's actually morning.' The words were more of a statement than a question and Kate nodded as she walked to the side of the bed.

'Here,' he said as he passed her the pyjamas she'd been wearing the night before.

Kate grinned and went into the en suite to change.

Ben had disappeared from the bedroom when she

returned, giving her time to slip beneath the duvet. The bed was familiar, soft, warm and cosy and she lay anxiously waiting for his return.

When he came into the bedroom just a few moments later he'd changed into jogging pants, a T-shirt and held a phone in his hand.

'Sorry, just checked in with the authorities. Still nothing.'

Kate patted the bed in invitation and Ben climbed in beside her. His strong arms pulled her toward him and wrapped themselves around her. Kate inhaled deeply. The musky aroma of his aftershave filled her nostrils and for the first time in weeks Kate felt surrounded by safety.

'Ben?'

'Yes?'

'Kiss me.'

Her words were a whisper as she turned onto her back suddenly realising that she was exactly where she wanted to be.

Ben's lips lowered and brushed hers with a single, soft, gentle kiss.

Chapter Thirty-Seven

Eric pulled up outside Eve's. The bungalow should have been in darkness, but a soft light came from a room to the front of the house and Eric smiled, knowing that the room was Eve's bedroom. He presumed that she'd either fallen asleep with the side light still on, or she was trying to finish reading *The Secret Keeper*, the book they'd started at the book club.

Eric looked down at his mobile phone. Should he text first, or knock on the door? If Eve were asleep, a sudden knocking on the door could scare her. It would take her time to get into her chair, get to the door and open it. Again, he looked at the phone and began to text.

Hey. Are you awake? Would you like a visitor?

He pressed Send, leaned back in his seat, closed his eyes and waited.

Where are you? Came the response just a few moments later and Eric smiled.

I'm right outside. x

He once again pressed Send and then thought about his response. What if Eve thought him to be stalking her? After all it was the middle of the night, and sitting outside someone's house in the dark wasn't exactly the normal thing to do, was it?

He quickly began to type on his keypad.

I'm not stalking you. Honest. Ben sent me. There's been an incident, but don't worry, Kate is fine. Could you open the door? I need to come in.

A few moments later, Eric was in the kitchen, while Max ran, jumped and bounced around his unexpected visitor.

'Oh, no, now I've got you all excited, Max, haven't I?' Eric said as he went to kiss Eve on the cheek, but she moved quickly. His lips caught hers and she responded hungrily. He broke off from the kiss. 'Okay, I … I … I think I should … you know, I think I should take Max out for a quick walk, I've got him a bit giddy and he probably needs to … you know …' He blushed, put Max on his lead and left through the back door.

Eve leaned back in her chair and watched as Eric left the house. She sighed, knowing that once again he'd done the gentlemanly thing and confusion went through her mind.

Had he left because he hadn't wanted the intimacy, or because he had and hadn't known what to do about it? Was it up to her to make the first move and was it too soon? She trembled at the thought. After all, they really hadn't known each other that long.

'Is time a factor when you love someone?' Eve whispered to herself. 'Would it really be different to make love now?' She thought of all the men she'd been with in the past; she'd been a wild child and sex had been the one thing she'd loved without thinking of the consequences. Or had she?

She wheeled herself back to the bedroom, threw back the quilt and inched onto the edge of her wheelchair.

'What do I do?' she said out loud. She looked at her bedside drawer and sighed. Opening the drawer, she began digging inside. 'Come on, where are you?' Eve finally laid her hand on the soft, pink nightie. It was satin, long and had the most delicate shoe string shoulder straps. She stroked the material and smiled. Taking a deep breath, she changed into the nightdress, rearranging the pillows, and pulled herself into a sitting position on the bed and waited.

'Wow. Slow down, Max. Eve, are you there?' She heard Max bounce through the back door, with Eric close behind.

Once again, Eve stroked the material and took a deep breath. 'Eric, come on in, I'm in here.'

Chapter Thirty-Eight

Roberto rummaged in the trees. He was looking for dry wood in the rain. Wood that he could burn. It was the best excuse he could think of, to keep him busy and away from Isobel.

They'd only been at the hideout for two nights and two days, but already he was sick of hearing her constant moaning, her constant criticism and her constant lectures. True it wasn't a palace, but it was practical and just what they needed while they waited for Giancarlo's instructions. But the longer he waited for the call, the more nervous he got.

Using the machete, he cut away the undergrowth, searching for what might lie beneath. He walked back to the hideout, checked for signs of disturbance or visitors and then entered with caution. He'd been out for an hour, but that would have been plenty of time for the authorities to have turned up, and he knew that they could easily be waiting inside.

He entered the dismal, candlelit room. He was wet from the rain, but his arms were full of wood and he saw the look of hope in Isobel's eyes.

'Is it dry? Can we burn it?' she questioned as he dropped the wood on the concrete floor.

He shook his head. 'Nah. It's piss wet through, everything out there's soaked. It's a good job I did what I could to set the place up ready.' He wandered out of one room and into the next.

The crude concrete property was on the edge of the woods, close to the coast, an old shack, disused and abandoned since the 1960s. The rooms had long since lost their décor and rough plastered walls could be seen through the old torn woodchip wallpaper.

Both he and Giancarlo had always known that one day they'd need a place to hide. The industry that they were in meant it was an occupational hazard and they'd always kept the place simply furnished, just in case it was needed quickly. It had an old piece of carpet on the floor, camp beds and shrink-wrapped bedding, but it was a far cry from the mansion that Isobel had been used to. It was cold, but dry, and the few possessions that Roberto had managed to bring had made it just about bearable for the short time they intended to be there, but a lack of electricity or heating made the days long and unpleasant, especially if the wood was wet and couldn't be dried in time to burn.

'Beans for tea,' he announced as he picked up a tin from the pile of food and threw it to her. 'You might be able to make enough of a fire to warm them up, just don't use too much wood. Once the food's cooked, bank the embers down a bit to stop the chimney from smoking.'

'But, Roberto, it's cold,' Isobel pleaded and he watched as she sat on the edge of the hearth, close to the embers and held her hands out over them in an attempt to get warmer. Half of him wanted to relent, to allow her the wood and let her be warm. But then he thought of the authorities, of how they'd be searching for them and hoped that they'd now be looking for bodies, rather than survivors.

Roberto shook his head. 'Not a chance. God knows how long we'll be holed up here. I don't want the police spotting the smoke and we need the wood to last. We can't leave, not until Giancarlo says so.'

'Why here, Roberto, why the hell did he send us here? It's freezing and you won't even let us have a fire that's big enough to keep us bloody warm.'

Roberto watched as she poured the beans into an old

metal pan. The pan was placed on the fire to warm and the last slice of bread was held over the fire on a toasting fork to brown.

He glanced across at the supplies piled up in the corner of the makeshift kitchen. Beans, tomatoes, dried pasta and packets of ready to make bread. It had all seemed a good idea at the time but now, he wondered how long even he could live on these rations. But he'd done his best in the small amount of time he'd had. There was the food, stacked in one corner, while in the other corner were toilet rolls and a small pile of clothes, all suitable for men. He sighed. There was no wonder Isobel wasn't happy. Not only had she been deprived from her warmth, shag pile carpets and luxuries, she'd also been deprived of all her clothes and now wore men's jumpers and jeans that were all much too big for her.

'Well, for what it's worth, Giancarlo can't get here soon enough,' Isobel smirked.

'What's that supposed to mean?'

'You don't think there was only ever you, Roberto, did you?' Isobel liked to tease him, liked to see him squirm. 'I like men, not boys, you were just a challenge, to annoy Giancarlo.'

'*What* are you saying? You're shagging my bloody uncle? Really? He's old enough to be your father. Plus, do you know what he'd do to both of us if he found out?' He kicked the wood pile. 'You really don't have any idea who you're messing with, do you?'

Isobel just smirked and poked the embers of the fire. 'You really didn't know, did you? Well, let me tell you, he really knows how to treat a woman. He'd have known what supplies to provide for me and, what's more, he's much better at it than you are, you know, the sex.'

225

Roberto exploded. 'You dirty little ...' His hand grabbed hers and he pushed it toward the hot embers of the fire.

'No, you don't.' She lifted the toasting fork with her other hand and held it up to his face, poking him with the prongs. 'One more millimetre, and I'll shove this through your face. Now get off me!' she screamed through gritted teeth as she waited for the pain, sure that Roberto would follow through with his threat and allow her to burn.

'It's no less than you deserve.' He threw her away from him and stomped toward the back door. 'Keep it locked,' he yelled as it slammed shut behind him.

'Don't come back,' she screamed, twisting around to make sure he'd gone. In poking him, she'd accidentally knocked the bread from the toasting fork. It now lay in the embers, ruined, dirty and burnt. Tears dropped down her face as she looked at the small packet of bread mix that stood on the shelf. It would take at least two hours to mix, knead and bake, that's if she could get the fire hot enough to get a rise from the dough or manage to use the old bread oven that was attached.

Turning off the beans she set to work. There was no corner shop to go to now. No baker, no butcher, and certainly no hairdresser; which reminded her, her long, lank blonde hair was still full of seawater. She disobediently threw more logs onto the fire and began to boil water in the biggest pan she had, knowing it would take some effort, but she needed to cook and more than that she needed a bath. Even if that did mean using more logs and making more chimney smoke than Rob approved of.

'What the hell are you doing?' Roberto slammed back through the door, dropped more wood on the floor and glared at Isobel.

'I needed a bath. Get over it.' The old metal tub stood

before the fire and Isobel moved the shallow tepid water round in an attempt to warm her body. Her arms automatically covered her breasts and she glared at Roberto through the corner of one eye. 'Anyhow, get out. Can't I get a little privacy around here?'

'You want privacy, do you? Do you have any idea how much privacy you're going to get when they catch you and throw you in prison? Zero, you'll get zero privacy.' He picked up a bucket, dipped it in the bath water and threw it at the fire.

'What are you doing?'

'I told you not to build the fire. They're looking for us; do you want to be caught?'

'Is that where Luca is? Have they caught him?' Isobel needed to know. Luca had barely been mentioned and she was aware of the tension Roberto showed every time she asked about him.

'He left us out there. Why would you care what happened to him? You were right, he was a traitor. And it's because of him that Giancarlo must have left the country.' He stamped over to the door. 'Now, get out of that bath.'

'I hate it here. I hate you. It's like camping in a concrete box. I need my luxuries. Even the bloody toilet seat is broken, it's disgusting.'

'Giancarlo calls the shots, you know that. You remember him, the wonderful Giancarlo, the man who is so good in bed, the man who gave you the best sex ever? Well, he told me to bring you here if things went wrong, and as soon as Luca disappeared on the dive, I knew that the force would be waiting and we had to get out of there.' He paused, smirked and looked her up and down with disgust in his eyes. 'You should thank him for his generosity, when and if you next see him. That's if he didn't leave us here to rot,' he said provokingly. He stamped around the room. 'Simon is looking for Luca, and once he's taken care of, we'll have no witnesses. At least we got rid of that damn fisherman. We had no choice.'

'No choice? We did have a choice, Roberto. I didn't want to get involved with murder.' She picked up the bar of soap.

'Involved? Oh, let's not go there, Isobel. You didn't seem to mind the drugs while they were paying for your luxurious lifestyle. Well, let me tell you now, drugs kill people. Do you know that?' He slammed his fist into the door. 'So, like it or not, you are involved with murder and if you hadn't been shagging half the Bellandini family, maybe your precious Giancarlo would be here, digging us out of the shit, instead of sunning himself abroad, probably laughing at our downfall.'

'How dare you blame me!' Isobel was furious and threw the bar of soap in her anger. It flew from her hand and hit the wall with the velocity of a bullet. It broke into a hundred pieces and dropped into the dirt on the floor.

'Oh, wasn't that clever?' Roberto shouted. 'That was our only bar of soap.'

Isobel burst into tears. 'You're lucky it wasn't a knife.'

'Really.' He grabbed her hair and pulled her out of the water. Isobel screamed and grabbed at her head. 'Stand up,' he growled, pulling her naked body over the side of the bath and throwing her to the floor. 'Pick it up, clean it, and when I get back, I expect it to look like a bar of soap, just in case I want to be selfish enough to use all the dry wood in one go, and take a damn bath.'

'I hate you.' Her words were venomous, as was the look in her eyes.

'Yeah. Well, I hate you too. Get some sleep. I might be back tomorrow. I might not.'

The door crashed shut behind him.

* * *

Roberto walked through the trees, towards the cliffs. He needed to get some air and to look at the sea. He checked his mobile for the hundredth time that day and moved himself into an open area in the hope of getting a better signal, when it suddenly sprang into life and Giancarlo's name flashed up on the screen.

'Giancarlo, thank God. What's happening?' Roberto sat down on the grass and took in deep breaths of sea air.

'Well. What's happening? That's a good question.' Giancarlo's tone was on the edge of aggressive and Roberto knelt up nervously and looked around.

'We did the drugs lift, Giancarlo, just as you said but we had problems, someone squealed. At first, we thought it was the captain, we got rid of him, over the side. But then, Luca, he disappeared and now, we're thinking it must have been him.'

'Is that what you think? Is it? Well, let me tell you now. I don't pay you to think,' Giancarlo growled down the phone.

'Right, sorry. We've made our way to the hideout.' He paused for breath and once again looked around, checking that no one could hear his conversation.

'At the hideout, good, good. I'm sure Isobel is loving the luxury? Is she?'

'Luxury, Giancarlo, are you serious? She's really not impressed, driving me insane. You've got to get us out of here and soon, because I swear another few days with her and I'll be burying her in the woods.'

Giancarlo laughed. 'Well then, that's good, everything turned out exactly as you both deserved and just as I wished.'

'Wished? Wished? What the hell are you talking about?' Roberto closed his eyes as the sudden realisation hit him: Giancarlo was not coming.

'My boy. Didn't I always tell you not to cross me? Didn't I warn Isobel that she shouldn't cross me either, that she

229

should stay faithful, that she was mine to have and mine alone? Well she was unfaithful, I knew over a year ago that she was sleeping with Luca and then more recently with you. And that's why I originally put a bounty on her head. But now, they have all of you.' He paused. 'Two hundred thousand was a small price to pay to bring you all to justice.' He laughed. 'Well, this is what happens to people who go against me. I get my revenge.'

Roberto pulled the phone away from his ear, and stared at the handset before carrying on. 'Giancarlo, I swear, I didn't know. You have to believe that. Isobel only just told me. I'm begging you, take it out on her if you wish, but you have to come get me.'

'Ahhhh, Roberto. That's where you're wrong. I don't have to do anything. You see, I'm clean. They have nothing on me. I've made sure of that. But, you my boy, murdered James Duggan and now the captain of the *Red Lady*, admittedly with the help of your cousin, Luca, and Isobel, which makes her a drug dealing, murdering accessory. Which means, one way or another, you're all screwed and you're all going to prison.'

Roberto could feel his anger boiling. He stood up and walked towards the cliff edge and looked at the sea which threw itself angrily up against the rocks. Giancarlo had stitched them up.

'Giancarlo. That's where you're wrong. I still have the drugs and drugs mean money. I can buy my way out of the country and when I do, you bastard, I'm coming for you. You'd better watch your back,' he shouted down the phone.

But Giancarlo just laughed. 'Do you think for one minute I'd have let you get your hands on the real drugs? The drugs you have, my boy, are made of talcum powder. They're worthless.' Roberto heard a sickening, high pitched laugh come from Giancarlo. And then the phone went dead.

'Bastard,' he shouted, and then cursed. He closed his eyes and kicked at the dirt. He had no money and no drugs to sell. He had no choice but to go back to River Cottage, find his passport and get as far away from here as possible. He needed to stay hidden and, when it was safe, he needed to get out of the country. He nodded. That's what he'd do. But what if Kate was there? He thought for a moment. Well, he hoped she was. It had all been her fault. If she'd been a woman to satisfy him he'd never have strayed with all those women, had sex with Isobel and annoyed Giancarlo. He nodded as though agreeing with himself. Kate was to blame for everything and he'd make her sorry for bringing him to this.

Roberto made his way through the trees and the undergrowth as he followed the track by torchlight, kicking at clumps of grass along the way until he got close to the beach, turned and followed the narrow path towards where he'd hidden the van.

Chapter Thirty-Nine

'You're both here then,' Elizabeth Duggan said as Kate pushed Eve's wheelchair through the door and into the substantial hallway of their parents' home.

'Yes, Mother, we're both here,' Eve replied, the sense of dread in her voice more than apparent and Kate felt sorry that she'd practically forced her into coming.

'I thought Ben was coming with you, dear.' Her mother looked past both her and Eve, as though expecting him to walk in behind them. 'I've heard so much about him and can't wait to meet him. He just has to be nicer than the last one you had. And where's Max?'

Kate took a deep breath. 'He's with Eric.' It had been two days since Rob had gone missing. During those days she and Ben had become very close. They'd eaten together, waited for news together and had slept in the same bed together. They'd held onto each other for constant support, and on more than one occasion, Ben had gently kissed her, without expectation of more.

No one knew where Rob was. Whether he was dead or alive, and if he was alive, where he'd turn up next. At Ben's insistence, Kate had stayed with him at all times, just in case Rob did come back, and the feeling of nervous anticipation surrounded them both. She knew she didn't love Rob anymore, and wondered if she ever really had.

Kate thought of Ben, of how he'd supported her when she needed it the most and if she were really honest, she was a little disappointed that things hadn't gone further. But then, after what he'd said, maybe he was biding his time and waiting for the right moment, or maybe, it could be that he was just being a friend and wasn't interested in romance at all.

They'd talked for hours. Ben had given her sensible advice. Advice she'd quickly realised was right. She knew that her mother was sick, she needed help, medical help. But also, Kate knew that the only way things would get better, for them all, was if she were to say what was on her mind, and tell them how she felt, once and for all. If things didn't change, if Mother didn't agree to get the treatment she needed, then Kate felt that she had no choice but to walk away. Permanently.

She sighed, loudly, and glanced over to where her mother stood, hands on hips, looking her up and down.

'Katie, wake up, dear. Now, what are you wearing?' she asked as Kate looked down at the clothes she'd borrowed from Eve. She sat down on the antique pew, and removed her pumps before dropping them into the wicker basket by the door and then helped Eve with her coat, replaced her shoes with slippers and then pushed her through to the huge antique oak kitchen with its array of units and colossal range, which put most people's cookers to shame.

'Mother. Kate's wearing my dungarees. I only bought them last week and they're the latest fashion. They look nice,' Eve responded before picking up a magazine and pretending to look at it. Kate had held her breath during the retort and now watched as Eve flicked through its pages hoping their mother wouldn't give out any more insults. The last thing either of them needed tonight was any sort of lecture.

Kate already wished she was back in Caldwick with Ben.

'I'll be there late tonight,' Ben had said as he'd hugged her goodbye.

'Now then, we have roast chicken, new potatoes, cauliflower with a cheese sauce, broccoli and carrots. Is that okay, girls?' Elizabeth's voice rang out as though nothing had been said. It was as though during any given emergency it was Mother's job to cook the dinner and nothing would ever stop her.

Elizabeth Duggan busied herself in the kitchen and Kate studied her, wishing she'd been blessed with the kind of parent who would at least be happy to see them, or at least give them a hug when they needed one. But unless something dramatic happened, that would never happen. Not in this house, it never really had, and Kate walked out of the kitchen and into the garden. The fresh air would do her good. Besides, she needed to think. Tonight was the first time she'd seen both of her parents together for months; it would be the perfect opportunity to speak to them both and she wanted to think carefully about what to say.

She sat on an old wooden bench and stared into space.

A robin settled on the ground in front of her seat and chirped at her while it dug for worms in the soft, well-tended soil.

'*Oh to be a bird,*' she thought as she wondered what sort of life the robin really had. It had to be less complicated than her life. But then again it must have its perils too and the idea of scratching around in the dirt for dinner didn't appeal.

She thought of Rob, of whether any of it had been real. Whether he'd ever loved her or he had just appeared in her life after the accident and hadn't left. Her mind once again drifted to the accident. She still wasn't sure what had really happened, whether there had been another car, whether they'd had to swerve to miss it, or had James simply lost control?

There were so many questions, with so few answers.

It was just after six o'clock when the front door opened and her father walked in from the golf club. It was Sunday, the one day that he didn't work. He looked older and more tired than he'd been the last time they'd seen him, but seemed to be happy when he walked in and saw them. But mother was

234

determined not to be outshone and she immediately ran to him, kissed him on the cheek, took his overcoat from his hand, and hung it up for him, just as she always had.

'Did you play well, dear?' she asked automatically as she closed the cloakroom door and returned to the kitchen to finish the dinner.

'Yes, dear,' came the customary answer. 'Now then, let me take a look at the girls.' He held his arms out towards Eve, as though waiting for her to run into them, just as she'd done as a child. Eve wheeled herself over without hesitation and hugged him affectionately, but Kate stood back, waiting to be invited, just as she'd done since the accident had happened. 'Come on, Kate. What are you waiting for, give your father a hug.' He looked up at her and she smiled with relief, knowing that all was not lost.

The dinner was served at the farmhouse table in the kitchen. Kate sat silently. She had nothing to say, not yet and she spent the whole time pushing vegetables around her plate, without eating a single one. Her throat was still sore and the thought of chewing and swallowing still filled her with dread. Looking up, her father simply stared at his plate and ate. Normally he'd have made conversation. He'd chat about work, politics, his golf game or the traffic, but tonight he also said nothing, which increased the tension that passed through the room.

Kate flinched as her mother suddenly jumped up from her seat, wrung her hands on her apron and snatched the plate from before her. She scraped its untouched contents noisily into the bin and then rinsed it carefully, before placing it neatly in the dishwasher. Collecting the rest of the dishes, she smiled at both Father and Eve, asking if they'd enjoyed all the lovely food that she'd taken the time to prepare.

Kate's eyes caught Eve's. She'd already told her that she planned on speaking to her parents and knew that Eve wasn't happy with the idea and would prefer to keep the peace, never ask the reasons why and stay surrounded by her own bubble, without fear of rupture.

Kate patted Eve's hand. 'It'll be fine,' she whispered as Mother approached with dessert.

Kate stood up and spoke. 'Father.' She kissed Eve on the cheek and then walked toward the lounge door. 'Could I speak to you please?'

Eve cringed as her mother tutted loudly, it was obvious she didn't like being left out of the conversation. Eve left her dessert untouched, excused herself from the table and began to wheel her chair into the lounge. She hadn't wanted to come and would have been happier at home, with Eric and Max, but Kate had needed her support and Eve knew she'd do anything for Kate.

Solomon, her parents' ginger tabby cat, jumped up onto her knee and pummelled her lap, before settling down to find a comfortable place to sleep. The cat was at least twelve years old and had always settled with Eve at every chance he got.

'Oh, hi, Solomon. How are you doing, my ickle puddy cat? Did you miss me?' She tickled the cat's ears and watched as he turned on his back, making himself more comfortable. 'I bet you did.'

'Eve, darling, he's just a cat. Cats are far too independent. They don't miss anyone.' Her mother's tone droned in from the kitchen and Eve sighed, deciding much to Solomon's disapproval that she might try and wheel herself further away, maybe make her way into the den, anywhere where her mother might never find her.

But it was Kate who came to find her.

'Eve, do this with me,' Kate's voice implored, but Eve shook her head.

'I ... I can't. Please, Kate, don't make me do this. She hates us.'

Kate knelt down. 'Eve. She doesn't hate us, she's sick. We need to help her, look after her, just as she did us as children.' Their eyes locked, and silently, but reluctantly, they agreed and Kate held out her hand to grip Eve's.

Kate stepped back into the kitchen. 'Mother, would you care to join us? I think you should, this concerns you too.' Her mother quickly wiped her eyes with a tea towel, before smiling and following her daughters into the lounge.

Her father pointed to the chesterfield, but Kate stayed standing. She paced up and down in front of him, whilst studying each piece of furniture in turn. It had all been at the old house and most had been in her father's study, a room she'd only ever been allowed to enter if there had been a need to discuss her school reports, her latest form of misbehaviour or the way she'd been fighting with one of her siblings. With a deep intake of breath, she turned and looked up, first at her father, then at Eve, and then at her mother, who had positioned herself on the settee opposite Father.

'The accident,' she finally spat out. She heard her mother gasp and Kate stared at her father, watched his reaction and hoped that he'd make the conversation easy. But Father was a master at concealing his emotions; being a barrister meant that his stern poker face had been practised to perfection. It was the trick of his trade, the one thing he could use to ensure that the opposing side found it difficult to read his thoughts. They couldn't know what he was thinking, couldn't know if he was happy with a defendant's answer or not.

'What about the accident, dear?' His words were slow and clear. 'I'm sure we've gone over this before,' he spoke dismissively and Kate knew that this was the one subject that he hated talking about the most. She watched as he flicked an imaginary speck of dust from his perfectly clean shirtsleeve.

'We all need help, Dad. Mum is sick.' Kate knelt down and stared into her mother's eyes. 'Mum, James is dead, he's gone and he isn't coming back.' She waited for a reaction, but her mother just sat, quietly, staring at nothing in particular. 'You blame me? You both blame me for his death, don't you?' The statement was direct and was meant to force a reaction. Kate knew that this was one of the only questions that neither her father nor her mother could wriggle out of.

'I … I don't think we do, dear. Now, why don't you go and help with the dishes? I'm sure your mother would appreciate it.' He looked at his wife who still sat, staring into space.

'Mum, are you okay?' Eve whispered, looking up at her twin. 'Kate.'

Kate was so busy studying her father, wondering if he knew that in one night she'd not only lost James, but she'd also lost both her mother and her father too, that she hadn't noticed the tears that now fell silently down her mother's cheeks. She hated herself for doing this, but knew that if the words were not said, right here, right now, nothing would change. Kate bowed her head. It was time they heard the truth.

'The last thing I'd have ever wanted was for James to die. He was my big brother, my idol, I loved him,' she began. 'I didn't drive the car that killed him.'

'We know that.' Her father wouldn't meet her gaze, he just looked at the floor.

Kate felt herself getting warmer. Her knees felt like jelly and they began to buckle beneath her. She looked around and moved toward the red leather chair where she perched, her hand gripping its edge, like a vice holding onto the wood. She couldn't think of the words to use and tears began falling down her cheeks.

'I ... I can't live like this, Daddy.' She paused and gulped for breath. 'Mother is sick, she doesn't know what she's saying half the time. She thinks that James has just stopped visiting. Everything she says is an insult, a dig, and I'm sure she needs professional help. You ... you have to get her some, you can't keep ignoring it.' Again she paused and her eyes locked with his. 'And you ... you can't keep blaming me either. I need you, Eve needs you and ...' She wiped her tears on the back of her hand.

Her father pulled a tissue from a box on the coffee table and passed it to her.

'Daddy, you used to love me. You used to want to be around me, but then James died and I feel as though I lost you too.' She saw his whole body stiffen and his fingers seem to sink into the leather of his chair.

Kate continued, 'I need you. I need you both and I need you back to how it used to be. Did you know that Rob tried to kill me? Did you? He tried to drown me and as I felt the life drain from me, do you know what I wished for? Do you know what I wanted more than anything?' She paused, felt the strength leaving her body and sobbed. 'I wanted to be with James. I could see his face, his cold, grey eyes, just as he'd looked that day when I went back to the car. I tried to get to him that day. I tried my best to save him. And do you know what? That day Rob pushed me under the bath water, I wished that I could die and be with James. But it hurt. I could feel the burning in my lungs and I began to pray.' Kate stifled a sob. 'I prayed that I was dead.'

'But, you're not religious, dear.' Her mother suddenly spoke and Kate left her chair and went to kneel in front of her again. She grabbed hold of her hands, staring into her tear-filled eyes, and waited until she saw some recognition there.

'No, Mum, I'm not, but that day I prayed like I've never prayed before. I just hoped that death would come quickly, because I never wanted to see that look of pure hatred in your eyes ever again.' Kate continued to cry, and couldn't stop. She looked back at her father who had stood up and was cradling a sobbing Eve in his arms, and then she looked back at her mother, whose whole body had begun to tremble and suddenly she saw the pain in her eyes.

'James ... James is dead?' The words were simple, but were followed by a piercing scream that filled the house. 'My boy, my baby boy, he's gone. Gerald, did you know? Tell me it's not true, Gerald. Gerald, please, please say it's a lie. Please tell me it's a mistake.'

Gerald Duggan let go of Eve, walked over to his wife and pulled her into his arms.

Gerald settled his wife on the settee, while Eve held her hand and stroked her face. And then, for the first time in over a year, he looked directly at Kate's face. He looked at the scar and at her tears. He knew he'd hurt her more than anyone else had ever done and slowly, he edged his body to stand close to her. He fumbled with his hands, and then reached out. He touched her cheek, wiped away her tears and then pulled her into a hug. With the grief of losing his son, he'd almost lost his daughter too. And for that, he was truly sorry.

At that moment she was a little girl again, curled up on his knee, hoping he could make her world perfect. She'd been right; no matter how grown up she appeared to be, she needed him. She needed her daddy back, she needed his love and what's more, he realised that he needed her love too.

'I'm so sorry, Kate. I love both you and Eve so much. I feel so guilty,' he whispered as his whole body crumpled and he too began to sob uncontrollably. 'I never meant to blame you, I swear to God, I never meant for you to feel that way. The only person I blamed was myself. You see, it was my duty to keep you all safe.'

'I know he was your favourite, Daddy. But he's gone and I can't live like this. It was nobody's fault.'

'He wasn't ...' her father whispered as he held her tight, her tears soaking into his shirt, but he didn't care.

'What ...?'

'He wasn't my favourite.'

Kate reached forward and pulled a tissue from the box. 'But you wouldn't look at me. You never kissed me goodbye or goodnight, not once, not after the accident. I thought you hated me, I thought you blamed me for killing James.'

Gerald Duggan shook his head. 'It ... it wasn't like that at all.' He knew how it had looked, knew how she'd felt, but the truth was he'd been too terrified that he'd lose her too. 'It's true, he was the only boy, the eldest and you're right, I loved him, but not more than you or Eve. I never loved any of my children more than the next. Surely ... surely, deep down you have to know that.'

Kate stepped back, but still held onto his arms. 'So why? Why couldn't you look at me?'

Gerald reached out and grabbed his wife's outstretched hand. 'Oh, Kate. I don't know ... Maybe, it's that we've both been just a little afraid to love you. I ... I feel ... Wow, how do I feel?' He paused and searched her face. 'I felt like I had to ... had to distance myself. From all of you. From your mother too, which is why I go away a lot. It was the only way to stop the pain.' He swallowed hard, looked across the room and then back at her. 'Oh, I don't know, I must have thought it was self-protection, just in case you were taken from me too.' He tried to smile, a slight reassuring smile. 'I came to the hospital, I came every day and I prayed so hard to the Lord that he didn't take you or Eve too.'

Kate thought back to the time in the hospital. She'd been sedated and everything had happened in slow motion, it had been as though a fog had taken over her mind, and had refused to dissipate. But now she thought about it, she could remember that her father had been sitting there. On the chair between the bed and the wall. It was true. He'd been sitting quietly, with his hands clasped and at the time she remembered wondering if he was praying.

Tears filled Kate's eyes at the memory. 'Daddy. I remember. I remember you being there. Thank you.' She looked across at Eve who still sat with their mother. Their eyes locked and for a few moments only silent words were spoken. Then, speaking for both of them, Kate said, 'Daddy, we need you. Me and Eve, we need you both.'

Chapter Forty

Ben pulled up on the drive and looked up at the Duggan mansion, which was lit up in the darkness. It was past ten o'clock. Much later than he'd expected, but Gloria and his father had gone on holiday, leaving him in charge of Parker & Son. Even though it was Sunday, work didn't stop and the surveillance operations they had going on had taken longer to organise than usual.

The front door opened and the light from the hallway flooded the drive to show Kate standing before him in a short black dress that hung closely to her hips. She was the coyest, yet most beautiful creature he'd ever seen. She stepped onto the drive and walked slowly towards him and he wasted no time in taking the three steps that he needed to reach her.

'Oh, Kate, I'm so sorry I'm late.' He took her in his arms and pulled her close. He breathed in deeply taking in the soft undertones of her citrus perfume. He'd never been to her parents' before, but the fact that Kate was there made it feel familiar.

'Mother ... the doctor came and gave her a sedative. She went to bed, and both Daddy and Eve are taking it in turns to sit with her. Just in case she needs them,' she whispered.

Ben laughed. 'Well, for what it's worth, I'm glad that I get you all to myself.' His eyes gleamed as he pressed his lips gently to hers. It had only been a few hours since he'd seen her, but the mere graze of her lips once again sent shock waves through his body. He sensed a change in Kate's mood, knew that she wanted more and began to kiss her slowly but passionately. It was a passion that left him burning with desire and without another thought he responded to her needs, with all the love he felt in his heart.

The kiss came to an end and Kate quickly stepped back, cheekily moved herself out of Ben's grasp and held her finger to her lips.

She beckoned him to follow her and stood, smiling seductively, as she grabbed his shirt and pulled him into the house behind her. 'This way, it's a separate annex, we can be alone.' She walked Ben to the side of the house, 'No one ever goes to the annex, it's kept for visitors.'

She was sure now that Ben wanted to be with her. Sure that all the innuendos had meant something and, before Rob had disappeared, he'd made it clear on more than one occasion that their friendship could have been more, but for the past few days, there had been too much going on, and far too much unfinished business.

But now, for the first time in over a year, she felt as though a huge weight had been lifted from her shoulders. The conversation with her parents had been heartbreaking, but she'd bared her soul and finally she felt as though her family had come together. She was sure her eyes were still puffy, but now both her father and mother were acting as though they cared. It was as though all the dirty washing had been made clean again and finally they could move forward with their lives.

Her only wish now was that Rob was found. He'd tried to kill her and she was sure that if Ben hadn't arrived when he had, he'd have succeeded. She'd come to terms with the fact that he could be found dead or alive and, after what he'd done to her, she wasn't sure that she cared which it was.

But at this very moment none of that seemed important. She was here, she was safe and she was with Ben. She caught the sparkle in his eyes and thought carefully before she

244

spoke. 'Take me to bed, Ben. Make love to me.' She lifted her arms up and hooked them behind his neck, pulling his lips back down to meet hers.

He stopped just short of kissing her. 'Kate, I need to know that you're sure.' He searched her eyes and watched her nod as she pushed open the door.

'I'm sure,' she whispered, pulling him roughly towards her, to land on the annex stairs. Her lips were crushed against his and she felt the contour of his body pressed passionately against her, his arousal now fully apparent. She wanted him so much that her heart pounded violently in her chest. She knew he'd been hurt before and knew that he'd patiently waited for her to come to him, for which she was grateful. But now she knew that desire would overtake them both and there would be no turning back.

Kate allowed her hands to move to Ben's jeans in response to his question, and she pulled at them with an urgency as her mouth repeatedly lifted to his. Their mouths and tongues moved in unison. Their hunger grew.

'Oh, Kate, I love you so much,' he whispered between kisses. He pulled her tightly into the curvature of his body and Kate felt his hand move under her dress, skimming her hips and thighs as the other began a gentle massage of her spine, sending currents of desire spiralling through her entire body.

Instinctively, her body arched toward him. Her dress was unzipped and dropped unceremoniously to the floor and she gasped as once again Ben pressed himself to her. His eyes locked with hers and without saying a word she gave him all the permission he needed as Kate moved him towards the bedroom.

Ben took his time to explore her, to arouse and give pleasure and without consideration Kate surrendered to his touch as Ben's fingers carefully moved over every inch of her, with an expertise she'd never known. The pleasure was pure and explosive, but Kate wouldn't be satisfied until she'd given the pleasure back and she moved her hands over him, touching him, caressing him until she knew he could take no more. And then, she moved away and lay beside him.

'Ben, make love to me. I mean ... really make love to me.'

Kate stared longingly and lovingly at his naked body. The deep sparkle of his eyes shone back through the darkness, as his mouth immediately took over hers. Pushing deep inside her, their bodies moved rhythmically together as one. A scream of ecstasy left Kate's lips as simultaneously a crescendo of multiple explosions escalated through them both. Ben moaned with pleasure and finally Kate allowed the release to leave her body with a long, surrendering moan.

'I love you,' he whispered in her ear as he pivoted above her. 'I loved you the first moment I saw you.'

Kate's eyes lit up like candles.

'But didn't ... didn't I call you a moron?' she murmured, as once again his lips tantalised hers.

'That'd be right. I loved the feisty sound of your voice, the way you almost launched yourself out of the car at me.' He smiled. 'I knew you'd be hot.'

Kate poked him as he curled up behind her.

'Do you need to sleep?' he asked, his arms protectively enveloping her body.

Kate turned to face him. 'Oh no, Ben Parker, don't you even think about sleep.' She giggled as her hands found their way under the covers. 'Now I have you, I want you again, and again, and again.'

Chapter Forty-One

'Would you like bacon and eggs, Mr Parker?' Kate's father asked politely as both Kate and Ben came down the side stairs and took their places at the kitchen table.

Kate avoided Ben's gaze in an attempt to suppress her giggles. It was quite apparent to everyone that they'd slept in the annexe. And for the first time in years, Kate felt fourteen again as the blush rose up her face as she watched her father awkwardly make his way around the kitchen, which was obviously an alien environment to him. Kate quickly moved forward to relieve him of the duties.

'Now then, Ben. Coffee, Eggs?' she asked as she switched on the kettle, picked up a pan and turned to collect eggs from a basket.

'No, no eggs.' He smiled and watched her at work. 'Coffee is just fine, thank you. I have to get back, you know, to the office. Eric will be tearing his hair out without me.'

Kate smiled and nodded. 'Dad, how's Mum?'

'She's sleeping, dear. The sedative, it really knocked her out.' He lifted his coffee mug and took a sip. 'The doctor is calling back later this morning to see how she's doing.'

Kate nodded. She was pleased that her mother was finally getting the medical attention she needed. 'More coffee?' she asked.

'No, dear. I can't drink coffee, not like you young folk do today, you all drink far too much, there's no wonder you don't sleep at night,' her father said, whilst picking up his paper and turning the page. He then looked up at Kate and gave her a knowing wink, making her quickly excuse herself from the table. It was good to have her father back, but she could feel herself getting hotter and hotter with embarrassment and this was one conversation she really didn't want to have.

'Eve, how about we go into town?' Kate asked, desperate to tell Eve about the previous evening with Ben. Besides, Father was going to sit with Mother until the doctor had been and then he'd made an appointment for them both to see a counsellor, in the hope that it would help them both come to terms and find a way of dealing with their grief.

It was important that life got back to normal, for all their sakes, and Kate felt that for her, the best way to do that was to go home and put her own home in order.

Kate took the handles of Eve's chair and pushed her through to the hallway. 'We could go into York and have tea and cake at Betty's,' she said as she saw Ben leave the breakfast table and walk up behind them both.

Kate pointed to the stairs. 'You, Mr Parker, should have been up there,' she said to Ben. 'I believe your room should have been the first on the right. You'll find an en suite in there, with a fully functional shower.' She laughed, making Ben raise his eyebrows.

'Yes,' he agreed. 'After last night I think a shower is more than in order,' he whispered. It had been a comment only meant for Kate, but Eve spun around in her chair, her head almost leaving her shoulders.

'What do you mean, after last night?' she squealed with the excitement of a teenager as she stared at her twin sister for clues. 'Come on, spill the beans, you can't say that and then go all quiet on me.'

Both Ben and Kate blushed. Kate looked at her twin, put her finger to her lips and pushed the wheelchair in the direction of Eve's room. 'You, Miss Duggan, need to go and get ready. Or I'll go without you and there will be no cake.'

They all laughed, but then Ben's phone rang and within minutes he'd left for the office, without the shower, but with the promise that he'd see Kate at home later.

Chapter Forty-Two

After dropping Eve off at her house, Kate had called at the supermarket to buy food for dinner. It would be the first meal she would cook for Ben and she took time choosing the ingredients. She even threw candles and scented reeds into the basket, determined to make it special.

Pulling up outside River Cottage, she sat for a while, staring. It looked different. It had been her home for two years and her grandmother's home before that, so why did it look so distant, detached and unfamiliar?

Mrs Winters came out of her house, waved and walked off towards the shops. The postman pushed his bike up the road and Jimmy from the farm was out walking his spaniel, Dexter. Jenny from the corner bungalow walked by with her pram and smiled. Everything was happening as it normally would, yet nothing looked the same.

The thought of going in made her feel sick. Her heart boomed in her chest and she resented Rob for making her feel this way, especially about a house she'd loved for a lifetime. She jangled the keys in her hand, walked to the back door, and let herself in.

Stepping inside, Kate gasped. Her mind spun and she held onto the door for support. The whole cottage was a mess. Her kitchen drawers were open, their contents scattered. The stools were tipped on their side and everything in the recycling bin, the fridge and the washing basket was spread all over the floor.

Kate fell to her knees. Everything was a mess and she angrily began picking up tins of beans, packets of rice and dried pasta from the floor. Packaged or not, she immediately placed everything in the bin, which she'd lifted upright and stood next to where she knelt. Her thoughts and her kitchen spun around her like flying saucers, making her whole body begin to shake and nausea took over. She heaved.

'So, you're home,' Rob's voice rang out and Kate screamed. She looked up and saw him in the doorway. 'I knew you'd come back eventually. I've been here two days. I thought I'd wait, after all, no one was going to look for me here, were they?' His voice was calm, deep, and emotionless.

'What … what the hell are you doing here? They think you're dead.' She looked around, searching for a weapon, desperate for something to fall into her hand, something she could use to protect herself. But everything had been moved. Knife blocks were empty, pans had disappeared and all that was left was the carnage that he'd spread all over the floor. She looked at her bag and wondered how quickly she could reach it. She needed to hit the panic code and get help. But the bag was too far away from her and she began inching her way towards it.

He walked towards her. 'So they think I'm dead, do they?' He smirked. 'Did you really think you'd get rid of me that easily?'

Kate scrambled towards the door, and towards her bag as panic overtook her. Rob's hand grabbed at her hair and then at her throat. The fear hit her before the pain, the pressure grew tighter and tighter and she gasped for breath. Terrified her eyes locked onto his. The blood pounded in her head. She couldn't speak, couldn't scream, couldn't breathe. The pain increased and everything turned to a blur.

'I'm gonna kill you,' his words were venomous and came through gritted teeth. The tip of his nose touched hers. His voice was poison and the look in his eyes was of hatred.

And then, as quickly as he'd grabbed her, he let go.

Falling to the floor she gasped for breath, whilst grabbing at her throat as the pain continued. She made a frantic attempt to drag her body across the floor and towards the door. Adrenaline rushed through her. She had to get away. The pain came from every direction, but fear kept her momentum as she pulled herself along, every second feeling like a minute. She needed to find safety, needed to get as far away as she could. Her heartbeat boomed in her head, and then she saw Rob's monstrous figure loom above her and the room was filled with his venomous laugh.

'P-p-please,' she begged, but Rob sneered at her. She no longer recognised the man she'd loved. The evil in his eyes had not been in those of the Rob that she'd known.

'*Please?*' The word spat from his mouth. His saliva showered her face.

Kate closed her eyes and prayed. Ben's face flashed before her and she tried to smile. At least she'd had that one night of passion. At least she'd known he loved her. She tried to focus on Rob and wished for the torture to end. If he was going to kill her, then she hoped it would be fast.

'You think you're so clever, don't you?' His voice hissed through his teeth. She felt his boot connect with her chest and she screamed. Her arms flailed all around, unsure what part of her to protect next. Then there was only darkness.

Chapter Forty-Three

Ben paced up and down the polished wood floor. He'd been home now for almost an hour, but Kate hadn't returned. He was anxious, and picked up his mobile and once again tried to phone her. A long continuous buzzing began in his mind and his whole body felt as though he were balancing on a wire, waiting to fall. Something was wrong.

Again, he looked at his phone. Checked his emails, text and messenger, repeatedly, while pressing buttons, and praying that the lack of notification was wrong.

Ben held his breath intermittently, and for what seemed like the hundredth time, he paced back and forth through the house, headed up the stairs, and stared at the bed. He imagined her lying in the bed at her parents' house, how beautiful she'd been the night before and how right she'd felt in his arms. Their lovemaking had gone on for hours, but then they'd both curled up together and he'd watched her sleep. She'd curled up, foetal, with her hands clasped together as though in prayer, whilst being tucked under her face, as though using them as a pillow. He'd stroked her face, kissed her jawline and wondered what it would be like to wake up with her every single day, and he looked forward to the day she'd be here, lying in his bed again.

He didn't know what to do. All he did know was that earlier she'd gone shopping with Eve, but she'd called him at midday saying she'd be home by five and it was now six thirty. Kate, the woman who was never late, was now unusually more than an hour late.

Ben tapped his foot to the rhythm of the radio, then suddenly sighed with relief. Of course, she'd said she'd be home by five and, to Kate, home was still River Cottage, where she probably was, waiting for him and cooking the meal she'd promised.

He kicked himself, ran upstairs and changed. Traffic permitting, it wouldn't take him long.

Chapter Forty-Four

Isobel stood on the doorstep of the hideout. It was late afternoon and the fresh air smelt of the sea and the warmth of the sunshine felt good on her face.

Roberto had been gone for two days and she decided that the shack was a nicer place without him in it.

She sat down on the grass and lay back, allowing the sun to warm her face. It shone through her eyelids in shades of amber. It was good to be outside, even though she knew that if Roberto came back and caught her, he'd be furious. He'd told her to stay inside. The authorities would probably still be looking for them and she knew she was taking a risk, but the hut had become claustrophobic with a cold and chilling atmosphere.

She lay and listened as the birdsong came from every direction. She could hear the gulls and knew that the sea was somewhere close by. They were good, beautiful noises. Noises that she'd missed while being caged up inside.

Isobel sat up, looked around her and picked at the flowers. She made a daisy chain and wrapped it around her wrist like a bracelet, just as she had as a small child. Closing her eyes, she thought of all the bracelets of gold she'd owned, all the diamonds, rubies and sapphires. Of the clothes she'd had and of how she now wore clothes only fit for men, and all far too big. She then glanced back down at the home-made bracelet that encircled her wrist. It was pretty and Isobel smiled. She was more than aware that it was the one and only piece of jewellery that she now possessed. Everything else had been left behind.

She sighed, wondering how long it would be before Giancarlo arrived or, after what Roberto had said, if he'd ever arrive at all. The thought of sitting it out and waiting for him was crushing her inside and she wished she knew where Roberto was. Was he with Giancarlo? With Luca? Had Luca betrayed them, as Roberto thought, and if he had, were they all imprisoned, dead or on the run? Were the police about to pounce? She looked up at the sun, wondering how long she'd be free. Whether they'd all escape or be locked up for life.

How had everything got so complicated?

She stared into the woods. They were thick and deep, but not impenetrable. She knew there must be a way to get to the beach. After all, after over an hour's surface swim, they'd come in on this shoreline. The kit had been temporarily hidden and, in the darkness of night, they'd made their way through the woods to get to the shack, which hadn't seemed so far away.

She looked back to the crude building, turned her back on it and anxiously walked along the edge of the trees. The further she walked, the louder the sea became and finally the trees gave way to a small narrow track. The grass was flat here, the bluebells, daffodils and daisies were unequivocally crushed and a bush or two had been roughly hacked back to create a wider path.

Was this the way through? The way that she and Roberto had walked?

She nervously looked back before stepping onto the path, and walking through what was left of the trees, until she saw them clear and open up. From here she could see the cliff tops, the beach and ultimately the sea. It was far below her and she tried to remember where they'd found the steps and at what part of the cliff they'd climbed them.

She walked along the cliff edge, and admired the view, as anger rose up inside her and she thought of how Roberto had left her alone. Giancarlo had said that Roberto would be the boss in his absence, but that didn't give him the right to leave her to rot. He went out. He got to chop wood, and he got to walk in the trees, but more than that, he hadn't come back. Not for days. 'You stay in and keep the door locked,' had been his final barked instruction before he'd left days before, but the fresh air had invigorated her; she liked it and she wanted to walk on the beach.

Chapter Forty-Five

'Eric, I need your help,' Ben shouted down the phone. 'I've called the police. Kate's house is a mess, ransacked.' He paused, pain flooding his heart. 'Kate's missing and I think Rob's been here.' He moved from room to room, searching for clues. 'And, Eric, I really don't need to tell you what that could mean. Call Patrick, tell him to go over to Eve's, she needs to know what's happening and we need to know she's safe. Get Patrick to take her back to the office. She'll be safer there with you.'

Eric gulped. 'Oh my God. I tried to call Eve a few moments ago. She didn't answer.' His voice began to shake. 'Okay, okay, deep breaths. Right, Ben, tell me what to do.'

'Follow procedure. It's proven. It works. Start with CCTV. Look at the roads going in and out of Caldwick. Also log in and try and get a signal on Kate's work phone.' Ben stepped over the kitchen carnage and walked into the living room at the front of the house. A passport lay on the floor and Ben quickly picked it up. 'Eric, I've got a passport. It's Rob's, he must have come back for it, but dropped it when he ransacked the place. Why else would it be discarded?'

Ben saw a police car pull up outside. 'They're here. Okay, look at all vehicles leaving Caldwick. He had to get here somehow and he can't be in his truck as it was impounded by the authorities. Phone me back if you find anything. If Rob is back, and it looks like he is, I need to know where he's taken Kate as fast as possible.'

Ben's words struck deep making Eric gasp for breath. He grabbed hold of the desk and held on. He felt as though he'd been punched and took just a moment to compose himself.

He knew how dangerous Rob could be, knew that he'd easily overpower Kate and, as for Eve, she wouldn't stand a chance.

Please. I've only just found her, please let Eve be safe, please let them both be safe.

Eric had never been to church, never really believed in God, but at that moment he prayed with all his heart and then kicked himself into action and began to follow Ben's orders. A quick phone call to Patrick had been followed by logging into every type of surveillance he could.

His phone rang again.

'Yes, Ben. I'm on it.' Eric took in a deep breath and stared at the computer screen. 'I've tried to find Kate through her phone. I'm not sure it's switched on.'

'She has to have it on,' Ben shouted. 'And if it isn't switched on then please keep watching that screen till it is. The only way that the phone will become inert is if it's been burnt or frozen. Other than that, I want a way of tracking it.'

Eric didn't respond. He just searched the screen and hoped. The surveillance was set up on a link. He could track every investigator that worked for Ben and twenty-three lights immediately lit up all over the map. Eric began to check each one for its identity.

Eliminating all other indicators, he stared at the screen, willing Kate's indicator to bleep. All he needed was one light; with that he'd be able to pick up her coordinates. He prayed for the screen to give him some idea of where she was.

'Eric, what do you have?' Ben growled.

Eric stared at the screen. 'Ben, her phone pinged up, it's at River Cottage.'

He heard Ben curse. 'Shit.' The sound of Ben moving things around came down the phone. 'Yes, it's here, Eric. Her bag is here and her phone's inside.'

Eric closed his eyes. Hope of finding Kate and Eve quickly slipped away.

Then, Ben spoke. 'Eric, try tapping into Eve's phone, see if you can locate it, just in case. Keep me informed.'

Eric grunted. 'Of course.' His glasses had slipped and he pushed them back into place, just as the door to his office opened. He looked up and held his breath for a moment, completely shocked and wondering what to do.

'Eric, are you there?'

'Ben, Ben, I think you should come back to the office,' he said, his voice quavering.

'Eric, what's happened?'

'Ben, it's Luca Bellandini, he's here. He's in my office. I'm putting you on speaker phone.'

Luca Bellandini shuffled nervously from foot to foot. 'You have to come quickly. Roberto, he has the girls.' He seemed to stop and think before continuing, 'And ... I know where he's taken them. I know where he's hiding out.'

Eric's stomach rolled 'Oh my God, Ben, I take it that you heard all of that?'

Chapter Forty-Six

Kate's whole body shuddered with the cold as she struggled to open her eyes. Her mind was dazed and everything around her was blurred. Her hand reached out to feel a rough corrugated metal floor and the sound of an engine made her quickly realise that she was in a vehicle, travelling at speed.

Where am I?

She tried to sit up but couldn't. Her whole body ached, every part of her felt bruised, her muscles throbbed and her head pounded. She tried to open her eyes, but the slightest amount of light sent shooting pains to the back of her eyes. She kept them closed and a deep, disturbing sob came from inside her as anxiety and trepidation flooded through her mind.

Again, she tried to open her eyes, but struggled. The piercing pain continued. But her need for survival took over and she peered around her, through the tiniest of slits. Kate tried to knuckle rub her eyes, but her hands were bound together and she awkwardly hit herself in the process.

'Oh, Kate, you're alive.' Eve's sob came from somewhere close by and suddenly the pain in her eyes didn't matter. She opened them wide to see Eve before her. She was curled up on the floor of the van, her hands and legs bound, and with a tear-stained face, her eyes pleading with Kate for help.

'Eve,' she whimpered, her voice weak and her throat sore. 'Eve, are you okay?' She breathed in short, shallow breaths, and watched for the gentle nod of Eve's head and the look of relief in her eyes.

'I … I thought he'd killed you,' she said, before bursting into tears, making Kate manoeuvre her body towards her twin, knowing that they'd feel better if they were close enough to touch. The power of two, they'd called it as children, knowing that together they had been and could be invincible. A sob reached Kate's throat. She knew she had to be strong, for Eve's sake, and wished that she could feel that sense of invincibility right now. But deep down, she knew Rob, knew what he could do and if he was happy to hurt her without a thought, then he wouldn't think twice about hurting Eve.

The van came to a halt, but the engine kept running. Kate kicked the side of the van, '*Helllllllppppppppppp!*' she screamed as loud as she could.

Rob spun around in his seat and looked directly at her. 'Be quiet, bitch. Or your sister gets it first.' He nodded his head and laughed. 'If you know what I mean.' His face was contorted with laughter and Kate knew that he meant what he said.

The look in his eyes was pure evil. She couldn't allow him to hurt Eve. Her mind went into overdrive. She looked around the van; she had to find a way to escape, she had to get them both to safety and if she couldn't save them both, then Eve had to come first.

Chapter Forty-Seven

The van came to a sudden halt and as Rob jumped out and opened the side door, Kate noticed that it was now dusk. Darkness wouldn't be far away and she had to work out where she was before that happened.

'Get out,' Rob barked as he reached forward to grab Eve by the arm, dragged her across the van floor and roughly picked her up, making her scream with fear.

'Rob, for God's sake, leave Eve alone. She's never done anything to you. Please, I'm begging you.' Kate tried to pull at his arm, but felt herself being pushed roughly away.

He stood back and let go of Eve, who dropped back to the van floor screaming. 'Begging me, are you?' he jeered. 'I remember begging you for another chance. I remember trying to be nice. I cooked you dinner and you were nasty and rude. What was it you said to me?' He paused and thought. 'I think "go to hell" could have been your words, Kate. So I did go to hell and I brought both of you "to hell" with me.' A sadistic laugh came from within him. He grabbed at Eve again, picked her up and carried her towards an old concrete shack. He looked around, checked the front and back, then kicked open the door and walked in. 'Now, get inside.'

Kate's hands were still bound, but she quickly dragged herself out of the van and followed Rob into the empty shack. It was crude, with whitewashed walls and an open fire that wasn't lit. She shivered and watched as Rob dropped Eve onto a camp bed that stood to one side of the room, before turning and throwing logs onto the embers.

'Bitch, where the hell is she?' He stamped around the room. 'Isobel, Isobel, get back in here.' He opened the back door, looked into the woods and slammed it in disgust.

'She'll be here, any second,' he said in a less than audible fashion, then stamped towards the door. 'Don't move, or I swear, I'll kill you both. And don't think you have time to run. I'll be less than two minutes. You wouldn't get far, not with the cripple.'

The sound of the van starting up could be heard and the smell of diesel filled the room. Kate knew that he'd gone, but knew he wouldn't leave for long. She crept to the door, looked out and watched as the van disappeared into the distance, and quickly took in her surroundings. They were in a remote area. Nothing could be heard, except, Kate tried to concentrate, was that the sea?

'Eve, listen to me. We have to run and we have to run now.' She heard the words fall out of her mouth and then looked down at her sister's crippled legs. 'I'll help you.'

Eve began to sob. 'Kate. You go. He'll be back any moment, and he shouted for that woman. She'll be here, she'll see us. We wouldn't get far enough. Please, get help, get help for both of us.'

Kate looked into her terrified eyes and knew beyond doubt that leaving her was the last thing she could or would ever do. 'No way, Eve. We're the power of two, right?' She shook her head and ran to the door. She could see a wood, trees and with them would be a hiding place. She took in a deep breath and turned to Eve.

'I have a plan.' She began pulling at the tape that bound her wrists. It was tight and strong. She was wasting time. She looked around. By the fire she saw a toasting fork and grabbed at it, and passed it to Eve. 'Hold it steady, I'm going to use the prongs to stab the tape.'

Kate ran through the darkness. Her heart pounded and her legs hurt, not to mention her feet that still wore high heeled boots after her day out with her twin.

She looked back into the woods, where only a few minutes before she'd left Eve, lying on her belly, cowering under a bush. Kate had managed to drag her to the woods, into the trees and to a place just off the main track where they'd both agreed it would be safe to hide. Even if Rob came back and ran down the track, the chance that he'd veer that far off the path while searching was slim. Hopefully he wouldn't stop to think that Kate would leave Eve alone. But after a tearful goodbye, both she and Eve had agreed that she'd be faster alone. She had to get help, had to get to some kind of civilisation and phone the police, Ben and an ambulance. Eve could be hurt and Kate was terrified that being dropped and dragged could have affected her paralysis, making it worse.

The darkness was dropping fast and Kate stumbled over shrubbery as she ran, but didn't dare stop. She could see the edge of the trees, a clearing where maybe someone would be, and she headed straight for it. Then she stopped as she saw the edge of the cliffs, the drop off and the sea beyond.

'No ... No ... No ... this is not happening.' She made her way to the cliff edge, looked along it and for as far as she could see it was a sheer drop, with boulders and rock pools far below. She looked back at the trees. How could she have gotten it so wrong? Why would there be a path through the trees if there was nowhere to go?

She turned, defeated, knowing that she'd have to go back. Maybe she could hide with Eve in the bushes until morning. But what if Rob was back? What if he was in the woods, looking for them? Surely by now, he'd have realised that they were gone. But she had no choice, she had to go back to Eve and find a way to keep them safe.

'Really thought you were clever, didn't you?' Came Rob's unmistakable voice from somewhere within the trees. Kate squinted, and spun around in the darkness trying to see where he stood. But then he emerged, looking both smug and determined.

'Rob, you're there. I ... I was looking for you,' she lied, while searching the grounds around him, looking for a way to escape.

He stopped in his tracks. Scratched his chin and held his hands out aloft. 'And why on earth would you do that?' He shook his head.

'Because ...' She had to think quickly. '... Rob, I love you. I thought we could talk, sort things out. Everything's such a mess and I wanted to see you. We had a good life together. We shared a home. Surely, that has to count for something?'

He walked closer to her, stared into her eyes. The look reminded her of the day he'd attacked her, the day he'd dragged her into the bath and the day she'd thought she was about to drown.

'A good life, is that what you think?' He looked over the edge of the cliff. 'Long way down, isn't it?' He laughed.

Kate tried not to look back over the cliff. She didn't want to see how far the fall would be. 'Look, no one has to get hurt, Rob. No one knows you are here. All you have to do is let me go. We ... we could go together, start again.'

'Do you think I'm that stupid?' he growled. 'I'm never going to let you go. Don't you understand that?' Once again he laughed. A loud, malevolent sound that made Kate's whole body shudder and her skin crawl.

Rob's hands were over his face. 'It's all your fault, you see. I was ordered to get close to you. Made to follow you, instructed to be around you. I didn't want to, but Giancarlo made me.' He continued to hold his head in his hands, and spun around on the spot. 'It's all your fault, everything is your fault,' he spoke as if in a daze. Lifting his face from his hands, he stared at the sea over her shoulder.

Tears ran down Kate's face. 'What ... why ... why me?'

He physically shook before her. 'I had to infiltrate the village, the women, the homes of the rich. I had to sell them the drugs and you ... your grandmother was well loved; you were the daughter of a barrister. Everyone trusted you, they trusted your family.'

Kate's world fell from beneath her feet and she dropped to her knees. 'So you only loved me because of who my family are?'

Rob nodded. 'I had no choice. I had to do the drug runs and sell the drugs or lose my family. I couldn't have one without the other, can you understand that? Yet now, here I am with no family.' He shook his head fiercely, walked towards her, knelt down and grabbed her by the shoulders, looking pleadingly into her eyes. 'You have to believe me. I didn't want to sell drugs ... you know how I hate them. What they do. I hated it, hated what it did to people, but I had no choice and I ended up just like my family: importing, selling, killing.'

She closed her eyes. It was as though she was hearing the story of her own life for the very first time. At last the truth was being told.

She carefully lifted a hand and risked touching his face. She was prepared to try anything to save both her and Eve, even if that meant seducing him right here, right now, in the darkness on the cliff top. 'Please, Rob. I love you so much. We can sort this out, I'm sure we can. It was real, wasn't it? We did love each other, didn't we?' Her mind spiralled out of control as the words fell from her lips.

For a moment Rob's eyes searched hers with a need almost too painful to endure. His lips lifted towards hers, brushed the side of her face, then his arms grasped hold of her like his life depended on him never letting go. 'Everything's such a mess, Kate.' He sobbed, his face nuzzled into her shoulder. 'Giancarlo, he's left the country, he's abandoned me and I

267

don't know what to do without him.' Pulling back his face, his eyes pleaded with hers. 'I'm in so much trouble. I know I've done wrong, but I can't go to prison. I'd never survive.' He nestled his face into her neck. 'No one was supposed to die. The car you were in, it should have just left the road, but the road was covered in mud, the car skidded too far and the water level was higher than I'd thought. I saved both you and Eve, but I couldn't get to your brother, not in time. I tried, I swear to God, I tried, but I couldn't save him too.'

Kate held onto the man that she'd loved, as her breath caught in her throat and her world fell into a million pieces around her. She couldn't believe what Rob was saying and her mind spiralled back to the accident. First to the car, to how it had swerved and then to how it had rolled, over and over, downward and into the water. Then she'd been on the grass by the side of the road, with Eve at her side ... and Rob ... she had no memory of him being there. But he had been. He'd caused the accident. He'd killed her brother and he'd crippled Eve. It had all been his fault, not hers.

Her breathing became shallow and rapid. She hated every millimetre of him and wanted justice for both James and for Eve.

She tried to calm her breathing and began taking deep, deliberate breaths, while she thought carefully about her next move. No matter what he'd done, no matter how much she hated him for what he'd done, she had to protect Eve and she was prepared to do anything to do that.

A noise came from deep in the undergrowth. It was too dark to see who it was and Kate began to tremble with nerves as Rob's demeanour altered. He spun around. 'Who's there?' he shouted, standing up and walking to the edge of the woods.

'Rob, just leave it, it'll just be an animal or something. Please, we need to talk.' Kate's eyes searched the woods, fearing that Eve had ventured out of her hiding place and dragged herself through the trees.

'Ohhhhhhh, so that's where your sister is hiding, is it?' He began pulling at the bushes and staring into the darkness. 'Now then, what am I going to do with you both?' He marched up and down, towards the trees, just as Isobel stepped out.

'Yes, Roberto. What are you going to do with them?'

Rob spun around on the spot. 'W-w-where the hell have you been? I've been looking for you. I told you to stay at the sh-shack,' he stuttered, obviously shocked by her sudden appearance. He pushed her out of the way and stomped back to where Kate was still on her knees.

'For God's sake, Roberto,' Isobel screeched at him. 'You've done some bloody stupid things in your life, but bringing her here has to beat them all. What the hell will Giancarlo say?'

'Don't you dare bring my family into this. My family love me ... do you hear that, they love me!' he screamed at her and his voice echoed through the trees.

Kate's anger boiled. It was because of his family that her brother was dead, that she was scarred and that her sister was paralysed. Yet still, all he cared about was what his family might think of him. 'Your family don't care, Rob. You just said it yourself. Giancarlo has abandoned you. He's left you both here to rot.' She could see him grinding his teeth, he couldn't argue with the truth and continued to pace up and down the cliff edge.

'Is that true? Has he deserted us?' Isobel screamed. 'Because if I've lost everything for nothing, I swear, I'll—'

'You'll do what, Isobel? I'll tell you what you'll do, you'll do nothing.' Rob stopped and stared at the sea.

Kate watched his movements. She knew he'd stopped watching her to concentrate on Isobel and took the opportunity to stand up, while she watched and waited for him to get closer. Then he turned.

'Ohhhhhhhhhhhh, you think you're going to push me over the edge, do you?' He marched towards her, grabbing her by the throat. 'Such a shame you're not that strong or clever. After all, it would be so easy for someone to trip and fall, wouldn't it?'

Kate screamed. 'Rob, p-p-please ...' she cried out as he physically moved her by the throat to the edge of the cliff. The heel of her boot caught in the undergrowth and she slipped and crashed to the ground, landing heavily on her back. But Rob easily moved her and now she lay, her head hanging over the edge, with his hand at her throat.

'One more squeeze, Kate, and you'll suffocate.' His body lay over hers. 'Or shall I give your neck just one little push? It would snap like a twig; do you know that?'

She stared at him. Her eyes felt like saucers, but she refused to close them. Refused to give him the satisfaction that he'd won. 'Then kill me,' she managed to whisper, her eyes still penetrating his.

'Rob ... stop ... I've told you before, I won't be party to murder!' Isobel screamed and Kate saw her launch herself at his back. 'You have to stop; you're going to kill her.'

Kate was aware of the thuds that vibrated through Rob's body and into hers, as Isobel struck him from behind. Drifting in and out of consciousness, she was vaguely aware that Isobel was trying to help and then as quickly as he'd grabbed her, his grip released and Kate once again found herself dragging air into her deprived lungs. She heard a scream and opened her eyes, just as Rob swung out, catching Isobel in the face. Isobel stumbled, screamed again and then fell backwards, her head hitting a rock. She was lying by the cliff edge and Kate watched as Rob walked towards her, ready to kick. But Kate summoned up every ounce of energy she had and kicked out, catching Rob hard on the ankle. She was terrified, but she had to do something to stop him from pushing Isobel over the edge. She tried to get up, knowing she had to escape, but also knowing that he'd follow.

'Oh, Kate, you were always stupid,' Rob said calmly.

Once again hysteria filled her body. Rob grabbed her by the hair and she felt herself being dragged up from the ground and into the air. Her feet had physically left the ground and Rob laughed in her face. 'Do you know what, Kate? I didn't love you. Not ever. Not really. Why would anyone love you, especially with you looking like that? You're so damned ugly.' Kate kicked out, catching him in the leg and he let go of her hair, allowing her feet to touch the ground, but then he sneered in her face. 'And that sister of yours, wait till I find her. I'll make her suffer so much. I want her to beg me to stop, right before I kill her. Besides, she can't fight back like you can, can she?' he snarled as, over his shoulder, Kate saw the outline of Eve loom up behind Rob.

'*Oh, yes she can!*' Eve's voice shrieked as she held a rock above her head and launched it in Rob's direction.

The rock fell short, hitting Rob on the shoulder, just hard enough to make him let go of Kate. They both fell heavily to the ground and Kate crawled away as quickly as she could to get to Eve, who was standing … standing a short distance away.

Rob raised himself to his knees, then slowly to his feet. He looked at the two sisters, standing with arms around each other, staring at him with fear and loathing in their eyes. He shook his head and started to move towards them, but his legs gave way, his footing was lost and he found himself falling backwards over the edge of the cliff, screaming as he fell.

'Arrrghhhhhhhhhh …!' His scream could still be heard and Kate ran to the edge. He was clinging on to the rocks below, terror in his eyes. Even after all he'd done, she couldn't allow him to fall and her instinct was to save him, to grab his hand, but as she held her hand out to him, he shook his head in defiance.

'Rob, come on, Rob. Take my hand. You're strong. I know you can pull yourself up from there. Please, for me?' Once again she grabbed at his hand, but he shrugged her off.

'I'm so sorry, I'm so sorry … for everything,' he blurted out, right before the rock gave way and she saw his body hurtle towards the sea.

Kate fell to her knees and immediately vomited. Then she turned slowly and stared in shock at Eve, who still stood before her, pale, wobbly, but standing, unaided.

Eve dropped to the floor and they both looked to the trees where a noise could be heard. Within seconds, they were surrounded. Ben, Eric and Luca Bellandini had all emerged and ran towards them.

'Ben, please,' she looked at where Isobel's pale, limp body lay. 'Help her. She tried to save us.'

Epilogue

Kate waited for the car to stop, before climbing out and unfastening her four-week old son from his car seat. 'There you go, go to Daddy,' she said as she passed him to Ben, who proudly hugged the baby close to his chest, his eyes immediately full of love.

They both turned in unison and looked up at the church.

'I can't believe we're about to christen him, Kate, here in Bedale,' Ben whispered as his arm went around her shoulders and pulled her to him. He kissed her lightly on the lips. 'Is it really only a year ago that you wound the window of your car down and called me a moron? Not two hundred yards up this very road.' He laughed and pointed to where Kate had pulled up that day.

'Well, for what it's worth, you're the nicest moron I ever met,' Kate said as she dug in the baby bag, pulled out a tissue and wiped her son's mouth.

'And you, Mrs Parker, you gave me everything – everything I thought that I had lost forever. I'm so happy and I love you both so very much.' His words were sincere and her eyes filled with tears as both she and Ben walked in through the church doors.

The sound of 'All Things Bright and Beautiful' echoed throughout the church, making both Gloria and Elizabeth smile at one another. Their mothers had become close over the past months, much to the disapproval of William and Gerald, who both counted the cost after each and every shopping trip, but who also benefitted from their hours now spent on the golf course. Eve and Eric sat together, hand in hand, and Kate smiled, knowing that the next time they entered this church would be in the summer, for their wedding.

The singing stopped and the vicar walked from the front of the church to the back, where he lifted a jug of holy water and poured it into the font.

'Could I have the parents, grandparents and the godparents please?' he asked.

Ben and Kate stepped forward, quickly followed by Gloria, William, Elizabeth and Gerald. Eve inched herself to the edge of her wheelchair, and Kate smiled with pride as Eve stood up and slowly walked the few steps to take her place at the font, with Eric by her side. It was a sight she'd never tire of. A sight that had happened more and more frequently over the last year, and Kate moved forward, placing a kiss on her twin's cheek.

The vicar then held out his arms. 'May I?' He took the baby from Ben and walked back to the font. He then paused and turned to Kate. 'We name this child?'

Kate locked eyes with Ben, who nodded. 'I know that up to now we've called him Benjamin after his daddy, but ...' She looked up and then individually at each member of her family, before turning back to the vicar. 'With my parents' permission, I'd like to name him James Benjamin Parker, in honour of the brother that I lost.'

Cries of delight filled the church and baby James was held over the font, where holy water was dribbled over his tiny head.

Kate's world was complete, but she sighed as she stepped out of the church. Rain had begun to fall and she moved quickly to put James in the car.

'Kate, wait.' Ben's words followed her and he held his arms out for their son.

'But he's getting wet.' She felt concerned but handed

James to Ben, who began spinning him around in the rain. 'What are you doing?' she asked and began to laugh as both of their parents began to join in, along with Eric, who spun Eve's wheelchair around and around.

'Come on.' Ben held a hand out to her. 'We're dancing in the rain.'

'But ...' Kate thought of all the nightmares she'd lived through. The accident, how her brother had been killed, Eve paralysed and the scar on her face; how Isobel had been killed; how Rob had fallen to his death; and how he'd tried dancing with her that night, before almost killing her in the bath.

'Kate, come on, trust me, it's fun,' Ben shouted. It was then she realised what Ben was doing. He was turning her worst nightmares into her happiest day. A day where her whole family was together. A day when they all danced in the rain.

Thank You

Thank you so much for reading my second novel *Tell Me No Secrets*.

This novel will always be my book baby, it's the second book of mine to be published, however, it was the first one I ever wrote and even though it's changed dramatically since it was first written, it will always hold a very special place in my heart.

I really hope you enjoyed following Kate's journey, through the smiles and heartache that both she and Ben shared during their search to find true love and I'm sure that you'll agree, that by the time they got it, they really deserved it.

I always get really excited (yet nervous too) when I know that someone is reading my work and I doubt that I'll ever tire of that feeling when I hear that someone has not only read it, but also that they've enjoyed it. They've taken the journey with my characters, empathised with them, cried with them, loved or hated them and more than anything else, believed in them.

As an author and like all other authors, I've been on quite a writing journey that has taken many years and I still find it surreal that my novels are now real, that they are 'out there' and available for readers to buy. With that in mind, I'd love to know your thoughts and I'd be delighted if you'd take just a few moments to leave me any feedback that you can. Reviews are so important to an author, they're a lifeline that not only helps them to improve, but inspires them to do better, to be disciplined and to keep going at times when it would be very easy to do other things.

If you do have the time to leave me a review on Amazon, Goodreads or any other reviewing platform, you'd make my day and I'd be forever grateful.

Please do feel free to contact me anytime. You can find my details under my author bio, or come and look for my author page on Facebook. I'd always be happy to hear from you and I always respond.

And … if you enjoyed *Tell Me No Secrets* and want to read another of my stories, then maybe you'd like to read my debut novel, *House of Secrets*, which is also available on all eBook platforms and in paperback.

Once again, thank you for reading my second novel, it was a pleasure to write it for you!

With Love

Lynda xx.

About the Author

Lynda, is a wife, step-mother and grandmother, she grew up in the mining village of Bentley, Doncaster, in South Yorkshire.

She is currently the Sales Director of a stationery, office supplies and office furniture company in Doncaster, where she has worked for the past 25 years. Prior to this she'd also been a nurse, a model, an emergency first response instructor and a PADI Scuba Diving Instructor ... and yes, she was crazy enough to dive in the sea with sharks, without a cage. Following a car accident in 2008, Lynda was left with limited mobility in her right arm. Unable to dive or teach anymore, she turned to her love of writing, a hobby she'd followed avidly since being a teenager.

Her own life story, along with varied career choices helps Lynda to create stories of romantic suspense, with challenging and unpredictable plots, along with (as in all romances) very happy endings.

She lives in a small rural hamlet near Doncaster, with her 'hero at home husband', Haydn, whom she's been happily married to for over 20 years.

Lynda joined the Romantic Novelist Association in 2014 under the umbrella of the New Writers Scheme and in 2015, her debut novel *House of Secrets* won the Choc Lit's *Search for a Star* competition.

For more information on Lynda visit:
www.lyndastacey.co.uk
www.twitter.com/LyndaStacey

More Choc Lit

From Lynda Stacey

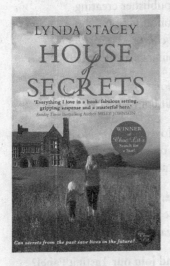

House of Secrets

A woman on the run, a broken man and a house with a shocking secret …

Madeleine Frost has to get away. Her partner Liam has become increasingly controlling to the point that Maddie fears for her safety, and that of her young daughter Poppy.

Desperation leads Maddie to the hotel owned by her estranged father – the extraordinarily beautiful Wrea Head Hall in Yorkshire. There, she meets Christopher 'Bandit' Lawless, an ex-marine and the gamekeeper of the hall, whose brusque manner conceals a painful past.

After discovering a diary belonging to a previous owner, Maddie and Bandit find themselves immersed in the history of the old house, uncovering its secrets, scandals, tragedies – and, all the while, becoming closer.

But Liam still won't let go, he wants Maddie back, and when Liam wants something he gets it, no matter who he hurts …

Winner of Choc Lit's 2015 Search for a Star competition.

Introducing Choc Lit

We're an independent publisher creating
a delicious selection of fiction.
Where heroes are like chocolate – irresistible!
Quality stories with a romance at the heart.

See our selection here:
www.choc-lit.com

We'd love to hear how you enjoyed *Tell Me No Secrets*.
Please leave a review where you purchased the novel
or visit: **www.choc-lit.com** and give your feedback.

Choc Lit novels are selected by genuine readers like yourself.
We only publish stories our Choc Lit Tasting Panel want to
see in print. Our reviews and awards speak for themselves.

Could you be a Star Selector and join our Tasting Panel?
Would you like to play a role in choosing which novels we
decide to publish? Do you enjoy reading women's fiction?
Then you could be perfect for our Choc Lit Tasting Panel.

Visit here for more details…
www.choc-lit.com/join-the-choc-lit-tasting-panel

Keep in touch:
Sign up for our monthly newsletter Choc Lit Spread for
all the latest news and offers: www.spread.choc-lit.com.
Follow us on Twitter: @ChocLituk and Facebook: Choc Lit.

Where heroes are like chocolate – irresistible!